# THE VERY MAN

Chris Binchy is a graduate of Trinity College Dublin,
has been a chef and is now a full-time writer.
*The Very Man* is his first novel. He lives in Dublin.

D1424728

To Lenna

# THE VERY MAN
# CHRIS BINCHY

Apologies for
bad words. Hope
you enjoy.

Chris Binchy

MACMILLAN

First published 2003 by Macmillan
an imprint of Pan Macmillan Ltd
Pan Macmillan, 20 New Wharf Road, London N1 9RR
Basingstoke and Oxford
Associated companies throughout the world
www.panmacmillan.com

ISBN  0 333 98978 3

Copyright © Chris Binchy 2003

The right of Chris Binchy to be identified as the
author of this work has been asserted by him in accordance
with the Copyright, Designs and Patents Act 1988.

All rights reserved. No part of this publication may be
reproduced, stored in or introduced into a retrieval system, or
transmitted, in any form, or by any means (electronic, mechanical,
photocopying, recording or otherwise) without the prior written
permission of the publisher. Any person who does any unauthorized
act in relation to this publication may be liable to criminal
prosecution and civil claims for damages.

1 3 5 7 9 8 6 4 2

A CIP catalogue record for this book is available from
the British Library.

Typeset by SetSystems Ltd, Saffron Walden, Essex
Printed and bound in Great Britain by
Mackays of Chatham plc, Chatham, Kent

For Siobhan

# THE VERY MAN

# 1

I stood at the door feeling sick. Shane answered.

'All right?'

'All right?'

He touched my back as I walked by and closed the door behind me. He'd got fatter since Christmas and his head was shaved tight like a potato.

'You look crap,' I said.

'You should see yourself.'

'I've an excuse.'

'Yeah well. Don't we all.'

My father was in the living-room with all the aunts. He stood up when I came in and shook my hand.

'Welcome back. Thanks for coming.'

'Yeah. Of course.'

'I know. I'm sorry.'

'Me too.'

'She's just gone. Gone, you know.'

'Yeah, I know.'

Aunts hugged me, all puffy eyes and snotty faces. Brian and Shane just sat there, looking into space.

'The removal is at five. Are you going to go to bed or what?' my father asked me.

'Is there anything else I can be doing?'

'Not really, no.'

'Well then, yeah.'

'I'll get you up later.'

I went up to my room. There was shit everywhere. Broken chairs and pictures and piles of papers and just crap. I sat on the bed and had a cigarette. I shut my eyes and reached out to her and she was there, smiling and gentle and funny.

Why didn't you wait?

She shook her head.

I'm alone. You've left me alone.

The cigarette burnt my fingers and woke me. I put it out and lay down. She was gone.

Three days before. Four of us were in a motel room in some shithole on the Cape, playing cards and drinking beer. Four guys from Dublin who'd known each other for ever. Codes and shorthand and slang and mumbling.

'Who did that?'

'Brennan, you mank bag.'

'You fucking minger.'

'You ming. Mercilessly.'

'Jaysus.'

'You absolute scum.'

We were mostly talking about old stuff, when we were in school and college, going over the legends which we all knew and had heard a thousand times but which brought us closer. Patrick was talking about the time we were walking through Dalkey trying to get a taxi into town, off our faces on Jagermeister and Holsten. Four English guys on Harleys or Triumphs came chugging through and I think it was Anto tried to flag them down like a taxi. Stupid but funny at the time, but one of the bikers gave him two fingers. Anto returned it thinking nothing of it, but then the four of them pulled up and started walking back towards us, taking off their helmets throwing them at us and I remember thinking, Oh fuck here we go. As we were all standing back waiting to see what we were going to do, Patrick walked straight at them on his own, went up to the roughest-looking guy and smacked him straight in the face. It was so funny. Your man had stopped and was standing looking so mean and hard and Patrick just belted him. He went flying back and the other bikers just looked at him on the ground. They said nothing and we all weighed in. We knocked them around the place and we were actually laughing as we were doing it, joking with each other as we kicked them. We left them lying in the middle of the road in Dalkey and got a taxi into town, laughing all the way. They didn't know what hit them.

Patrick told the story well. He performed it and at the end we were all in stitches. A wave of euphoria passed over me. Sitting in a motel room on the edge of America talking about the old country like a bunch of mafiosi.

'I love you guys. I love you all, you all mean so much to me. I always thought you were a bunch of wankers but I've seen the light,' I said and the others laughed. I was so happy. I felt safe. Then I got back to New York and Jim told me the news.

I couldn't breathe. In the back of the Merc with a black tie and shades. I always thought I couldn't feel enough to care at funerals, just end up posing, but I couldn't breathe. She was everywhere. Everywhere I looked, every time I blinked, all I could see was her, suffocating me. My stomach and chest full of pain. Arriving at the church and through the crowd outside, all moon eyes and long faces. You'd almost laugh. What the fuck is it to you? So many of them. Into the church up to the front. Standing at an altar that I hadn't seen in fifteen years. My mother is in a box. Cold and alone and dead. Gone. I stood and sat and kneeled and heard nothing and sucked air into my lungs and wished I was dead. Better than this. Quiet and peace and emptiness better than being eaten by this pain. And then they came. Hundreds and hundreds, for what seemed like hours. Neighbours and relations and school friends, guys I hadn't seen in years and loads that I didn't know, but all the same, sorry for your trouble, the firm handshake, looking you in the eye and I was thinking, My mother is dead, but all I said was 'Thanks very much', always nodding bravely. What else can you do? Then my lot in a group, all hugs and looking at me, all trying to tell me something but stopping short, as if being there wasn't enough. Can you get her back to me or make this different or just put an end to it? Because if you can't there's nothing to say. We left her on her own. I hated that.

We drank that night. There were loads of them back in the house, all the old pals and the cousins and all. I sat on the couch and drank cans and smoked. Everybody talking and then someone would laugh and I'd hear that and think of her and I couldn't handle it so I'd just shut up. I was drunk and couldn't follow anything, they all talked about the time she did this and that and fuckers I didn't know saying she was always a very proud woman, proud of her family, and I didn't know whether they were full of shit or if I just didn't know and it made me worse to think that, that I didn't really know her any more but then I thought of when I was a kid and the others used to take the piss out of me and she was the only one who'd make them stop. I was still me and she was the only one who knew what that meant but then I was too drunk to think and I just started crying and when I woke on the couch it was nine o'clock and we had to go.

In the morning it was more of the same, more people and nodding and smiling though your heart feels like it stopped beating two days ago and it's just rotting. We carried her out, me with Shane's arm over my shoulder, and I thought, This is going to kill me, it has to end. Then the graveyard with a pile of earth where my mother belongs, walking over gravel with the sky that takes the colour from your face. They lowered her down and it wasn't her, I knew that, I knew she was gone but I said goodbye. Over and over. Goodbye. I had no mother. I was alone.

Phil and me were out in the back of my house looking out over the sea at six in the morning. He'd got a back payment from the dole and we'd been drinking for two days when he said it to me out of nowhere.

'Let's get out.'

'What? Where?'

'Out of here. Dublin. There's nothing here for us. What are you going to do? What are you going to work at? Are you going to cook burgers or line up and take a shit job in a bank for a hundred and fifty quid a week if they stoop so low as to hire the likes of you?'

'I don't know. Where do you want to go?'

'Anywhere. New York. Why would you hang around being an arsehole here, when you could be a richer happier arsehole there? What would keep you here?'

'Friends. Family. I don't know.'

Shit weather. No work. Living for Thursday, broke by Saturday, waiting for Thursday again. Watching videos with the same bunch of idiots all the time. Getting drunk on cheap cans. Stumbling around Leeson Street in the rain. Family. Brothers. Not having a notion what to do to get out of this. Lining up. Pricks everywhere.

'How much would I need?'

'About a grand.'

'And how do I get that?'

'Get a job and save. We say now we go in August and we do. We just fucking go.'

'OK. We just fucking go.'

I could feel a shiver pass through me at the thought, the end of the old life, the start of something new and I put my hand on Phil's shoulder and he just laughed. We were hammered.

I worked in a restaurant six nights a week for six months. I saw no one. I worked and slept and rang Phil every so often to make sure he was still on for it. Dirty greasy work serving dirty greasy people. From six in the evening until four, waking up every day feeling jet-lagged and hungover, without having travelled or been drunk. Living on twenty-five-pence packs of noodles. Fucking a waitress who had an arse like a duck but a flat around the corner and smoked so much hash she never wanted to talk. Arguing with the boss every week about my money because he always messed it up.

'There's plenty of others will do your job,' he told me.

'So hire them.'

He never did. Arsehole. He knew he was on to a good thing. Every week I checked my bank balance and the number eventually got to four digits. I rang Phil. I hadn't spoken to him in about a month.

7

'I'm ready now,' I told him.

'For what?' he asked.

'New York. I've got a thousand quid. How much have you?'

'Oh fuck, yeah. I can't do that.'

'What? Why?' I felt a sick panic.

'I don't have the cash.'

'Well save it. I did.'

'I know, yeah. No, I just can't do it. I've got a job starting next week.'

'Where? What job?'

'In the bank,' he said. He had the grace to sound ashamed.

'You went and got a job in the bank?'

'Yeah. Well no. My dad got it for me.'

'Your dad? Your fucking daddy? You useless prick. I don't believe this.'

'Yeah, well I'm sorry.'

'Well I'm sorry I listened to you, you wanker. I've been breaking my arse for six months and now this.'

'I said I'm sorry. I can't do any more. You go to New York. Why not?'

'On my own? What would I be doing going on my own? It was supposed to be the two of us, you know that. You've let me down badly here and now you say "Go on your own." Fuck you, I just might.'

'You should,' he said. He sounded very calm. It was doing my head in.

I hung up.

He was always like that. I should have known. Big talk when he was pissed but it was a different story when it came to the sober morning. Hanging around bitching and pissing and moaning, always on the verge of something but never actually doing anything. It got so tired. There's nothing very sharp or ironic about your dad getting you a job, but he'd do it and he'd spend Friday nights talking about how crap it all was. I couldn't stand it. It was such a small town where everybody was totally comfortable, knew their place, knew what was expected of them and played it out. There had to be more. There was and I was going to see it.

My mother cried when I told her. Not at first. But when she knew I meant it.

'You will come back, won't you?' she said.

'Of course I will,' I said but I didn't know. How could I?

We all went out the night before I left. Another one of those nights. There was one every other week, another one of us bailing out, leaving the rest behind and heading to Boston or London or Chicago or Sydney. We'd all sit around and tell them they were a prick and no good and nobody cared that they were leaving, that we were only out for the drink and then when we were pissed, we'd tell them how great they were and everybody would go home and forget about them. You might start ringing someone you hadn't seen in a while to make up the deficit but they were gone, only to feature again in the twelve-day binge at Christmas.

We went to a pub in town and they were all there. It was a week-night so there was nowhere to go afterwards.

'Jane Murphy's having a twenty-first,' Patrick said. 'You know her, don't you?'

'I don't know her. I've met her about twice.'

'That'll do.'

It was in some kippy hotel on the quays. The others waited around the corner as Patrick and myself tried to get in. The hotel porter kept the door shut, asking us who was having the party and were we invited and I'd told him it was Jane Murphy and of course we were, and the old bastard went and got her. She didn't know what to do when she came out, smiling, expecting some late arrival, a friend or family member, and she saw us. She knew who I was all right but she pretended she couldn't see us, craning her neck, still smiling, her face six feet away through the glass, looking out. I was looking straight at her, waving, going, 'Jane. It's me. Come on. Stop messing around,' but she just walked off and the porter came up to the door shaking his head and shooed us away. We went back around to the others and we were going to leave it. But then Patrick went off down this lane behind the hotel and found a way in through the fire exit. We all piled in and went straight to the bar and got a drink. We were standing around trying to look unobtrusive when Jane saw me. She stared at me for a second. I thought about waving again, to get her back but I just turned away. She went and started talking to the barman and to some of her pals. Three of them came over. They went straight up to Patrick, not me. He was having a ball.

'How are you, lads?'

'Guys, this is Jane's night. Don't wreck it on her.'

Patrick was deadpan.

'What you mean? We're doing nothing. Just having a drink.'

'You're not invited. Will you just go?'

'Is that what she told you? Jesus. She must be locked. She told us we could come down. She used to work with us. She can't have forgotten.'

He called her across the room.

'Jane. Jane.'

She looked around at him and turned away.

'Ah, Jane. Jesus.'

He looked at the three guys, laughing.

'She's such a dope.'

They were confused. One of them went off and brought her back. She was mortified. We all started shouting at her.

'Hi, Jane. How could you forget? She's messing, isn't she?'

Her pals were looking at her.

'I don't know them. I don't.'

'You know me, Jane,' I said. 'Rory.'

She didn't seem too sure.

'Oh no.'

'I don't believe this.'

'She's blanking us.'

Jane spoke.

'Get them out. Make them go.'

I thought there could have been trouble but Patrick wandered off towards the door. We followed, the whole party at a standstill watching us go, wondering, waving goodbye to our disloyal friend.

'That was fun. At least we got a drink out of it,' Patrick said as we were outside waiting for taxis.

'My last night in Dublin I get thrown out of a party. What's fun about that? It's typical,' I said.

'It's not your last night,' he said. 'And anyway I'll probably be there in a few months.'

'You should,' I said, knowing he'd never get it together.

'I wish I was going with you,' Phil said.

'You could have been, if you hadn't . . .'

'I know, I know.'

It wasn't the time to be giving him grief.

I said goodbye to them all standing there on the street.

'It won't be the same without you,' Patrick said, which was a lot for him.

'I think it will,' I said.

Coming home along the Rock Road at five in the morning, the sky already brightening above Howth, I felt something. A wrench or a pull, like I was losing something. I could see the comfort of the familiar, but this hadn't been enough for twenty-odd years and one beautiful morning wouldn't change it.

I went to the airport alone. Everybody else was in work. Driving across the Northside, all grey and dirty and boring, full of slack-jawed, track-suited, bleached, grey-skinned, poor, lost fuckers. I was glad. I was getting out of this place, because all the nice girls in debs dresses and coffee in Bewley's and the sun rising over Killiney Bay couldn't change the fact that at its core Dublin was a shithole. It was dead and I was getting out.

I knew New York was for me from the first day, my heart thumping, my breath catching in my throat as I felt the life and the pace and the heat and stink. Dublin was a village asleep on a stream. This was God's city, mine from the first. I crashed with a friend of Shane's, a fat alcoholic who managed a bar on Third Avenue. On the street the first day, looking for work, I couldn't hold back the smile, the thrill that this was New York. Nobody cared about me. I could be anyone and nobody cared. I could do anything. I was free. I got a job that day, working as a waiter. Nobody knew me. I was quiet and kept working. The customers were snotty, loud, rude fuckers who would start barking when they arrived and would tip five dollars on a twenty-dollar bill. I worked and worked and took no shit off them. After two weeks I moved in with a guy who worked in advertising and got a boxy little room with no window for a hundred and fifty dollars a week.

I worked with a bunch of thieves. I would drink with them sometimes but would get out before it got messy. The bars with shamrocks in the windows and ridiculous names made me sad sometimes. I missed something. I reminisced about a life I had never lived. Simple, rural, quiet. Stupid but what can you do? Pogues records, teabags, crisps, chocolate. The true cultural expression of Ireland. Dingy holes full of construction workers from Mayo. I didn't travel three thousand miles to drink with bogmen. There had to be more. I asked my roommate was there work in his place. I had a degree, I was legal and that. Anything to get me back in touch with humanity. He said he'd check and came back with a name. I sent in a CV. My interests include advertising. My interests include anything that allows me to wear a suit and not come home at four a.m. smelling of grease. I rang him, wrote again. I scourged him until he gave me a trial working as a dogsbody.

All I did was work and sleep. I'd been there two months and I knew no one, hadn't been drunk since arriving. Going home at night, I would hear the Dublin accent on the subway and look over at people so familiar that I knew if I'd asked in ten seconds we'd discover that we had common acquaintances. I thought about doing it, about saying I know no one here, I'm normal and I'm sick of people who don't know me, don't understand what I mean when I say I'm from Ireland, but I never did because we were in New York and that wasn't how things were.

I worked differently. I was smart. I didn't keep my head down. I wasn't polite or modest or diffident. I worked my arse off and I made sure the relevant people saw me. I watched as my co-workers turned against me, one by one, as I went from being the new boy to being the competition. Fuck them. I could work harder than anyone. I worked and slept, slept and worked. New York was there, outside, but I left it there, unexplored and untried and watched my career progress as I went from a nobody to an account manager in a year. Every month the money would lodge and I'd buy cigarettes, coffee and pay rent. It piled up. I moved in on my own, a bigger place with windows. I saw who the big guys were and worked them. The Irish thing was a help at first, for the conversation starter, marked me out as different but then I saw that any chance of hitting it off with these guys was going to be on their terms. I couldn't have that languid ironic conversation that we had at home, where everything was just put out there for discussion, whether it was ridiculed, debated or just disregarded didn't matter. Here it was all straight. This is a good cigar. That basketball match was great. That girl wants to fuck you. Where did you get that suit? Straight straight straight. They went to bars where a martini was fifteen dollars. They went to strip clubs and leched communally and would drop $1,000 and then talk about it all the following evening. They never had normal conversations with women. They competed with each other but always in a familiar slaggy way. I struggled. Nothing that they did made sense to me. They all had the same background, had a language and a history that I could never fully understand. But I could emulate and I did. My accent faded, the mannerisms and the stock expressions changed. I worked like a dog all day and at night I worked them hard. I dropped the hand in strip clubs, I got people at home to send over Cubans and I took tennis coaching and they noticed and over time I became one of the boys. When I spoke to anyone at home they heard it straight away.

'What's happened to your accent?'

'It's a temporary thing. I'm going undercover.'

'To be understood?'

'For the money.'

The money came. The suits got better. I got used to eating in good places. We drank in new bars, sometimes funky, never weird. I met girls I couldn't imagine. They were a set, a group who cared only about money and the higher the money went the better looking they got. Everything mattered – shoes, hair, cologne, what you drank, how much you drank, where you lived. They were whores really. I didn't care. I could pay.

At Christmas I would come home to Dublin and nothing ever changed. It was like going back in time. Shit roads, congestion, a half-finished look to everything. Ugly people all sniffing and coughing. No public transport, no taxis. The same people hanging around the same bars having the same conversations wearing the same clothes. Fun people. Yeah. It was nice to take the piss and have it taken, but what had they ever done or seen? There was always a new bar or restaurant that everyone was talking about, every year, and when you eventually went it was like three years ago in New York. They talked about how things were getting better, how there were jobs and better times coming, but if you looked in the paper nobody was getting paid. I could do it all. Catch up with everyone, meet the new girlfriends, do the rounds and drink solidly for two weeks. It was too deep in me to have gone, but it wasn't the same. Or it was the same. I had changed.

My brothers asked about girls and drugs and money. I showed them photos and told them stories and they tried not to be impressed. My father asked about burnout and where I was going and coughed and growled. My mother asked if I was happy.

'Of course I'm happy. I live in Manhattan. I make two grand a week. What do you want?'

'I don't know. You've done so well and you work so hard but you look older. You know, I don't know if you should think that you'll always be there. Most people come home. You should be enjoying yourself. You're too young to go down that road. Get a bit of experience and think about coming back here.'

'I make ten times what I'd make here. I'm having a good time. Too good, a lot of the time. Relax.'

'I know but it's not all about money, you know. That's all. There's more to it than cash.'

'Yeah, I know that.'

She was so wrong. It was all about the money. In Ireland we tried to convince ourselves that there was more, something else deeper and more important, but there wasn't. We thought that way to console ourselves for the fact that we were poor. All the things the Irish thought were their virtues – a slow pace of life, friendliness, hospitality – were symptoms of poverty. I had seen what there was in New York. There was work and money and benefits. Anything you wanted you could get if you had enough and all those guys sitting around spending their Christmas cheques in Neary's, talking about stupid Americans and the quality of life in Ireland were kidding themselves. If they had ever lived in Manhattan, eaten in the Rainbow Room, drank in Halo and got blown by an eighteen-year-old Brazilian model they'd know a bit more about quality of life.

It wasn't so bad for the first few days after the funeral. There were a lot of people around and they were trying to make sure that I was OK, hanging around all the time. But after the first week, it got quieter and I started spending more time on my own. I didn't know what to do. How do you behave a week after you've buried your mother? You still have to eat and drink and wash. Then the office called from New York. Jim came on the line. He didn't mess around.

'Rory, I'm just wondering when we're likely to see you back here.'

'I don't know, Jim. I'm thinking about the start of next week.'

'That's OK. You are aware that you're using your holiday time at this stage?'

'I'm aware of that, yes.'

'And also, Rory, I've got to tell you – and forgive me if I'm overstepping the mark here – but when my mother died, I didn't feel like going back to work, as if in some way that would be disloyal or would indicate that I hadn't given myself time to grieve, but after four days I just made myself do it and in hindsight I think it helped. I was back to doing what I do and while it was desperately sad, it put it in perspective that life goes on. Your life has to go on.'

'That's very true. I wouldn't argue.'

'But anyway, Rory, I don't want to tell you what to do, once again you have my sympathies and take as long as you like, but at this stage you're thinking next week?'

'Next week, yeah.'

'Well I'll talk to you then but keep me posted, OK?'

'OK. Thanks for calling.'

I could imagine him sitting in the office. I could smell it, the mix of coffee and perfume and hot office machinery, could hear the background sounds of keyboards clicking and phones buzzing and a low hum of one-sided conversations as people schmoozed on the phone with clients. That was my life and at a remove of three thousand miles it seemed faintly depressing. My desk would be there unattended and unnoticed. My phone calls would automatically be diverted to one of my colleagues. Jim's conversation with me would be gone from his mind already, as he worked his way through the rest of his to-do list. The pulse of the streets, the nights out with booming men and beautiful women seemed far away and empty. I wasn't ready to go back. I was scared.

I went out with Patrick and I said it to him.

'Should I bother going back to New York?'

'Why? Why are you asking me this?'

'Because when I'm here looking back, I know what I've got over there, and it's all good but I don't know. What's it like being here now?'

He stayed silent for thirty seconds before speaking.

'I know you're in New York and I know you've got the job and the life and all that, but have you friends in New York?'

'I've friends. What do you mean? Yeah, of course I've friends.'

'Because I've never heard you talk about them.'

'Well, by definition I've only known them six years or whatever, I can't have known them as long as all the guys here but they are friends. I go out with them, we hang out, meet girls and all that.'

'Then how come not one of them came back for your mother's funeral?'

'Oh come on, you know what it's like in America with two weeks' holidays, and in what I do it's even worse. Some of these guys wouldn't even take the day off for their own mother's funeral.'

'I know, yeah, but have they been ringing you or checking to see what the story is?'

'It's not really like that. They're more people I socialize with than anything else. I don't even know anything about some of them. They are people that I hang around with, it's a different type of friendship. Try as I may you can never have that same bond in New York, there are languages for everything and the one for work friendship doesn't involve much about the past or your family or that.'

'What's most important? Do you need the money and the job and the life in New York or do you need other people who know where you're from?'

'I had that before and that's why I left.'

'No, you left because that's all you had, all there was at that time to keep you was people who knew you, nothing else. But now there is more and you can get a job and you can get a flat and you can live in town and whatever you think from what little you see when you're home at Christmas, that is a hell of a lot more than it used to be.'

'So basically you think I should stay.'

'I'm not taking responsibility for anything, if you come back and hate it, that's your problem, but if you ask me what I would do if I were you then yes I'd come home.'

'You'd come home.'

'Yes.'

'That's all I wanted to know.'

I waited. I waited and thought and looked around town and

bought the papers and talked to other people. I spent nights out with friends, evenings at home with my family and days just wandering around in town and I made my decision. I rang Jim and told him I wouldn't be back.

# 2

It was as if the changes had happened over night. That was exactly how it was. All the cranes and new buildings and pubs, builders in hard hats everywhere. Streets with no names. Everybody on Grafton Street and in the pubs wearing the clothes but never quite getting it right, great smells coming out of cafés but when you went in it took twenty minutes for them to get to you and when they did they could never understand you. People in shops were sloppy and rude. It was like all this money had just landed out of nowhere and nobody really knew what to do, or they knew what they should be doing, they just didn't know how and they could only make a half-assed attempt at sophistication. There was an edge in the way people dealt with each other. Everywhere you walked on the street you could hear it – fuck him, fuck it, fuck off, fucking prick, cunt, bitch. Everywhere and everybody. Phones ringing all the time and stupid inane conversations, too stupid to have face to face. Everybody smoking hard, all lighting, sucking, pulling, blowing. Skinny girls in skinny jeans with no arses hanging around with loutish young lads in shit tracksuits looking like they're only hanging around long enough to get her fags. Rubbish everywhere, piled up at the sides of buildings and in doorways, streets lined with puke. Everybody shoving past tourists who wandered around lost and bemused. They came from Manhattan to Ireland and it was too busy for them. Traffic going nowhere. People who couldn't drive delaying people who couldn't wait. One person in every car. People beeping when you crossed the road in front of them because they were going to break the red light and now because of you they couldn't. You fucking prick. Nothing ever arrived when it was supposed to, nobody ever came when they said and if you got snotty they'd start getting up on their high horse.

'Why didn't you come?'

'I don't like your tone.'

'Yeah, well I don't like being lied to.'

'Are you calling me a liar?'

'You said you'd be here. You're not. What would you call it?'

'I think it would be better if you took your business elsewhere.'

What could you do? They didn't care because they had never had so much and nothing anyone could say right now would cop them on to the fact that when all this ended and the shit eventually went down, they'd go with it.

I started working as an account manager with a crowd called Talisman. The guy who interviewed me had worked in New York. He knew some of the same people that I did. I asked around and found out about him. He was a tough bastard but he'd told me that himself. He let me know what he expected, talked about the board. When he told me I had the job I thanked him.

'Fuck that,' he said. 'You better be worth it.'

We went for a drink then. He just took off at three o'clock and we stayed in a crappy little place around the corner until seven. He was a foul-mouthed, rough bastard but he knew his stuff. I liked him a lot.

I got a flat in Temple Bar. It was a stupid amount of cash for a place the size of it, but it was where I wanted to be. I paid Ciaran's girlfriend Jane to furnish it. She was a designer or going to be and she'd done some course and she knew what I should be getting. She took me in and showed me all the stuff she was getting in these funky places around town. All very cool but she made me pay for it. When it was finished, I let the boys in to see it. They were impressed.

'If you can get a girl in the door of this place it's a done deal.'

And all that, presuming that all I'd be doing would be shagging.

There were girls. Better looking than when I'd left, trendier, more knowing. At weekends we went to wherever was new, there was always somewhere new and there were always the same kind of girls, in black and beige and stupid-looking clothes that didn't fit together or maybe did in some sort of ironic way that just looked crap. Girls with pigtails and dark-rimmed glasses with little bags on their backs and girls with pierced tongues and eyebrows and bellybuttons sucking lollipops and I just didn't get it but it was OK. It was OK because they drank, they got drunk and they did lines and pills and everything that was going and they got as messed up as we did and they didn't talk just about themselves and their tragic lives like they did in America, they didn't talk about the difficulties faced by strong, young, intelligent women, they just talked bollocks like we did and they'd go to bed if you made them laugh and when everything was going well I could make them laugh.

Most of my friends had girlfriends. They all tried to set me up. They did it with the sad and lonely and boring, the girls who had slipped through the net and who these guys' girlfriends presumed I'd be glad to get, or so it seemed. Not for me. I didn't want anyone and was having a better time just doing my thing every weekend.

'You need to settle down and get yourself a girl. Good-looking fellow like you. You could find someone no problem,' said a very drunk Phil when we were out slaughtered one night. He met Catherine in the bank when he was twenty-three and was still with her, all settled down.

'I get girls all the time. You need to back off and leave me alone,' I told him.

'No, seriously. I know it's all a laugh and great fun doing what you're doing but do you not get a bit bored of it?'

I just looked at him.

'Sex? Do I get bored of sex with different girls? That's what you're asking.'

'No. Not that. I'm asking and I know I shouldn't presume that you're the same as me, but do you not get tired of it all? Do you not want to just forget about it some Saturday night and just stay in and watch telly and do nothing with someone who knows you?'

'Well, if I do I can always call you.'

'You know what I mean.'

'I know what you're saying and I'm choosing to believe that you're saying this out of concern for my well being and not warning me that I'm getting too old for my chosen lifestyle.'

'Mostly concern. It is becoming a bit unseemly though. People are starting to talk,' he said, smiling now.

'Bollocks to that. You know you're getting a kick out of living it up vicariously through me.'

'Yeah I'd love to be you. All that wanking.'

'And I'd love to be you, snuggling up every night with your missus. I bet she goes like a train.'

'Oh yeah. You'd want to see her.'

They did it because they cared. That's what they would say. Or did they do it so that we would all be the same? Was it that they could see what I was lacking, or that they saw what I had and couldn't handle it? Was it a quest for happiness or conformity? I felt it when I went out with them all, queering up the table plan, the odd one out, treated with affection and amusement and indulgence like I was doing something wrong and they were ignoring it.

We were out for Anto's thirtieth in some Italian place. It was all the usual with a couple of Léan's friends who I didn't know.

'If you've set me up . . .' I said to her when I arrived.

'The world doesn't revolve around you, Rory.'

'Not for you maybe. Anyway I know what you lot are like. Who's that one?'

'Which?'

'The dark one.'

'Niamh. Why?'

'Just you know.'

'Are you expressing an interest?'

'No. I am emphatically not.'

'Well, she's free. Just so as you know,' she said smiling.

'That's nice. I hate paying.'

Do they pull it out of the air? Do you smell different when you're on the market? Léan must have told her by some sort of girly telepathy, but the next thing was me and her were throwing these crafty little glances and never looking straight at each other and after an hour of this messing around I went over and it was easy. She knew what was going on and I played it cool and asked would she like to meet during the week for a drink and she said OK. That was it.

Léan rang in the morning.

'So what's the story with you and Niamh?' she asked. She sounded like she was going to explode.

'What story?'

'The story. I don't know. What happened?'

'Nothing happened. Nothing happened. I'm going to ring her during the week and we may do something.'

'Great.' She actually squeaked.

'Well, I don't know if it is yet.'

'It will be. She's really nice. Seriously. You're going to love her. I said it to Catherine, that you'd get on well with her.'

'I bloody knew you were setting me up.'

'I wasn't. No I wasn't. This was—'

'I knew you were,' I interrupted her.

'This was after. That's all. OK? Afterwards.'

'Yeah. I don't know if I believe you.'

'Well, go out with her and see how you get on. And have fun if you're capable.'

'Stop grinning. I can hear you grinning.'

I made an arrangement with Niamh a couple of days later. The first night we went out I was nervous. It made it harder that I thought I was going to like her. If I wasn't sure, then I could just do the usual thing. Eye contact and asking loads of questions and open receptive body language, not drinking too much and pulling out her chair and all those stupid formulas for making a girl like you. But I didn't want any of that. I didn't want to trick her into liking me. I didn't want to play games. What I wanted was to try and be like myself and that made me nervous.

I met her in the bar of the hotel where we were going to eat. As

soon as I saw her I relaxed. From when she said hello, I knew it was
going to be fine. She was so smiley and open as if we already knew
each other.

She was studying for a Master's in Art History at Trinity. She
talked about the course and the artists she was into. I knew enough to
ask the right questions to keep her talking. She was interesting about
it but anyway, I liked watching her talk. Her face was totally open, it
was impossible to believe that there was anything going on in her
mind that wasn't there written on her face. I had to stop myself from
staring. After always striving to conceal myself with girls, to show
them only the person that I thought they would want, this was so
much easier. She asked about me and I told her about the job and
how I'd just started but it was going well and the people were cool. I
told her I'd been working in New York for years, about the job and
all that.

'What brought you back?'

'I don't know. I got fed up with my life being split between here
and there. I had to settle somewhere and in the end, I don't know, all
my friends were here. I suppose I just made the decision.'

'Do you regret it at all?'

'Not really. Not yet. I do feel more at home here, more like myself
and you know money isn't everything. Money and respect. And a nice
apartment and the world's most exciting city at your front door. And
power. All that power. I don't know. I don't know why I came back.
But I'm glad I did. We'll see how it goes.'

We went downstairs and ate. We didn't stop talking. She made
me taste what she'd ordered and I gave her bits of mine, forks being
passed over the table and back. The food was great. It was all great. I
was thinking all through dinner, Do not fuck this up. This is so good,
don't let it go, and then she asked about my family.

'Do you have brothers or sisters?'

'Two brothers. No sisters. They're both older than me by a few
years.'

'So you were an afterthought?'

'A mistake, I think. I don't know. I never asked.'

We went for a drink afterwards. We were talking about the people we both knew. She knew a lot of my old crowd, Léan and Jane and Ciaran.

'And you came out with me despite what they told you?'

'No, I knew you were all right.'

'How?'

'Just the way Léan and the others talked about you.'

'Yeah, but they've all known me for ages. They have to think I'm OK. They have to believe I'm worth hanging around with.'

'And are you?'

'Of course I am. Can't you tell? Hasn't this been the best evening ever?'

She smiled.

'It'd be up there. What did Léan tell you about me?'

'She said you were lovely. I think that was it.'

'I am lovely, amn't I? I think she got that right.'

'You are. You're very beautiful,' I said and she looked at me like she was going to laugh.

'Well you are,' I said. 'It's not my fault.' I could feel myself blushing.

'Thank you,' she said.

I walked her to a taxi rank. The nervousness I had felt earlier came back, not badly, but just there in the pit of my stomach.

'I really enjoyed that,' I said when we got there.

'Yeah, it was great.'

'I'll see you again?' I said.

'Yeah.'

'Well. Goodbye.'

'Bye.'

She stood there and I leant in and kissed her on the cheek and held her hand. We looked at each other for a second and then we kissed. It was lovely. I put my arms around her and hugged her and rested my chin on her head for a second, holding her. I was so happy. I looked at her and she smiled and I kissed her again quickly.

'I'll ring you tomorrow,' I said.

'OK,' she said. 'Bye.' She got into the taxi and I watched her go. I walked off towards the flat. My legs were shaky and I started laughing.

I rang her the next day and we met again that weekend and then a couple of times the following week. Then she came back to the apartment.

'I can't believe this place. Where did you get this stuff?'

'Some design company.'

'Well, I like your taste.'

I kept my mouth shut. She liked it all. She liked the glass I gave her wine in. She liked the towels in the bathroom, the sound system and when, inevitably, we went to bed she liked the sheets and I think she liked me. I wasn't trying too hard because I felt like I'd get another chance so I chilled out and it was great. It was nice that she was there the next day and that we could go out for breakfast. Then she started coming over midweek and just hanging around and I still went out with Patrick and them but I enjoyed the time with her more anyway. It was good to have someone to fuss over. I gave her things and told her she was beautiful and I started to love her and I think she started to love me.

We started getting invites to things together and all my friends liked her a lot. We got on without even thinking about it. Same humour. Both of us acting like none of it really mattered but then sometimes, I'd look at her and I knew there was something happening. She called me on it once.

'What are you gawping at?' she said without turning to look at me when I was watching her watch telly.

'What?' I asked, innocently.

'What are you looking at me for? Am I doing something wrong?'

She turned to me half-smiling, waiting for me to say something funny or throwaway. I couldn't say anything to her. I couldn't get it out. I didn't know what she'd say if I told her that I was staring because I was totally smitten. I just didn't know. So I stammered, trying to think of anything to say but I couldn't.

'You're not so smooth,' she said and I laughed at that.

'I'm really not.'

'That's all right,' she said. 'I can teach you.'

After two months of this, the lease ran out on her flat and I told her she could stay with me. I hadn't even thought about it.

'I don't think so. It's not really fair,' she said. She looked worried.

'Fair? What's fair?'

'I should get my own place.'

'Well, you can pay me rent if it makes you happy.'

'Not that so much. Do you mean just until I get somewhere else?'

'Whatever. The flat is big enough for two. You spend most nights here anyway. If you want to, it seems to make sense that you move in. You can earn your keep.'

She still didn't seem sure.

'Is it a bit soon?' she asked.

'Hey, look. I'm not proposing to you. If you want to the offer is there.' I smiled but she wasn't looking at me.

'I'll have a think and let you know.'

I'll let you know. Afterwards I felt like I hadn't put it strongly enough or that I'd come on too strong or that I hadn't told her what I wanted, but then I wasn't sure of that myself so how could I? Just trying to do the right thing. She rang me later that week to say that if the offer was still open she'd like to take me up on it. I said great and she moved in.

We went out for cocktails the night she arrived. I wanted to make a fuss of it so that she would know I was happy to have her there. I was talking about how great it was to be in town. How we'd be able to go for breakfast downstairs at the weekends and we'd never have to queue for taxis and all that. She was smiling and nodding but her heart wasn't in it. I was throwing back drinks trying to get the pace moving. If she got a bit buzzed, I thought she'd relax and get into it but she didn't. In the end I started getting edgy. She was making me edgy. It was stupid. I wanted her there. It felt like we were putting in time until we had to face the fact that we were going home together.

I'd had about six drinks and she'd had about two. I'd run out of things to talk about so I just thought, Fuck it.

'Let's go,' I said and we went.

I was trying not to wobble as we crossed back over to the Southside. Bloody cocktails. Like drinking juice and then you can't walk. My head was together though. I was holding her hand. She wasn't saying anything and then I just thought it was ridiculous.

'What's wrong with you?' I asked.

'Nothing,' she said. 'I'm fine.'

'Are you worried about this? About moving in?'

'No. Not at all.' She said it but she wasn't sure. I could tell.

'Because there's nothing to be scared of. It's going to be great.'

'I know.'

'And it's your place as much as it's mine. You can do whatever you want to make it feel right for you.'

'It's your apartment, Rory.'

'No. That's the point. It's ours now. It's not mine any more. There is no mine. There's only ours.'

She was laughing.

'You're drunk.'

'No I'm not. Or yeah, I am, but it doesn't matter. I'd be saying the same thing if I was sober, I swear to God. I just want you to be happy. I want us to be happy and I can't stand the idea that you wouldn't be completely comfortable, that you wouldn't feel at home in your own life. You know what I mean? I just couldn't stand that. You must be happy. You must do whatever you want. I don't care. Nothing else matters.'

I'd started out serious but by the end I was joking because she was smiling at me like I was mad.

'I'm serious,' I said.

'It's very nice,' she said and she kissed me. 'I just hope you remember this conversation in the morning. When I get the builders in.'

'Fine by me,' I said. 'I just want you to be happy. Because I really love you. And I'm not that drunk.'

'I love you too,' she said. What else could she say? She was laughing at me but she seemed happier after that. Sometimes the big dramatic gestures are what's needed. Easier with a skinful but I meant it all so I didn't mind. We hadn't known each other all that long and maybe it wouldn't work, I couldn't know for sure. But I had to go with my instincts. There was no logic to trusting her. That was what made it so great. When we got back she put on the telly and I made tea. It was like she'd always been there.

The others joked about it. Tamed, they said. Packing in the single life. Too tired to go on, too old, but actually they were glad. I was as well. It meant that at the end of the day there was someone there for me. It was great to be able to relax after spending the day at work trying to convince everyone that I was a tough bastard. I needed to switch off, let my guard down with someone who would listen and tell me I was OK. When I came in she'd be on the couch watching TV or in the bath or ordering food. When she was going out she'd ring me at work and I'd meet her in town. I never had to go home on my own, eat on my own, sleep on my own. Sometimes you want to but more often you don't.

I met Patrick after work a couple of weeks later. I hadn't seen him since she'd moved in.

'It's a bit of a cliché, isn't it?' he said. 'Dropping your friends when the girl comes on the scene.'

'She has particular attractions which you've never offered.'

'You've never asked.'

He didn't say much at first. It wasn't like him. I was talking about work, just general moaning, and then he got going. He was talking about a tax bill he'd got that week. He worked as a sound engineer in theatre. He'd just finished one show and was looking to start another. The timing was bad.

'I swear to you, I'm almost contemplating becoming a PAYE nobody like you. Suit and tie, the whole job thing. The slow drip feed of tax is much less painful.'

'It still hurts. And you'd have to get up every morning, spend the day looking at the same sad shower of wankers. You'd go mad.'

'Right now the security looks pretty good.'

'Yeah, but when you get this thing sorted out, it won't seem so appealing. You'd have to shave, you know. It really wouldn't be you.'

'Maybe.' He was chewing his finger. I went to the bar. When I was waiting, I got a notion. It was probably because of Niamh and how well that was going, and because I'd got paid a couple of days before. It might have been because I felt I'd been neglecting him. I don't know. It just seemed like the right thing to do. I wrote out a cheque for two grand and folded it up. I brought the drinks back to the table.

'That was quick,' he said. 'I could have died of thirst.'

'Shut up,' I said, 'and take that.'

He looked at it and then threw it back at me.

'Oh no no no—'

'Stop. Take.'

'No way,' he said. 'That's not what I was after. I was just talking.'

'I know. But I don't need it. You do. It'd be in the bank otherwise sitting there. You may as well.'

He looked at it lying on the table where it had fallen.

'Just take it and let's pretend it never happened,' I said.

He picked it up and put it into his wallet.

'Thanks,' he said. 'You're an awful man.'

'Enough.'

'I'll get it back to you.'

'You better. If you like your kneecaps.'

It was a bit embarrassing but I was glad I did it. After that we tried to have a normal conversation. He started asking about Niamh and how all that was going.

'Grand,' I said.

'You're getting on OK.'

'Yeah. No problem. Easygoing, you know.'

'She looks like she's in good shape.'

'Yeah. Definitely. Everything.'

'Good to go?'

'I'm not going to tell you that. But yeah. Very much so.'

'Bastard.'

'It's great. It's worth it. You know.'

'And if it doesn't work out?'

'Why wouldn't it work out?' I asked.

'Just if?'

'I don't know. I'm not thinking like that.'

'Well, I don't think she's going anywhere too soon,' he said.

'I don't think so,' I said. 'Not unless she's told.' I laughed at my own joke.

'Well, we'll see.'

'We will.'

She wasn't going anywhere. We got on fine.

She was redoing the flat.

'I just spent ten grand getting this place done,' I told her.

'But there's two of us now.'

'Well I like it,' I said.

'So do I but there're things I want to change. Nothing major,' she said like it wasn't anything.

'What in particular?'

'I don't know. Nothing. Small things. I'll pay for the work.'

'It's not about the money,' I said.

'Well what's it about?'

'It's just a waste.'

'Of what?'

'Of time. Of effort. I don't know.'

She was just looking at me like I was an idiot.

'OK,' I said. 'Of money as well, yeah.'

'I said I'll pay.'

She changed everything: the curtains, the flooring, the lights. The place was torn apart and put back together again. She'd read all the magazines. This green was better than that one. Shag pile is back. Up-lighters and acrylic eggshells. To me it looked the same, but when the others came round they made the right noises. I didn't know anything about it so it was easier to let her get on with it.

'Is this ever going to stop?' I asked after a while. 'Not that I mind.'

'Just another couple of things.'

'And then?'

She smiled at me.

'Then it will be perfect.'

She started on the kitchen, the food that we ate, the coffee that we drank, the shampoo that we used, the moisturizer I put on my face after shaving.

'This one is better,' she would say.

'The old one cost four quid for a bottle, this stuff is twenty.'

'It's better. Your skin looks clearer since you've started using it.'

'It's my skin and I can't see any difference,' I said. She sighed like I was a child.

'Well there is. Trust me.'

Trust me. Why would I care?

I took her out to meet my father. I thought it was only right. She was living with me and I knew that would mean something to him. I rang him to arrange it. I told him that I wanted to come out and see him and I'd be bringing a friend.

'A female friend,' I said like a fucking idiot.

'Does that mean she's a girlfriend?' he asked.

'Kind of. Yeah.'

'Right. Bring her out on Sunday for lunch. The boys will be here.'

'Sunday's not the best day, actually . . .' I said.

The horror of her meeting my brothers was too much.

'Have you something on?' he asked.

'No. I just think Niamh might be going out to her parents.'

'Where are they?'

He'd never admit it but he was checking.

'Howth.'

'Northside,' he said.

I laughed. 'Oh come on.'

'What?' he asked.

'Howth's hardly Northside.'

'Howth is on the Northside. I'm not implying anything, sorry, don't get me wrong. I was just saying.'

'I know what you were saying,' I said.

'I wasn't saying anything,' he said and he started laughing. 'Come out on Sunday and bring the female friend if she's free. I'll have a look at her.'

He was winding me up. I had to do it.

She was totally cool when we were driving out. I could hardly speak when we had met her parents in a hotel out near where they lived a couple of weeks before, trying to smile and unable to think of anything to say. I could talk fifty grand out of a complete stranger's pocket in a one-hour meeting and I couldn't tell my girlfriend's mother whether I wanted tea or coffee. When her dad asked me what I did in my free time I thought, You mean apart from sleeping with your daughter? and then couldn't think of anything else so I said I read a bit.

'Everybody reads,' he said. 'Everybody says reading when they're asked for a hobby. It's ridiculous.' That was the end of that conversation.

'You're very quiet,' she said when we were getting near the house.

'I'm OK,' I said. 'Just don't ... listen to these guys. They're wankers.'

'Who?'

'My brothers.'

'They can't be that bad.'

'They're fine. They'll be perfectly OK to you but they're wankers.'

Brian's wife Rebecca opened the door. It was better that she was there. We went into the living-room and did the introductions. Niamh was nice and smiley with everyone. I hugged Dad and nodded at the other two. Shane was laughing already. The conversation was going on, all polite and how was the drive and what a nice day it was, and all the time Shane was sitting there his hand on his chin trying to look serious but his shoulders were shaking. When Niamh was telling my father about the course she was on, I asked him, 'What's funny? What are you laughing at?'

'Nothing,' he said and he looked at Brian. 'He thinks I'm laughing at him.'

'Nothing funny about him. He's in advertising,' Brian said.

'What does that mean?' I asked him.

'Stop it,' Brian's wife said to them. She knew what they were like. Brian shut up, but the two of them sat there giggling like a pair of eight-year-olds. You wouldn't think it, but I was the young one. The two of them were less than a year apart and then there were five years to me. I never understood what was going on with them. They laughed at everything I said when I was a kid. They spoke in this code that I could never crack. It was like everything was an incredibly complicated joke and it was always, always on me. It was better when I got older, when I could have a normal conversation with either of them on their own. But the two together were always the same.

We sat at the table and it was all going fine. My father and Niamh sat beside each other. I sat beside her on the other side in case she needed me but she didn't. Brian asked her how she'd met me.

'Friend of a friend,' she said.

'And the rumours didn't put you off?'

She just laughed. 'A bit. It was more a sympathy sort of thing.'

I looked at her.

'How long was it before he told you how much he makes in a week?' Shane asked.

'What the fuck?' I asked. 'Jesus, can we stop this.'

'It was his opening line,' she said, ignoring me.

'Wow,' Brian said. 'He's been using that for years. It didn't work so well when he was a hamburger cook but he's stuck with it.'

'And it's paid off now,' Shane said.

They were all laughing now. I looked at her.

'Please don't encourage them,' I said. 'Seriously, this could go on for hours.'

'I'm enjoying it,' she said.

'I like this one, Rory,' Brian said. 'Much better than that last one with the big hands and the frog in her throat.'

'I'm going to go and bury myself in the garden. Let me know when you're finished,' I said and I went out and had a fag.

I had to take it. I didn't really mind because she was getting on so well with all of them. When I was in the kitchen making coffee my father came in with plates.

'Nice girl,' he said. 'Very nice.' I didn't need him to say it but I was glad he did.

We left after six. The two brothers made a big show of hugging me.

'I love you, man,' Shane said.

'I love you too, man,' Brian said.

'You're both wankers,' I said. 'I told her before we came out.'

'Niamh doesn't think that,' one of them said.

'I don't,' she said. 'I love you guys,' and then they all hugged. It was ridiculous.

'That was fun,' she said when we were driving home.

'I'm really glad you had a good time,' I said. 'You were great. My father liked you a lot and you seemed to be enjoying yourself.'

'I was. At your expense, of course, but yeah I absolutely was.'

'I wasn't.'

'They're only messing around.'

'It never stops. Never. They just go on and on.'

'But it is really funny,' she said.

'Why? Why is it funny? I don't get it. I have a sense of humour but it just goes over my head.'

'That's why it's funny. You know, normally you're Mister Cool and chilled out and with these guys you're completely different.'

'They just really wind me up.'

'I know. It's great.'

'Why is it great?'

She put her hand on the back of my neck.

'Because it proves you're human. You're not always so bloody casual.'

I didn't know what to say. I was just glad she'd got on with them. It was a relief.

'Thanks for doing it anyway,' I said.

'It was fun.'

We drove on for a while. When she reached forward to turn on the radio I spoke.

'I can be very passionate, you know. Very emotional.'

She just laughed and I saw it was better as a joke so I laughed as well.

We were in a bar, loads of us on a Friday night. Just getting going and I was talking to Anto, some old shite, and he started staring at me. I stopped.

'What? What are you looking at?'

'You're different.'

'What?'

'I don't know.'

'My hair. Have I got fat? What?'

'No. You're different since Niamh moved in. You're more settled into yourself. I don't know. You're very lucky.'

'Am I?'

'Yeah. You're only back six months and you've got it all.'

'What are you talking about?'

'You've got it all. You have everything.'

'Jesus, I don't think so. Not yet.'

I looked different because I had what he wanted. He was such an idiot.

I was going into a new place on Wicklow Street on a Thursday night and a girl walked up alongside me on the street. I smiled and waited for her to ask for directions or a light and she asked did I have forty pence for a cup of tea. Nice looking, dressed OK, not on heroin or drunk, just jaded and bored. What was her problem? She could have worked anywhere, there were fifty places hiring within two hundred yards. What happened? Why could she not work? Bored. Lazy. Lost. Couldn't be arsed. These people from huge estates on the west side, areas you'd never have heard of, came into town like a different breed, tracksuits, jaws hanging loose, sloping along smoking, spitting, eating crisps and chocolate, empty bags in their wake.

I met Phil and Ciaran. I asked them about Anto's girlfriend.

'Have you met her? Have you seen her?'

'Who?' said Phil.

'Anto's girlfriend.'

'No,' said Ciaran.

'Who?' Phil asked again.

'What's she like?'

'Who? For fuck's sake. Who?'

'Anto's new girlfriend. Jesus Christ.'

'What? Not good?' Ciaran asked.

'No. No, very good,' I replied. 'Surprisingly.'

'Oh, come on,' said Phil. He was always kinder than us about people. I think he worried about what we said behind his back.

'Ah, now in fairness, Phil, you have to say, he's been fishing the shallow end of the pool for a while. The fat girl's friend,' I said.

'Doctor Dolittle,' said Ciaran.

Phil winced. 'Well, apparently not any more,' he said.

I changed the subject.

'He was telling me the other day that I've got it all.'

'You have got it all,' said Ciaran.

'All he wants maybe. Girl, money, my own place. I think that's what he's talking about.'

'I think he fancies your chick.'

'Well, maybe we could swap for a while.'

'He might go for that.'

'Hey, he's welcome to her. He can pay the bills. Save me some money. The last thing. I couldn't believe it, and I've got used to it. Seriously. I know what she's like, but two grand on a fridge. A fridge.'

'What does it do?' Phil asked.

'I don't know. Keeps things cold. Whatever. It's enormous. You could fit a pig in it.'

'Two grand.'

'Two grand. We don't even cook. It's got a bottle of wine and some coffee in it. I think she's going to fill it with a whole load of stuff just for appearance.'

'Accessorizing at Tesco.'

'Marks and Spencer. Please. For fuck's sake. Tesco.'

'So what's she like?' Phil asked.

'Who?'

'Anto's girlfriend.'

'I told you. She's fine.'

'No, but what's she like? Is she nice?'

'Nice. I don't know. Maybe. She seems to like him.'

'Who cares? Nice, for fuck's sake, Phil. Who wants a nice girl?'

'Yeah, cop onto yourself.'

We had to knock him around a bit to show him we were joking.

The two guys started talking about work and I was looking around. At a table in the corner two girls were sitting beside each other talking, their faces inches apart. One smiled and then the other smiled back but then I saw that it was wrong, all wrong, and one girl grabbed the other by the hair. They were both still smiling. The girl whose hair was being pulled swatted at the other girl's face and found her head pulled lower and then picked up her glass and I said, 'Fuck me, look at this,' and the two guys stopped and looked over and throughout the room the conversation dried up but the music kept thumping and she slashed at the other girl who let go as a line of red opened along her arm. She threw a punch as the other pulled back to cut her again. A bouncer grabbed her arm and twisted it back until she dropped the glass and another guy grabbed the other girl who was still trying to get at her.

'What happened?' Phil asked me.

'I don't know. I looked over and they just started fighting and then the dark-haired one picked up the glass. When did girls start fighting with glasses?' I asked.

'Twenty years ago in some places,' said Ciaran. 'Family tradition.'

'When the bouncer won't let you bring in your slashhook.'

'Scumbags.'

'Yeah, but they don't look like scumbags,' said Phil.

'It's getting harder to tell,' I said. 'I swear to God, on my way in tonight a girl stopped me. I thought she was looking for directions and she asked me for money for a cup of tea.'

'A cup of tea?'

'Yeah, jack it into me vein. I'm strung out, bud. Know what I mean,' Ciaran said.

'No. She wasn't a junkie, she didn't even look poor, she was just begging.'

'Why? Why would anyone do that?' Phil asked.

'I don't know,' I said.

Ciaran spoke up. 'There's too much money around when you can't tell the difference between beggars and the rest of us.' I nodded as if I understood.

Patrick rang me to say he had some Italian guy he'd known when he was in college in Holland over for the week. He'd been with him for two days and they were running out of conversation.

'It's like having an exchange student or something. I don't know what he wants. We've been to the theatre and we've seen all the sights which took about ten minutes and it's all grand and that but he just smiles all the time. It was different when we were in college. There was loads of us. I don't think I ever spent more than five minutes talking to him.'

'At least he's smiling.'

'It's starting to freak me out. I've got him for the week.'

'Take him to Glendalough.'

'I took him today. It was raining. We ran around the lake and then went and had two pints and the locals were staring at us because he was wearing red trousers so we got the bus back. He's a nice guy, you know, but I don't know what to do.'

'Book somewhere and the four of us can eat and then have a drink. I'll book it.'

'I don't know what he eats.'

'Why? Is he vegetarian or something?'

'I don't know. He's just weird.'

'Well, he must eat.'

'Probably. I don't know. OK.'

'What's his name?'

'Andrea.'

'His name is Andrea?'

'I told you. He's Italian. It's just weird.'

I rang him later and told him where and when. Niamh laughed when I told her about it.

'How old is Patrick again?'

'The same as me.'

'What's his problem? Why is this is so hard for him? Why does he need us to bail him out?'

'I don't know. Wait and meet this guy. Maybe he is a bit strange.'

Andrea was lovely. A nice smiley guy. He ate the same thing as the rest of us and was happy with everything. Himself and Niamh and myself got yapping about Italy and his work and his family and how he'd wanted to come here because he heard it was great fun.

'And then this fucker brings you to Glendalough for the day. In the rain,' I said. 'That must have been a barrel of laughs.'

'Bit of culture,' Patrick said. 'That church thing is really old.'

'It was very nice,' Andrea said.

We went to a pub afterwards. I bought a round. It was a Tuesday so it wasn't busy. He was looking around.

'This is a new place,' I said. 'It's not really typical.'

'We were in an old place last night,' he said.

'Which?' I asked.

'The International,' Patrick said.

'Did you like it?' I asked Andrea.

'Yeah. Very nice. Lots of Spanish girls.'

'Well, that's good,' I said. 'Traditional.'

He went to the toilet. Myself and Niamh both lit into Patrick.

'What are you like?' she said.

'What?'

'He's lovely. He's a really nice guy.'

'I know. I didn't say he wasn't.'

'You told me he was weird,' I said.

'No I didn't,' he said. 'I was getting a bit hassled having to entertain him.'

'You were getting hassled because you had to do something,' I said. 'You couldn't just lie around in your jocks all day eating biscuits getting stoned.'

'Good old Patrick,' Niamh said, rubbing his head. 'The world's best tour guide. "And here is the fridge."'

'You can have him tomorrow if you like him so much.'

'I just might,' she said and looked at me. 'Show him some sights.'

'Calm down,' I said. 'His mother wouldn't like you.'

When he came back he bought a round.

'Thank you, Patrick,' he said, lifting his glass. 'Thank you for inviting me here.'

'You are welcome,' Patrick said. 'Did I really invite you?' he asked after a second and Andrea laughed.

'What do people do here for fun?' he asked later on.

'Well, if you're these guys, this is what you do,' Niamh said. He looked confused. 'Other people play sports or go for walks or to the theatre, loads of different things, but these guys sit around in places like this and drink for days on end.'

'That's not all we do,' I said.

'Name two other things you do every week,' she said quickly. I looked at Patrick and he looked back and shrugged. Andrea burst out laughing.

'You've made a good point,' he said to her.

'No, hang on,' I said. 'That makes it sound shit. It's not about drinking. It's about talking and meeting people and socializing. It just happens that social life in Dublin revolves around pubs but it's not about alcohol.'

'So why don't you meet in cafés?' she asked.

'How many coffees can you drink?' Patrick said. 'More than three and I'd be going up the walls.'

'You don't have to have coffee,' she said.

'You can have tea. Or ice-cream,' Andrea said.

'Ice-cream?' Patrick said, baffled. 'What?'

'I think there is something culturally distinctive about it,' I said. 'Irish people tend to keep their homes private, not like in Italy, so pubs are the outlet for people to meet and get together and talk. Go into one of the old places with no music on a Saturday night and you have to shout because everybody, everybody, is talking non-stop. It's about talking.'

'I never knew I was expressing my cultural identity so often,' Patrick said. 'I'm so patriotic.'

'So how come you guys get drunk so much?' Niamh asked.

'Because it's fun,' we said in unison.

'Which is where we came in,' she said. 'What you guys do for fun.'

In the taxi on the way home I was slumped against Niamh.

'So are you going to leave me for a sober Italian?' I asked. 'He had very nice hair.'

'Beautiful,' she said. 'You'd want to be careful.'

'I'm OK. It's like the driving test.'

'What?'

'All you have to do is drive properly for ten minutes and you've got your licence for life. It's the same with you. I put the effort in. I've got you now. I don't have to try any more.' I looked up at her to see if she was smiling. She looked profoundly depressed.

'Joke,' I said. 'I know how lucky I am. You know I love you.'

'Don't presume too much,' she said.

'I don't,' I said. I was getting worried. 'Jesus, I don't.'

'Got you,' she said but afterwards I wished I hadn't said it.

\*

We settled in together. I hadn't lived with a girlfriend before and it surprised me how easy it was. There were things she liked and things she tolerated and things that just stopped happening. It didn't bother me. We ate healthily. We went for walks. We didn't go out during the week. At the weekends we met the others for meals and films and sometimes drinks and then went home, back to our own space. Weeks passed. I thought she'd just moved in and then I realized she'd been there three months.

She'd get home before me and more often than not she would have changed by the time I came in. She'd be there flopped on the couch eating carrots ready for bed at eight o'clock. She talked about how tired she was, how college was exhausting. I found that a bit rich, seeing as I'd have just worked a twelve-hour day and was raring to go, but I never said anything.

That Friday I was going to meet up with Anto and his sister in a restaurant at about ten. She'd just got back into town from Berlin after two years and I wanted to see her and for Niamh to meet her because she was one of the old pals. Anto was supposed to ring me during the day to tell me where, but he didn't and then my mobile died on the way home. When I got in I asked Niamh straight away had he rung. She said yeah.

'So what's the story?' I asked her.

'He was talking about going out for dinner at ten o'clock or something.'

'Right.'

'I said no.'

I just looked at her.

'What?' she asked me, looking all innocent.

'Why did you say no?'

'Because I'm knackered, you were out with Ciaran last night and I don't know, I didn't think you'd want to.'

'But I said I would. We would actually.'

'Well, you didn't tell me about this.'

'His sister is home and I thought you could meet her.'

'But you didn't tell me.'

'No, I didn't. I meant to but I didn't.'

She settled back down on the couch.

'Is she home for long?' she asked me.

'For good, I think.'

'Well then. We can meet her again.'

I thought about it for a second. I was still standing in the doorway, my bag on my shoulder.

'I should go,' I said.

'Don't go,' she said looking up with a wounded look on her face. She was joking but there was something there. 'Stay.'

So I did.

I didn't have the balls to ring Anto and listen to him go on about how she'd broken me and all that crap, so I left my mobile off and had a shower. We spent the evening watching telly. She lay on the couch her head resting on my lap. Sitting together, feeling her breathing beside me, listening to her laugh, another human being so completely comfortable with me that she seemed oblivious to my presence. I sat there and I told myself over and over, This is very nice, but all I could think was, I'm kind of bored. I had it all and I was bored.

It was immaturity. It was an inability to relate properly to her. It was a misunderstanding of what life was about. That was what I heard, what the others said. To find this life wanting meant that you were wanting, that you were too stupid to appreciate what mattered. It was time to settle down, to shift focus from what was out there, to what was in here, within these walls. I'd had my fun and now it was time for the next stage.

But to look at the others who were at that stage was not inspiring. All these guys who looked like they'd given up. They talked about their girlfriends and wives with a jokey fear and respect that seemed to conceal a genuine capitulation. The women, all charm with everybody else, would snap at them with a cold discipline, and the men could either take it or start a row. Get Rory an ashtray. Don't put that glass on that table. Did you walk that mud in here? What in God's name are you talking about?

# THE VERY MAN

Conversation about houses, decoration, cars, kids. That was what I saw. We had it all and this was how we aspired to live. This was what Niamh wanted, what I thought I wanted. But now that it was there in front of me, I knew I wasn't finished yet. What could I do? I loved her. I didn't blame her, but there was plenty more to be done. It was not over. I would not surrender. I would do what I wanted and that was my truth.

# 3

Anto rang me at work the next week.

'I'm having a party.'

'When?' I asked.

'Next Friday.'

'What for?'

'Don't know. Nothing. Just a party. After the pub. I think it's going to be fancy dress.'

'You're joking.'

'No.'

'You're having a laugh. Whose idea is this? Whose bone-headed notion?' I knew it wasn't his. He wasn't that much of an idiot.

'Rachel's.'

'Who?'

'Rachel. You've met her. The girl I'm seeing.'

'Oh yeah. Right. And she thinks this is a good idea.'

'It is a good idea.'

'Why?'

'It's fun.'

'I have plenty of fun at parties without having to dress like a pirate. Seriously.'

'Oh, come on.'

'It's just a killer, making the effort and then always two thirds of the people don't bother which means they feel bad and the other third feel like a pack of arseholes. It's a no-win,' I said.

'Well, thank you for your concern but it's going ahead. Tell Niamh and anyone else you want to bring and personally I don't give a shite what you say, you curmudgeon. It's going to be fun.'

'Fun. Fun. Fuck me, what do you know about fun?'

I told Niamh.

'That's a great idea.'

'It's not. It's stupid.'

'Just because you don't like it.'

'It's not that. It just never works.'

'It does if everybody does it.'

'They never do.'

'So make them. Ring up all your little friends and make them dress up. You and Ciaran and Patrick could go as the three musketeers. Or the three little pigs.'

'Or the three little maids from school. In kimonos.'

'Perfect. My little geisha.'

'I'm telling you it's a fucking nightmare.'

I went as Robert Smith.

'Shocker,' she said. 'Who would have seen that coming?'

'What? Why?'

'Well. It's dressing up without dressing up. It's putting on make-up and a suit and messing up your hair. If it backfires you can wash your face and stand with all your friends talking about how stupid it all is.'

'No. No. That's not it. We're not like that. That makes us sound awful.'

'You are awful.'

'No really. I just like the make-up.'

I did. It was all a bit queeny but I liked it. I wore an old suit. I looked ridiculous. She said I looked great. She would. We arrived late because she couldn't get her hair to stay up. It was packed and the place was jumping. Everybody looked stupid. It was liberating. I met Anto. He hugged me.

'What did I tell you?' he said, beaming.

'OK. *Mea culpa.*'

'I told you.'

'You did. You were right. I was wrong,' I said.

'I was right and much more importantly you were wrong.'

47

'Yeah, OK, don't milk it.'

'You've met Rachel,' and he pulled her over to meet me.

She was done up like Cleopatra with a wig and a robe thing. It wasn't bad. She looked well. I kissed her on the cheek and left a mark.

'Wow. I don't think I've done that before,' I said. She looked at me confused. 'I've got lipstick on your face.'

I wiped it off with a finger and smudged it. She reached up and our hands touched and we both laughed. She blushed and looked up at me and I knew she fancied me. She wanted me. It was just there. Anto didn't see it, too hyper and happy with the party.

'I'll see you later,' I said and went off. I looked back a second later and she was watching me go. I shook my head and laughed.

It was a good party. A great party. I stood around yapping with all the pals and then danced a bit, myself and Niamh getting it on on the dance floor. She was in good form.

'See what you can do when you let yourself go,' she said.

'I'm holding myself together. You don't want to see me letting it go.'

At the end of the night I was sitting in the living-room, only a few people left, Niamh was somewhere around, Anto had crashed. I was talking with Patrick who was getting all upset and confused, talking shite, and I was saying yeah or no or whatever. All I was doing was looking at Rachel. She was talking to some friend of hers and we were just staring across the room at each other. Niamh came in and said the taxi had arrived. I stood up and walked to the door with her.

'I'm looking after Patrick, he's a bit down,' I said.

'He's just pissed. He's just drunk and morose,' she said.

'Yeah, well I think it helps him to talk to someone.'

'Talk to someone? What are you, his counsellor? Come on, let's go. He'll wake up in the morning and hold his head when he remembers whatever he's said. If he remembers.'

'Maybe. But anyway. What's the harm? I'll follow you later.'

She was pissed off.

'Since when did you give a shit about Patrick's feelings? He's just drunk, for Christ's sake. He's always drunk. Why do I have to get a taxi on my own because of him?'

'It's not because of him . . .'

'Are you coming with me or not?'

I just turned around and went back inside. I heard her slam the door. I tried to convince myself that I'd been telling her the truth. That Patrick and I were going to have some great bonding moment, but I knew why I'd stayed. I tried to stop myself but I couldn't help feeling the thrill of it. Inside Patrick was asleep and Rachel was laughing.

Anto would never do the same to me but that was hardly the point. Different people, different rules. I didn't even mean to. But I was drunk and she definitely was into it, so why not? We went into an empty bedroom. I'd never seen anyone get out of their clothes quicker. I don't know, was it a Robert Smith thing? I closed the door and turned around and there she was. I laughed and then she started taking off my clothes and within minutes we were at it. She was so up for it. I was half-drunk, but she kept it going. She was in charge.

'What's Anto going to say about this?' she said in the middle of it and I just stopped.

'He's not going to know, is he?'

She laughed. I kept going but I had to keep my head in the right place. As soon as we finished we both got dressed and left the house. We walked down the road and stopped a cab. She was going north.

'Well, that was fun,' I said.

'We should do it again sometime,' she replied.

'I don't know. Maybe it's a bit dodgy,' I said smiling.

'Maybe.'

'I don't know. I'll see you around anyway.' It was totally inappropriate but for some reason I shook her hand. She got in the cab and left.

I went home and slept on the couch. When I woke up it took a minute to remember how I'd got there and then it came and it was bad. In six hours it had gone from being a bit of stupid fun to being sordid and cheap. I thought of how happy Anto was when we arrived, how much fun it was dancing with Niamh. I couldn't remember why I'd done it. I couldn't even imagine. Turned on and drunk? I went into the bedroom to wake Niamh. I sat on the bed and she turned over.

'I'm so sorry. I'm sorry. I shouldn't have let you go on your own,' I said.

'What time is it?' she asked, still asleep.

'Nine.'

'It's Saturday. Let me sleep.'

'I'm just sorry.'

'It's OK. Just stop talking. Sleep. I need sleep.'

I got in beside her.

I couldn't undo it. I could have told her about what had happened and hope that she might forgive me. I could try and explain that I was just too drunk and that I would never do it again. But I couldn't undo it and that was the only thing that would have been enough. I loved Niamh. Anto was a friend that I would do anything for and in one stupid night, with one stupid drunken fuck-up, I'd jeopardized my relationship with both of them. Neither of them would ever forgive me. It was all my fault. It was my mistake but there was too much to lose.

There is a way that some things once done, finished, need not ever have happened. They belong to the past and that was something plastic that I could remould and reshape in a way that made as much sense, was just as believable, just as real as anything. I made my decisions as a mature adult and I had to deal with the results in a way that caused as little pain to those involved. I knew it was a cop-out but it was also the right thing to do, so that's what I did.

That day she went into town in the morning to meet Léan and Aoife to get her hair cut. I was in bed and I called her into the room before she left.

'What's on tonight?' I asked her.

'Nothing. I haven't planned anything.'

'Me neither. Keep it free. Let's stay in.'

She looked at me half-surprised, half-amused.

'You want to stay in on a Saturday. What's up? Feeling your age?'

'Just don't make plans.'

She left. I lay there, my head aching with tiredness, my body feeling the excess of the previous night. I thought of Rachel and how easy it had been, how clear and clean. I felt a thrill pass through me that I could still do it. I still had it. I lay there and thought of her, her body, nothing special but charged by its availability and the fact that she wasn't Niamh, and as soon as I thought of Niamh, it changed into something else. I went back to sleep.

I woke in the afternoon and went into town. I bought food and wine and was heading back when Patrick rang me. I met him in a café. He looked rough, eyes red and hands shaking as he drank Coke.

'What happened to me last night?' he asked me.

'You were hammered. That's all. Why?'

'Was I talking to you at the end?'

'You were, yeah.'

'Was I making any sense?'

I laughed. 'Not that I remember, no.'

He held his head in his hands.

'Jesus. Sorry. What happened to you?'

I weighed it up for a second and then just went for it.

'Well. It was terrible. You know Anto's girlfriend?'

'Rachel. Yeah.'

'We. We ended up . . .'

'What?'

'Well, when I arrived I just got this look from her, and then at the end it was just me and her . . .'

'And?'

'And Anto wasn't around so . . .' And I looked at him.

'No!'

'Yeah.'

'No! Are you mad? Have you lost . . . ? What the fuck? You're joking?'

He seemed angry. Not what I'd expected at all. I didn't pause for a second, not an instant to let the thought grow in his head. I burst out laughing.

'Of course I'm joking.'

'You didn't?'

'No, you idiot.'

'Christ, my heart. I'm not up to that kind of thing today. Fuck me. Could you imagine?'

'I just did.'

'You're sick. Is that some sort of bizarre fantasy thing, screwing your friend's girlfriend?'

'What? You've never had that one?'

'Stop it, for Christ's sake. I can't handle it.'

I started again.

'So anyway. What actually happened was I got a taxi home at about four, leaving you asleep and dribbling on the couch and not having gone anywhere near Anto's girl.'

'He would kill you. You know that.'

'No, he wouldn't. I'm his best friend.' I laughed before he had a chance to say anything else. I was such an idiot. It was true. I was Anto's best friend.

When I got back to the house, I started getting a meal ready. She came in at about six.

'This place smells great.'

'Look at you.' Her hair was cut short. It was nice.

'I hate it,' she said shaking her head.

'You look great. It's lovely, really.'

She looked around.

'What's all this in aid of?'

'What?'

'You've tidied up. Made dinner. What's going on?'

'Nothing. I just thought we could stay in for a change.'

'Wow. And on a Saturday night. Well, great. I don't know what you've done but it sounds good to me. I'm going to have a bath.'

'This'll be ready when you finish.'

When she came in I poured out wine and sat with her and let her talk. She talked about her haircut, that the stylist that normally did it who she'd actually booked two weeks ago was on holiday and that they'd told her that one of the other stylists would do it for fifteen quid less and she'd said it wasn't about the money but had gone ahead with it anyway and it wasn't as good as Jeanette would have done but it was OK. I was trying to think if I'd ever told her about the old lad who'd been doing my hair since I was about ten and then I copped on and told her that of course her hair wasn't OK, that it was lovely. I got up and served the food. We were in the middle of eating when she said, 'I know why you're doing this.'

'Why?'

'Because of last night.'

I kept it cool and just said, 'Because I let you go home alone.'

'Yeah.'

'Yeah. I know.' I took her hand.

'I'm sorry. I was just having a good time, you know, I was pissed and I didn't want the night to be over.'

'But there were only about five people left and the only person you knew was nearly passed out.'

'I know, it was stupid. I won't leave you like that again.'

'I felt so alone leaving there. I mean, why would you stay? Why wouldn't you come with me?' Her voice was cracking, the effects of two glasses of wine pushing her close to tears.

'I'm sorry. Never again. OK?' She nodded. 'I love you so much. I can't bear for you to be sad. I won't do anything to hurt you or upset you. OK? I promise you,' I told her.

She hugged me and right then it became real. It was true. I felt it. I was very much in love. The past was gone and in the future everything would be OK.

# 4

A couple of weeks later I went out with Patrick on a Sunday night. There was something conspiratorial about drinking on a Sunday. You could feel it in the pub, see it in the faces of those around you, all shaking from a heavy weekend, or heading off the inevitable gloom of a Monday morning with drink. We were among our own. Patrick and I only ever had one conversation, which we picked up every time we saw each other and it didn't go anywhere or do anything, it just wandered in wide slow circles as we laughed ourselves into a stupor. I should have gone home at eleven but he bought another two and then it was my round, so we had to go to Renard's to get it and once we were there it seemed a crime to leave while they were still serving.

After that we went back to his place and listened to fucking Christy Moore and drank whiskey. I remember setting the alarm on my phone for seven, so that I could go home and shower and get a suit and still get into work for half-nine, which wouldn't be too bad and then the next thing was Patrick was giving me a cup of tea and it was bright outside. He sat beside me and lit a cigarette.

'Shouldn't you be in work?' he asked.

'What time is it?'

'Ten.'

'No. Fuck no.'

'Are you late?'

'Of course I'm late. I should have been in an hour ago. What happened to my alarm? I never heard it.'

'You must have turned it off. Or did I? I can't remember.'

'Bollocks. What size shirt are you?'

'I don't know. Thirty-two?'

'You're not thirty-two, Patrick. Nobody's thirty-two. Fuck it, I don't have time.'

I had a shower and put on his shirt. I couldn't close the top button and I had to roll up the sleeves but it would do. I left and got a taxi straight away. I turned on my phone and rang the office. I got put through to Anne.

'I'm on my way. I was up all night puking. Food poisoning, I think. What's the story there?'

'Did you get my messages?'

'No, I've just put my phone on.'

'Where are you?'

'Mount Street. I'll be there in five minutes. Why?'

'The people from FitzPatrick's are here, they're waiting for you to pitch. Your meeting was supposed to start at ten.'

'That's on Wednesday.'

'No, it's today. Do you remember? I told you last week that they were rearranging for today.'

I could feel the panic spread through me.

'No, I don't remember. It's not in my diary.'

'Rory, I told you and you said you'd remember.' She used my name like I was six years old. 'You said you'd write it in.'

'Anne. I don't remember this conversation at all. Look, tell them I'll be there in a couple of minutes, we'll sort it out then.'

'I definitely told you, Rory—'

I hung up. I remembered all right. She had told me. They had rung to reschedule, and I'd forgotten to write it in. If I wasn't already late I could have admitted it and it wouldn't have been a big deal, but now it looked too bad. It was easier to play dumb until it all died down. All I could do was brazen it out. The taxi driver spoke.

'I'll tell you one thing.'

'What? What?'

'You don't smell like a fellow has food poisoning. I'm half-jarred with the fumes off you. You'd want to sort yourself out before you go anywhere near an office.'

I got him to leave me at Spar and bought Polos. Anne was waiting for me when I went into the office.

'Who's in there?' I asked her.

'A guy and a girl, Tom Lyons and Angela something. Are you eating mints?'

'Rennies. We're going to have to rearrange. This is a mess.'

'Well, it's not my fault.' She was almost shouting.

'Don't worry about it. It doesn't matter. I'm going to sort this out and we'll talk about it later.'

I went in. They were pretty frosty at first, but I worked them with apologies and talked about a breakdown in communication. I got the impression that they hadn't been involved in changing the original plans, so they couldn't be entirely sure that the fault was at our end. I said I'd be over to them the following morning to present, that I would be ready then, apologized a bit more and sent them off. When they had gone I was walking back to my office and Anne called me over.

'Gerry wants to see you.'

I went into him. I tried to take control.

'Gerry.'

'What happened this morning, Rory?'

'OK. I was up sick all night. I was going to ring this morning but my alarm didn't go off. I woke late, was on my way in and then Anne starts telling me I'm half an hour late for a meeting that I thought was on Wednesday.'

'It was rearranged for this morning.'

'Apparently so.'

'So why weren't you here?'

I couldn't see any way around it. I didn't want to land her in it, but he was standing there in front of me and it was my fucking job on the line. Rap on the knuckles for her, dole queue for me. What could I do?

'I wasn't told.'

'But Anne says she told you last week.'

'She didn't. It's not in my diary.'

He picked up the phone and called her in. I could feel the blood pulsing in my head. She came in. Gerry spoke to her.

'Anne, Rory says he didn't know about the rescheduling of this morning's meeting.'

'Well, I told him.'

'When?'

'Thursday. Thursday last week.'

'I don't want to mess you around,' I said. 'I'm not saying you didn't mean to tell me, I'm not even saying that you don't think that you told me, I'm just saying you didn't actually tell me.'

'Rory, this is my job. This is what I do. I told you and you said OK, that you'd write it into the diary.'

'Did anyone else hear you tell me?' I asked her. It was a cheap shot. I knew she'd have already mentioned it if they had.

'No,' she said.

'Anne, will you leave us,' Gerry said. She walked out, her face red.

'Gerry, I'm telling you. I think she's wrong on this one.'

'I don't really care, Rory. The fact is that that meeting was fucked-up and it looks shit.'

'OK, well I've rescheduled for tomorrow,' I said. 'I'm going over there to pitch and I'll get the contract. That's all there is to it.'

'Yeah, well I'd advise you to wear a shirt that fits and have a shave before it. You look like shit. Whatever about whether Anne told you or not, you were late today and that's where this whole problem started. It's not good, Rory.'

'Gerry, I've been here nearly six months, I've never missed a day, I've been late about twice. I was sick. Genuinely.' I sounded pathetic.

'Just sort yourself out with Anne and don't fuck the meeting up tomorrow. We need that account.'

'I won't. I won't.'

I left and went over to Anne's desk. She didn't look up when I spoke.

'I'm sorry, Anne, but I have no recollection whatsoever of you telling me about this. Honestly.'

She didn't speak.

'I think you could at least admit the possibility that you made a mistake,' I said. She lifted her face and I could see that she was livid.

'No, Rory. I don't admit that possibility. I don't believe that you don't remember the conversation and I'm quite sure that you're covering your ass at my expense. That's what I think is going on and I'm not happy about it. Not one bit.'

It was hard to know what to say, but then I thought for a second. If what I was saying were true then I would have been scandalized by what she'd said. Up on her bloody high horse. I let her have it.

'Jesus Christ, Anne, I was trying to give you a bit of slack here, let you back out and allow neither of us to lose too much face, but obviously you want to escalate things. When I get back from meeting FitzPatrick's tomorrow, I suggest we go in to Gerry and discuss it. I'm not sure I can work with someone who makes these kind of accusations to my face.'

'Fine.'

'OK.'

I was shaking when I went back into my office. If anyone else had heard her talk like that to me, I would have lost it. I didn't know what she was playing at. The reality of the situation was that if I came back the following day from FitzPatrick's with a contract worth fifty grand, Gerry wasn't going to give a damn about the accusations of a surly bloody secretary. I just had to be sure to get it. I could make it up to her after.

I got working on the package for the meeting. I spoke to Frank in creative and got him moving on it. I skipped lunch and by the middle of the afternoon I was on top of it. There was a whiskey sweat on the back of my neck, but I felt great. All the adrenalin had cleared me of any hangover. At four o'clock Anne put a call through from Niamh.

'So where were you?' she started, pissed off.

'I'm sorry. I meant to ring. It's been mad today, just mad.'

'Last night. Where were you last night?'

'I was sick.'

'Sick where? What are you talking about?'

'I was with Patrick and I was sick, so I stayed in his place.'

'Were you drunk?'

'No, I only had about three pints and we were in his house watching a video and I started feeling shit so I just stayed there and at that stage it was too late to ring.'

She was silent.

'Look, I'll talk to you later. It's not a great time just now. I'm busy. I'll be home at seven and I'll talk to you then, OK?'

She still didn't say anything.

'OK?'

'OK.'

I left my office and walked out by Anne's desk to check if she'd been listening. She was in the middle of a call. I went to the water-fountain, had a drink and went back in. Anne came in at half-five and told me she was leaving. I said nothing.

I got home at eight. Niamh turned off the telly when I came in. I went over to kiss her. She turned her face away.

'So what happened?'

I sat beside her.

'Well, I was out with Patrick for a drink last night, as you know.'

'Yes, I know. And?'

'And we got a bit hammered and I crashed on his couch. I meant to ring, but it just got too late.'

'So what was all that stuff about getting sick? I didn't know what you were on about.'

I smiled.

'It's a bit involved. I was late for work and I missed a meeting which Anne, the secretary, told me about but which I forgot. I told them I was sick and that's why I was late and that Anne hadn't told me about the meeting, and I think I pulled it off. But when you rang she put the call through and I had to tell you that I'd been sick in case she was listening. But she wasn't. So it didn't matter.'

She looked confused.

'She said she told you about the meeting and you said she hadn't.'

'Yeah.'

'But she had.'

'Yeah.'

She shook her head.

'Why did you do that?'

'Because I had to. I would have been in shit if I hadn't.'

'Did you say this directly to her or what?'

'Yeah. Well. And to Gerry.'

'Jesus, Rory.'

'I had to. It's not like I had an option. It was her fuck-up or mine and it wasn't going to be mine.'

'But it was yours. I mean, it's no fun having to take responsibility but it was your mistake.'

I was getting pissed off with her now.

'It was a small mistake that would have been blown out of proportion. So a secretary forgets something. Big deal. But if it's me, if it's my mistake then my job's on the line. She can afford to have this one go against her. I can't.'

'I don't think it's fair.'

'I know it's not fair but what can I do? Go in tomorrow, sort it all out and collect my P45?'

'You're being stupid. I just don't think it's right.'

'Yeah, but you don't know what my work is like, what I have to put up with. There have been literally ten times where Anne has screwed up, small things, but fuck-ups nonetheless and I've never ratted her out. I've covered for her. I don't see why just this one time she can't take the blame.' She was looking at me with an expression that I couldn't identify. 'What? What's that look?'

She shook her head.

'That's just wrong. I don't know what's up with you, how you can think like that?'

'It's the real world. It's what it's like when you work in this industry, any business. It's you or the next guy and if you're not up to it then you shouldn't be there.'

'Well, I don't ever want to work in that kind of atmosphere. It's horrible.'

'I know but it's what I do. I have to look out for myself.' She walked out. 'Niamh?' I called after her. 'It's not my fault.'

She stayed away from me for the rest of the night. I was up until one working on my presentation. She was asleep when I went to bed.

We walked into the FitzPatrick's building five minutes early. The secretary showed us to the meeting room and brought in coffee. By the time Lyons and Angela arrived I was in charge, welcoming them to a presentation in their own building. It was a dream. Frank was inspired. We could have sold them anything. I'd worn a new suit. I joked with them. I even got them involved, like they were children in a kindergarten. I was not the person they had met the previous day. I went through the whole presentation but by the end it was a formality.

Handshakes all round, backslaps and big laughs. Fifty grand in the next twelve months. Not bad for two hours' work. Frank and I had a coffee standing at the counter in a place on Leeson Street, clinking our cups in celebration like a pair of arseholes.

'To the brains,' I said to him.

'To the mouthpiece,' he said.

'Without whom you'd be in a fucking garret somewhere eating candles,' I said.

'Fair enough, yeah,' he said. 'It's your deal.'

'It's our deal.'

'Well, whatever. Gerry's going to be eating out of your hand. He needed this one. I believe he's been having a rough time of it with the bosses.'

'I wouldn't know.'

'That's the word.'

I shrugged.

'I don't get to hear the word. I'm surprised you guys do. I would have thought you'd all be floating around the clouds being artistic.'

'All we do is smoke and bitch about everybody.'

'Sounds good.'

He went off to meet someone for lunch and I walked through the Green back to the office. It was my deal. He was right about that. It's not the guy who makes it, it's the guy who gets the signature and that was me. The sunshine had brought out the med students and mothers with kids, lying around on the grass, feeding the ducks, playing on the swings. Normally all I would want would be to stay there among them and lap it up, the sound of kids, the smell of grass, freedom hiding in the middle of town, but I had to get back.

I was practically whistling when I walked in. I went straight over to Anne.

'We slew them. I swear to God. You should have seen them. They were like performing seals. Frank was brilliant. I was inspired, not to blow my own trumpet or anything.' She looked at me stone-faced. 'What?' I asked her.

'Do you want to go in and see Gerry?' she asked.

'Too right I do. Have a little talk about me and my bonus.'

'No, I mean about yesterday,' she said.

'Oh. Oh yeah. I don't know, Anne, I mean to be honest, at this stage what's the point? I got the contract, you know, that's what was important and I got it so can we not drop it? I'm sorry, I was just totally wound up yesterday.'

'No. I'd rather we dealt with it.'

I spoke quietly.

'Come on, Anne, what's the point? Life goes on, you know. Gerry will have forgotten about it anyway.'

'Yeah, but I haven't.'

She walked straight into his office without knocking. I stood there for a second like an idiot and then followed her in. She was standing in front of him, saying nothing, just waiting for me. Gerry was sitting there looking confused.

'What's going on, Rory?' he asked me. I was at a loss.

'Anne has a problem,' I said after a second.

'I thought it was you had the problem,' she said. 'That's why we're here, isn't it? You can't work with someone like me calling you a liar.' She'd obviously been storing this up. She was shaking with anger. I put my hands up.

'Can we calm this down a bit? I don't have any problem with you,

Anne. I was a bit pissed off yesterday, but I know you're a great worker, you're great at your job. I'm sorry.'

'I told you about that meeting and you know I did and it's completely unprofessional of you to try and blame me for your mistake.'

Gerry looked at me.

'I thought this was resolved yesterday.'

'Not entirely, no, but at this stage I think it's irrelevant,' I said, talking slowly, keeping my cool.

'It's not irrelevant. It's just not.' She was shouting. I was driving her mad, I could see that.

'Calm down, Anne. What's the problem? What exactly is the problem you have with Rory?'

She took a deep breath before speaking.

'I think he's trying to blame me for the fact that he forgot about yesterday's meeting. I feel I'm being undermined and that he feels that if he makes a mistake, he can just pass it on to someone less important like me.'

'You know we value you very highly,' said Gerry, 'and I want this issue resolved. What would satisfy you, Anne?'

'If he admits it was his mistake.'

'So?' he asked me.

'I can't do that. I mean, I honestly have no recollection of Anne telling me about it, but if she's absolutely certain that she did, then maybe she did. I don't know.'

'Nobody is blaming you for anything,' Gerry said to her, his voice soft and reassuring. 'OK?' She nodded. 'And everything's OK with you, Rory?'

'Absolutely, yeah, no problem.'

Gerry smiled.

'OK. Problem solved.' Anne walked to the door. I stayed put.

'Actually, I wanted to tell you about the meeting with Fitz-Patrick's,' I said to him as she left. He walked over behind her and closed the door.

'Yeah?'

'We got it.'

'You star. You fucking star. How much?'

He was practically jumping up and down. I told him all the details. He lapped it up, the whole spiel. He loved all that cut-and-thrust shit. He loved all that money. By the time I was walking out, he had his arm over my shoulder, talking about getting me out with Niamh on his yacht in Dun Laoghaire at the weekend. Before he opened the door I stopped him.

'By the way, all that stuff with Anne? I've no idea what's going on. I think she's just a bit hassled at the moment.'

He patted me on the back.

'Yeah, well just go easy on her.'

'I know. I know.'

That afternoon I was playing solitaire and Anne walked in. She handed me a piece of paper.

'What's this?' I asked.

'I'm giving you my notice.'

'What? Why? I thought you were OK. I thought you were happy with my apology.'

She smirked.

'It wasn't an apology. I've been thinking about it and I don't think I can continue working with you.'

'Oh come on, Anne. For fuck's sake. Water under the bridge, you know.'

She just shook her head.

'Well, I don't know what's going on, but if you want to go that's your decision. I wish you luck and I'll give you a one hundred per cent positive reference.'

'I'll get my reference from Gerry. And you know exactly what's going on, Rory.'

She went back out. I talked to Gerry that afternoon and he was a bit shocked, but he said there was probably something going on in her life that was upsetting her. He said it was easiest to just let her go.

We went out after work, a whole gang of us to celebrate the new contract. I was keeping as low a profile as I could. I wanted to get out early and try and sort things out with Niamh but Gerry kept on buying round after round and I could hardly leave. He was doing it all for me. I eventually got out around ten and took a taxi home. All the lights were off. I went into the bedroom and could hear her breathing, asleep. I sat beside her and turned on the lamp. She woke and looked up at me. I pushed her hair back.

'Hello.'

She looked at her watch.

'Where were you?' she asked.

'I was out with work. It's not late. I got a big contract today and Gerry insisted on taking me out.'

'Right.'

I couldn't tell if she was being stroppy or if she was just half-asleep.

'I'm sorry about last night. I don't want to argue with you. I hate it,' I said feeling the emotion rise in my throat.

'Me too. I just didn't like that you'd blame someone else for your mistake.'

'I know, I shouldn't have.'

She was awake now.

'It makes me wonder how well I really know you. That's not what I thought you were like,' she said.

'Yeah. Well. Yeah. I don't know . . .'

I always thought that when someone apologized to you, you should either take it or refuse it, never take it and insist on putting them through the wringer again. But I knew I was drunk so I said nothing.

'It's not fair. That's all,' she said.

'I know. It's OK. I know.'

She reached out and held my hand. I buried my face in her neck and lay there holding her. After a minute or two she spoke again.

'So what happened?'

'With what?'

'With the girl.'

'She quit.'

'What?' She pushed me back.

'I mean, I tried to apologize to her and I don't know. She gave notice.'

She sat up in bed.

'That's awful.'

'Yeah well. I don't know what the problem was.'

'Oh for God's sake, Rory. I wasn't there, I don't know the girl, but I know why she quit. Because you made her out to be a liar.'

'I didn't. Not deliberately, it just happened. And I apologized.'

'How? How did you apologize?'

I was too drunk for this.

'Sorry. I said sorry. I mean, what the fuck?'

'Did you tell your boss that you had forgotten the meeting?'

'He wouldn't have cared. I closed a huge deal today and all you're concerned about is a girl that you've never even met who gets all melodramatic over a bit of office politics. Somebody will take her place tomorrow. End of story.'

'All I'm concerned about is you. That's all. You and us.'

'I don't know what the problem is. I could do with a bit of support, you know. "Well done." Something like that. That's all I wanted. Not this.'

I went through to the living-room and fell asleep on the couch. I hoped she'd come through and get me but she didn't and when I woke I had to leave straight away.

# 5

Anto rang me later that week. I hadn't spoken to him since the party. He sounded hassled.

'Can I see you this evening? Are you free?'

'I don't know. I think so. I don't know. Why?'

'I'm serious. I really need to talk to you.'

'OK. Where?'

'I don't know. You decide.'

We met at a sushi bar. I used to eat it all the time in New York. This one had a conveyor belt. There was nobody there. I sat at the counter. He arrived late. I was so nervous. While I was waiting for him I couldn't figure out if I wanted him to know what had happened with me and Rachel or not. At least if he knew about it, I could stop worrying. I wouldn't feel sick every time I thought of him. I could let him beat the guilt out of me. As soon as I saw him I knew he had no idea.

'Sorry. Thanks for meeting me.'

'No problem.' I waited and let him sit. 'Are you hungry?' I asked him.

'No. No. I just want a drink.'

'I love this stuff. I could eat it all day.'

'I just want a beer. How do I get a beer?' he asked.

'Ask a girl. Do you even like sushi?'

'No. I don't know. What are these things?'

'Fish with rice and seaweed. You mix this stuff with soy and use it as a dip. It's great.'

'Jesus. I'll take your word for it. I just want a drink.' He looked around nervously. He seemed edgy. I lifted a plate off the belt.

'You've got to try this. It's salmon caviar. It's fishy but it's great. The Japanese love it. It's one of my favourites. Try.'

'No. I'm not hungry. Can I smoke here?'

'No, you can't.'

'Can we move to a table? Do you mind? I want to smoke and just have a drink. Is that OK with you?' he asked.

'Just give me five minutes. I need to eat and then we can move. Can you give me yellowtail sashimi and sea urchin and smoked eel?' The chef didn't speak, just nodded. I knew what I was about. 'So what's up? What's the problem?' I asked him.

'You know Rachel? The girl I've been seeing.'

As I chewed I could feel my heart beating. I swallowed.

'I've met her. Yeah, you know when we were at that thing in the Russian place.'

'And at my party.'

'That's right.'

'What did you think?'

'Very nice girl, I think, I couldn't say though, Anto. I don't know her. Why?'

He waited a second. His voice was low and shaky when he spoke.

'I don't know what to do. I don't know. She's losing interest and I thought everything was going well.'

'How long have you been seeing her?'

'About six weeks. Two months maybe.'

'And what's changed?' I asked.

'At first she was ringing me every day, trying to arrange to meet up and do things all the time and now she never rings. I have to always call her and she's busy a lot of the time and when we do meet, I don't know, she's not as affectionate.'

'So she's cooled off a bit.' I was trying to be casual.

'Yeah, but why? I mean, when we started going out it felt like we were really getting on, you know. Why would she change?'

'Has she said anything to you? Have you asked her what's going on?'

'Kind of. She says it's nothing, but there's definitely something. I mean, what would it be?'

'I don't know. I'm not sure that I've got anything I can tell you. I don't know her.'

'Yeah, but you're good with girls.'

I laughed.

'I'm no good at understanding them. I'm pissing Niamh off at the moment. Try this. It's the roe of sea urchin. It looks like shit but it tastes amazing.' He looked away.

'I don't know what to do.'

It was awful. I really wanted to help him. I felt responsible. I didn't know if what was going on had anything to do with me, probably not, but I thought that I could make amends by advising him. I tried to be as objective as I could.

'There's nothing to do. Ignore it. If she's being a pain in the arse forget about her and find someone else. Come on, Anto. Just stop agonizing.'

'So you won't help me?'

'I am helping you. I'm trying to. I'm telling you to just move on and stop worrying about it. There's lots of girls.'

'Yeah, but I like this one. Should I not try and sort it out?'

'No. If she's fucking you around like this after two months I don't think it's going to get any better. Oh, I don't know. Do what you like. I just can't stand that hot-and-cold crap.'

'What am I doing wrong?' He was almost in tears. I felt like shit.

'Nothing. Jesus. Cop onto yourself. There's nothing wrong with you. You're fun and kind and you're a nice, good guy but you can't let people walk over you. If there's a problem at all, it's with her, and if she has a problem she should tell you what it is and not leave you coming to the likes of me. It's nothing to do with me. I mean I don't mind, you're a friend, but it's not my business.'

'So what?'

'It's not my place, you know? You have to make your own decisions. Come on. Let's go and have a fag.'

At the end when we were outside and I was going into the car park, he thanked me and touched my arm. In a second I thought I should tell him. Just straight out. Bang. But for what? To make me feel better and him feel worse? There was no point. He didn't deserve to know and I didn't deserve to be forgiven. I'd made my bed. I gave him an awkward kind of hug and patted him on the back. I felt awful, but I knew he'd finish with her. It was for the best. Anto and I could just start again.

When it started to go wrong with Niamh, everything acted like a trigger. I had a shit time in work the next day. When I walked into the flat, she called me and I didn't say anything. She came into the hall. When I saw her I knew I wanted the row to be over, I didn't have the heart for it.

'What's wrong with you?' she asked, but I just turned and walked away. I could feel the wrench in my stomach, but when I thought of the previous night, how happy I'd been coming home a couple of nights before and how she'd spoilt it, how I'd slept on the couch, I thought. Fuck it. She can come to me.

She could have come to me at any stage. She could have said I love you Rory or I'm sorry or anything really and I would have hugged her and that would have been it. We could have just moved on. But she didn't and days began to pass. The longer it went on the more determined I became. The more determined and the more desperate. I felt sure that to do the wrong thing would mean losing too much. She was able to continue as if nothing was wrong. She could smile and say hello and ask did I want a cup of tea. It was as if she was putting on a performance for an invisible audience. Nothing is wrong. Everything is OK here. But it wasn't OK. She had withdrawn and left me on my own. It was horrible to sleep beside someone who wasn't there. To sit beside a ghost watching TV. To look at the person you loved and have them look through you. I couldn't bear it. It felt like she was better at this than I was. I felt outclassed.

After three days I went out to see my father. I hadn't seen him in a month or two and anything was better than going home. I rang to tell him I was coming out.

'What for?' he asked.

'For dinner. To see you. I don't know.'

'I don't have anything to eat,' he said. 'I only eat those frozen yokes, ready meals. That wouldn't be your thing.'

'That's fine. That'll be fine.' I bought pasta and chicken on the way out.

He looked old when he opened the door. The distance of a couple of months showed him to me with starkness, his features faded, his movement slower than it was in my memory.

'I brought food. You haven't eaten yet, have you?' I asked him.

'Ah, don't. I'm grand with my own thing. Don't bother yourself.'

'It's no bother. Come in and talk to me while I cook.' I walked into the kitchen. He called after me.

'I'm watching the news. I'll be in to you after.'

The kitchen was spotless. Cleaner than it had been when Mum was around. It smelt of disinfectant. I looked for signs to see if he had cleaned it because I was coming but it didn't look like it. The fridge was organized. One tub of butter, one packet of rashers, six eggs and a litre of milk. It was sad. He had the oven on and two plastic trays on a baking sheet ready to go in. I put them back in the freezer and started cooking. When it was done, I brought a tray in to him. He was asleep. I woke him and went and brought my own through. I sat in Mum's chair and we ate, watching telly in silence. I made tea after and when I brought it in he turned the volume down.

'So how have you been?' he asked.

'Great. Grand. Yeah. Work's going well. Everything's fine.'

'That's good.'

'And you?' I asked.

'Ah, you know. Very quiet. I'm only going in now for the mornings and to be honest for all the difference it makes, I think even that may be too much.'

'It's good to get out of the house, though. Is it?'

He shrugged.

'I suppose so, yeah.' He looked away for a second. 'How's Niamh?'

'She's fine. She has exams coming up in about six weeks or something but I think she's OK. I think she's on top of it.'

'She's very bright I'd say, is she?'

'Oh yeah. Definitely.'

We sat looking at pictures flicker silently across the screen. I didn't know what to say. I didn't know why I was there. I asked about the brothers and he said they were OK, that he'd seen Brian yesterday. No news. He picked up the remote to turn the sound up and I leant forward and breathed in. He looked at me. I shook my head.

'What?' he asked me.

'I'm not sure if I should ask you.' He shrugged and waited. 'I've had a row with Niamh and I don't know how to put it right. I just don't know. It's doing my head in. I think she was wrong but at this stage I can hardly remember. She's acting like everything is OK but it's not and I want to get back to normal but I don't know what to do.'

He folded his arms and sat back and then sat forward again.

'I'm sorry,' I said. 'It's just getting to me. I shouldn't have said anything. I'm sorry.'

'You're OK, Rory. It's no problem.' He sat looking out the window, his gaze fixed. I didn't know if he was about to speak or if he was waiting for me to say something else, anything else. I waited for a minute or two and was about to start talking when he spoke.

'You just have to keep plugging away, you know? That's all there is. All the crap that life throws at you, you have to take it and deal with it and keep going because that's what we do. It's what we're here for. It never gets any easier, you think it does when you're young, but it doesn't. All the same fears and anxieties and uncertainties and you have to just keep the head down and get through it. It's not great advice but it's all I can give you.'

'No, thank you. Thanks, Dad. I shouldn't have bothered you. It's nothing anyway. I'm sure it's nothing. But thank you.'

He laughed quietly.

'That's all I can tell you,' he said again, and he turned the telly back up.

I didn't really know what he meant, but it was nice sitting there with him. He'd tried to help and I'm sure what he had said could be useful at some stage and the silence between us now was a happy one. I stayed until he began to fall asleep in the chair and then told him I was off. As he stood at the door he called after me.

'Good luck,' he said.

It could have been nothing, just another way of saying goodbye, but I wanted it to be more. It felt like he was telling me to resolve things, to try and put it right, and I drove home determined.

I didn't hang around when I got in. She was still up and I went straight over and stood in front of her.

'I can't stand this any more. We've got to get back to normal. I can't take this war of silence. I'm sorry. I've been stupid. It was stupid of me to start this over nothing and I just want us to be back to normal.'

'What's so great about us when we're normal? Why do you want it to be like normal? We're always arguing about something. Is that what you mean by normal?' She was completely calm. She was ready for this conversation in a way that I wasn't.

'I just want us to get on.'

'What do you think I want?'

'Yeah, I know. I'm sorry. I will try to sort myself out, I know I'm a bit all over the place, but you have to give me a chance. I do love you and I want us to stay together. You've got to bear with me.'

'I've heard this before, Rory. You know?'

'Yeah. Well, judge me on how I am from now on, that's all I'm asking. I can't even remember what we're fighting about, it's ridiculous.'

'About that girl you had fired.'

'I didn't . . .' I stopped myself. 'I think you may have misunderstood or I may have told it wrong or something, but that was nothing. It happens every day. The new girl is part of the furniture already. I didn't do anything wrong, I don't want to start all that again. The problem is that I was stupid to get pissed off about it, but this has gone on too long and I'll do whatever it takes to get back to how we should be. Anything. Is that fair enough?' I was trying as hard as I could.

She sat there looking over my shoulder.

'Yeah. Fair enough, yeah.' Then she looked at me. 'What's wrong with you anyway? You don't seem happy at all. You're on edge the whole time. You're not yourself.'

I didn't know what to say.

'Work pressure. I don't know. I'll be all right.'

'If you don't talk to me I can't help you,' she said.

'I don't need your help,' I said. I only meant that she didn't have to worry but it seemed to piss her off. She went and had a bath and left me there alone in the living-room. I wanted it to be right. I wanted to atone for whatever I'd done. I had tried everything to bring it about, but I felt like I'd laid myself open and she'd walked all over me. I'd done plenty of bad things but nothing had made me feel as bad as I did right then.

It wasn't her fault, what happened next. I wouldn't ever blame her for what I did, but I was confused and upset by what was going on. I didn't know what to do to sort it out. I'd tried my best and it hadn't worked. I couldn't talk to anyone about it or ask advice. The brothers? That's a laugh. I thought about asking Phil but he'd tell Catherine and then she'd tell Niamh and then she'd know and I wouldn't be sure. I began to think that we'd moved in together too quickly. I didn't know her that well. I didn't know she could be so stubborn. I had thought she would begin to warm up again. But she seemed to be taking her time. I gave her the space I felt she needed and she walked through it without even noticing. I would spend the day at work with everybody lining up to kiss my arse, still the big man after the FitzPatrick's thing, and then go home to make polite conversation with a woman who seemed to have forgotten that we were supposed to be in love. Weeks passed with no real change. It's not an excuse but I didn't know what to do. I wasn't sure.

# THE VERY MAN

I went to a pub after work. An awful little shithole that you'd walk by without seeing – too dark and the smell of burnt coffee and smart-arse barmen who would never know what they were, never see themselves without that awful self-aggrandizement that usually belongs to the stupid and powerless. I sat at a table and read the paper. Without the paper I was a young fellow in a suit drinking on a Tuesday. With the paper I was going about my business, purposeful. A man is entitled to a pint with his paper. Even me. The stress and anxiety of the day dissolved as the drink sank in, the warm feeling in my stomach, telling me that it was OK. It would be OK. It would be fun again. The information in the paper took on extra significance, I was reading it, really taking in the information, my relationship with the world, Israel, Ecuador, England, was important.

She arrived with a friend. Students, country girls, not bad but very straight. They stood at the bar, all hair and laughing, looking sideways around the room. I looked down as I felt them look at me and laugh unrelated. Barman throwing shapes – what can I get you lovely ladies? – puke. They had bottles of some sugary concoction for kids, maybe trying to be slick in the city, maybe because this was not a place to pose, maybe because they were kids. She was the taller one, nothing remarkable until you looked at her again and her face had something. Cheekbones and a mouth that was full and smiling. I noticed her. They sat two tables away. I looked at the sport pages and listened. Inane country-girl chat, thrilled at living in town, big nights out in Rathmines, asking after some pal from home who was supposed to be in Dublin. All very young and clean, small hints about fellows in class that they liked but try as they could they were out of their depth. It was too much for them and they were very far from home. Talking about Saturday nights at the Oasis and Francie Leddy and Sean Brady. Another country. They were tourists. I looked over and she saw me. I held it and she continued talking, reddening slightly, becoming self-conscious, touching her hair and quietening her voice. I loved her just then and she knew it.

I didn't know what was going to happen. I didn't know where it would go. I could feel the adrenalin pumping. My hand was shaking when I picked up my glass. All I wanted was for this to be my life, to be the smart-arse messer trying to pick up a girl in a pub. I didn't want all the other stuff, the uncertainty and worry and always trying to do the right thing and always getting it wrong. I'd had enough. I was sick of being the bad guy. I just wanted to have fun. I wanted to know that I could still do it. I put Niamh and the apartment and work and the rest of my life to the back of my mind and tried to forget about them.

I waited. I drank slowly, aware that I would have to have my shit together. I waited hoping they wouldn't leave. When she went to the toilet I moved in on the friend.

'Sorry, I couldn't help overhearing, but where are you from? It's driving me mad. I know that accent.'

'Monaghan. Clones.'

'Clones. OK. Yeah. I've been there. What was it, Ulster Final?'

'Could be.'

'My name is Rory.'

I warmed her up. Stared straight at her, kept it light and easy. When she came back, and I was introduced it was like we were pals.

'Róisín. This is Rory.'

'Róisín. Hi.'

I shook her hand. I looked at her and she knew what was going on. She was scared but she wasn't running.

I spent an hour, working the conversation. I asked about everything, bought the drinks, made them laugh. I didn't push it at first, but I let it go after a while, using her name all the time, staring straight at her whenever she spoke. When her friend said it was time to go, I asked her straight out. Stay. Have another drink. Where do you have to go at this time? She said OK. Her friend left. I made a fuss over her as she was leaving but she knew what was going on.

She was almost drunk, holding it together but barely. I asked about her home, whether she missed it, and she started talking. She loved it in Dublin. It was big and exciting and so much going on and Trinity was like a city in itself and so many people to meet. But every day a

hundred times she thought of her home and her mother and father in
the house always there, always the same, doing the same things at the
same time. It was warm and quiet and it was home. So however good
Dublin was she would always be a bit lonely. You shouldn't be lonely,
I said and I kissed her. She was so young.

We got a taxi to a house in Phibsborough. My hand on her leg,
her head on my shoulder holding on to my arm. The perfect couple.
She had a bedsit on the top floor. Full of posters and photos. We
drank coffee and I kissed her some more. She was shaking. I would
have walked away. I told her.

'I'll go if you're not sure. I'm not going to make you do anything
you don't want.'

'No. No. Stay. I want you to.'

This was what she was supposed to do. She was supposed to go to
college and become an adult and live her own life and go home with
guys she didn't know and fuck them and hope that she could come
at least once, before they scarpered or, if you were lucky, stayed.
She didn't know what she was doing, all hands and awkward. It is
awkward. I don't care how often you've done it but getting it on with
someone you don't know is always going to be hard, what they want,
how much they trust you. I knew what I had to do and took control.
I put her on her back on the bed and lay on top kissing for about five
minutes, then undressed her, kissing her all the time, took off my
shirt, got her down to her underwear. I could feel her nervousness,
then her excitement as she forgot herself. What I was doing felt good
but she needed to let herself go. I talked to her, made jokes to relax
her all the time kissing, caressing, until she was turned on. I went
down on her and she groaned, tried to push me away but her heart
wasn't in it, she let me go on and I could feel her tense, hear her
breathing catch as she came closer to coming, I slowed and she pressed
against me encouraging. I picked it up and she came hard, her back
arching, pressing against me, and then pulling away. She lay there and
I moved up and pushed the hair back from her face. When I went
into her, her breath caught but she didn't say anything. I fucked her
slowly for a while until I felt her begin to press again. All the time I

kissed her deeply and she looked up, not scared any more, but not knowing what was going on exactly. She came again and then I let it go. I was regretting it before I even came. I felt empty lying there. I could feel her need for something – affection, gentleness, warmth. I could give it to her, rub her arm, kiss her head, anything small and meaningless, but I couldn't feel it. I was faking.

Her smell was on my skin as I walked home at five in the morning, sick with guilt and drink. You spend so much time trying for something, chasing it, and then when it happens you wish it hadn't, the confusion and inconsistency of my life. The shirt and tie and the manners. I could talk to anyone, make them see me as cultured and sophisticated. I could hold the door for ladies, light their cigarettes but it was like putting a gorilla in a suit, unnatural. Hello my name is Rory and I am a sophisticated man of sparkling intelligence and impeccable taste and given half the chance I'll fuck your sister or your girlfriend with not a thought for the consequences. Not a thought for this poisonous addled guilt which results. Not a thought for your feelings or his, hers, theirs. Only mine. My poor girlfriend at home in bed, unaware of me out prowling around, waiting in our bed which I had cajoled her back to the previous week, down on my knees begging her to stay with me, to work with me, that it would be worth it. And now walking home with another girl's smell spread over me. Marked. What was I doing? It didn't seem like fun any more.

The hall light in the flat was off when I went in. I closed the door and took my shoes off. As I walked across towards the bathroom, I could see the light from under the bedroom door. I could hear her moving, sitting up in the bed.

'Rory?' She said my name.

I stood there not knowing what to do. I waited for what felt like ages trying to decide and then opened the door and went inside.

# 6

She was lying in the bed propped up on her arm. She looked like she had just woken up, her eyes were bleary and she wasn't entirely together. I was more on the ball than she was. I needed to be. I sat beside her.

'Where were you?' she asked.

'Out.'

'Where?'

'Pubs. Clubs. I don't know. Around.'

'What time is it?'

I could have told her any old time and she wouldn't have checked. But what if she did?

'Half-five.'

'And where were you?' she asked again.

'In town. I don't know. I had a bad day and I just couldn't handle coming home so I went to a pub on my own and then a club on my own and now I'm back.'

'I was worried. Your phone was off. I was trying to call you. I didn't know what was going on.'

She didn't. She still didn't. She sat up and put her hand on my back. I looked away from her, afraid of what she might see in my face. Sympathy, self-disgust, frustration. I wasn't ready to let her know what had happened because I hadn't decided yet what it was.

'What's wrong? You look so upset.'

I could feel myself welling up, the drink getting out of my system, I could feel it in my throat and I knew if I started talking I'd just fall apart completely. She didn't deserve this. It wasn't her fault.

I was there knowing that whatever I did in this situation would

79

matter, that I had to get my story right, and then this feeling just washed over me, so tired and exhausted, so fed up and spent and it was just tell her. She deserves to know. It'll be easier. It'll be better, just be done with it. Wake up tomorrow and a new day begins. Go to work, come home, and it's my life and my space and I don't have to worry, I don't have to try any more. I smiled and looked at her, ready to open my mouth and let it all come out. She had no idea what was coming. She looked concerned and for a second I hesitated, stupidly, and then she started talking and I realized that she must have been awake all along. She had been thinking and she was ready.

'I hate to see you like this, Rory. I can't stand it.' I should have interrupted her but I couldn't. It would have been easier if she was angry. 'You just look so lost and sad and I don't know what the hell you're doing out until this kind of time on your own. But I don't care. I just don't care, whatever it is that you need, whatever it is that's upsetting you I will be here and I will help you. I know we haven't been getting on great but, you know, people fight, couples fight all the time, different people deal with things in different ways. You're too idealistic, wanting everything to be perfect all the time, but it's just not. I'm not always going to be in great form and neither are you but as long as we stick together and don't worry too much, support each other, it'll be OK.'

She sat up on her knees and put her arms around my neck and kissed me. I froze, terrified that she would smell the other girl off me. What was her name? There were tears coming down my cheeks, dripping off the end of my nose. I knew it was the fucking booze getting to me and guilt and remorse and I knew it would make her more sympathetic and that would make me worse, but I couldn't help it. I couldn't stop. The moment to tell her was gone. I knew that. There was no way I could say anything to her now, it would be such a rejection of what she'd been saying and of what she was thinking. Even though she was wrong I couldn't tell her. It wasn't fair. Later maybe, some other time, I was saying to myself, but even then I knew I wouldn't. Forget about it. Put it behind me and move on. That was all I had to do.

I pushed her off me gently and keeping my head down I went over to her table and got a tissue and blew my nose and then went back and sat beside her and held her hand. I coughed a bit to steady my voice and I said, 'I'm sorry. I'm just so sorry. I don't know what's wrong with me . . .' Guilty as fuck. Disloyal. Cheating bastard. 'But you're probably right,' I said. 'I will be fine. We'll be fine. I am getting myself back together, but it has been hard, you know, for me and I'm sure, I know, for you as well and it's very difficult to just pick up and go on without thinking about what's happened. But we will.' I stood up and kissed her. 'Thanks for being so great.'

'Where are you going?' she asked.

'I'm going to have a shower. I'll have to get up in the morning and just go.'

'I'll probably be asleep when you come back.'

It was my problem and I'd deal with it in a way that didn't hurt her. That's why I didn't tell her, it was for her sake.

Standing in the shower, washing another girl's smell off me, the pain of guilt there in my stomach, knowing I was going to be in bits the next day, I leant against the door and let the water beat down on the back of my neck. I could feel my shoulders loosen, the pounding in my head lighten, the tension wash away. I didn't know how but I was doing all these stupid things, things you're not supposed to and nothing bad was happening. I was lucky. I looked at myself in the mirror, hair plastered against my head, my body loose and relaxed.

'This is me,' I said out loud. I said it again, but I didn't look too impressed. I didn't look too convinced.

When the alarm went at half-seven there was no way I was going to be able to go to work. It took a couple of minutes before I remembered the night before and I felt desperation and then hope as the conversation with Niamh only two hours before came back to me. I sat on the edge of the bed staring at the floor trying to get myself moving. After a couple of minutes I could remember that nothing major was going on at work and that calling in sick was the only thing to do. I reset the alarm and went back to sleep. Niamh woke me at eight.

'You're going to be late,' she said. She was speaking so close to me I could feel her breath on the back of my neck.

'Sickie. I'm not going. I can't. I'm in bits.' I waited for her to tell me to get up, that I'd feel OK in a couple of hours but she didn't. Instead she put her arm around me and held my hand.

'We should stay in bed all day,' she said.

I got up. I made my call to Carol, Gerry's PA, and turned my phone off. We slept until eleven and then I went and brought in tea. We stayed in bed all morning just dozing. We got up later and had breakfast. I hadn't seen her like this in ages. She was just relaxed. We were getting on. It felt strange. One day you can barely be in the same room as each other and then you get it back. I didn't understand how it had happened, what I'd done to bring this about but it seemed that I'd managed without really trying to end up as happy as I'd ever been. I said it to her.

'What has happened?'

'I think we both know that we're right together, but we hardly see each other and it's easy to forget. I think we've remembered that we need each other.'

'We do.'

'I think so,' she said.

'So that's it. Let's not forget.'

'Let's not forget.'

The rest of the day we slobbed around the apartment, watched telly, ordered an Indian, read for a while. The whole day we were in the same room, my head resting in her lap as she read. The world was so changed in only a few hours. All the time I had been running away from this, lying around feeling at one with someone else, relaxed and comfortable. The world outside seemed random and ugly, in here was safe and meaningful. This was something worth living for, something worth working for. We could go out and do what we had to do in order to maintain what we had in here. That world of drink and girls and impressing people seemed stupid and empty. I had everything I could possibly need in here. I looked up at her, holding my stare until she felt it. She looked down.

'What?'

'I'm an idiot.'

'You are,' she said. 'I've always thought so.'

I don't think she knew what was going on with me, but I could see she was hopeful. She wanted this to last. So did I.

We slept for ten hours that night. I woke up feeling better than I'd felt in months. I had a shower and made coffee and was standing in the kitchen when she came through from the bedroom.

'You're up early,' she said.

'I've a lot to do after yesterday.'

'Well, I hope it was worth it.'

'It was,' I said. 'I know already that it was.'

She smiled a sleepy, groggy kind of smile.

'I'll see you tonight,' I said.

I was in before anybody else. When Gerry arrived he stuck his head around the door.

'You all right?'

'Yeah, I'm fine.'

'What was up?' he asked.

'I don't know. Just sick all night and I didn't sleep. I was totally zonked in the morning.'

'Were you out?'

'No, I wasn't.' I could hear my voice rise, phoney indignation. 'I was just sick.'

'OK. I'm just asking. It's not unreasonable.'

'Well. I wasn't out. I was at home with Niamh.'

'You're OK now?' he asked again.

'Yeah, I'm fine. I've got a bit to do though.'

'I'll leave you to it. See you later.'

I settled down and got stuck in. I felt like I could do anything.

I made a list and worked through it, phone call after phone call, email after email, until I was ahead again. My body felt great, I could hear a confidence in my voice that hadn't been there for ages, I was focused. I cared about what I was doing. Every call that went my way felt like corroboration that I was back on track. I was a success, this was my life and I was living it and I could do anything that I wanted. Anything was possible for me. A good night's sleep, a happy day at home with my girlfriend. That was all I had needed. Look at me now. I could feel it as I walked down the hallways. Anybody looking at me would know how I felt. I was on top of the world. I was on form. I was the shit. I went into Gerry's office.

'Got a minute?'

'Yeah. Sure.'

I closed the door behind me and sat down.

'What's up?' he asked.

'Have you noticed anything odd about me lately?'

I could see him trying to work out what was happening. He shrugged.

'What? No. Not really.'

'I'm glad to hear it.' I waited before continuing. 'I haven't been having a very good time of it at home, things haven't been working out very well and I hope it hasn't impacted too much on my working life.'

'I don't think so,' he said. 'I haven't noticed anything.' He seemed edgy, unsure of where I was going.

'I hope you're not being polite to save my feelings,' I said.

He laughed and then said quite sharply, 'I wouldn't. You should know me well enough for that. What's the point?'

'The point is that it's OK now. Everything is OK. I've sorted out what the problems are and I'm back. I feel great and I'm totally committed to my work. You should notice a change. One hundred and ten per cent.' I knew it was dorky but I wanted him to know. He smiled and then sat forward, resting his elbows on his desk.

'I'm glad everything has worked out for you and I look forward to seeing evidence of your new-found enthusiasm. I do ask myself, though, why you would bother sharing this with me, Rory. Why are you telling me that you've not been concentrating on your job? It seems a bit weird. Why would you tell a story that goes against yourself?' His tone was relaxed, very informal, but there was a question there.

'Because you're my boss and I want you to know what's going on in my life, to explain why I haven't been totally focused and mostly because I want you to understand why I'm going to be around here a lot more. I feel now like I can do anything and I want to be pushed and to push myself. I want to do the absolute maximum for the company, for you and for myself. And as well we're friends, I mean I drink with you so we'd have had this conversation at some time or another anyway. You know what I mean?'

He shook his head and laughed.

'I think so. I'm not entirely sure.' He paused. 'But yeah, that's fine. Good news. Glad you're happy. I'll look forward to seeing this new you.'

'OK then.'

I went back to my office and spent the rest of the day putting together a strategy thing that I should have done about a month previously. I was still there at seven when Gerry came to the door.

'Does this new regime allow you to go to the pub on a school night?'

'Not really. I'm going home in a bit.'

'Oh come on. We haven't had a drink together in ages. Just the one.'

'It's never one. Never.'

'Ah go on. On me.'

I could feel the pull. A good day's work done, a happy evening, me and the boss having a couple of quiet ones. Telling him enough about me and Niamh's problems and how I'd resolved them to show me in a good light. But then what would happen after? Getting home late smelling of booze, and Gerry and me if we got going, it could be all hours, it could be messy. In some basement in Leeson Street and anything could happen then. I'd wake up late and my new regime would have lasted one day. It was just stupid.

'Any chance of an answer before closing?' he asked. I woke up.

'Sorry. No. Not tonight. It's the improved me. No pub midweek,' I said.

'That doesn't sound very improved. That just sounds boring.'

'Aren't you my boss? Shouldn't you be supporting me in this?' I asked.

'Only in work. You walk out that door and you're your own boss and I'm just some guy until nine o'clock tomorrow morning. Twist your arm?'

'No. No. I'm going home.'

King of all I surveyed. Happy at home, happy at work. I was sitting in my office a week later and between now and then it had all been good. I could feel looseness in my muscles, see a glow in my skin. I was getting up early, going to bed at ten. Sleeping. Not answering the phone to Patrick or any of the other pissheads. They'd still be there whenever I wanted to let it go, but that wasn't now. People were commenting on how well I looked after only a week. What kind of a state had I been in before? Gerry had seen it in me. I was sure he'd thought I was losing it when I went to him with my little mission statement or whatever, but he noticed the change. Every day when he came in he would put his head round the door.

'Do you still have positive mental attitude?'

'Yes I do,' I said in reply and he just laughed. He was taking the piss. He hated the idea that we were just a bunch of salarymen who really cared about the work. He could talk like this, being ironic, but I knew that he would only do it if he felt happy that I was onside, if he thought that I was really committed. I was and he knew it.

That day I had nothing to do. I was drawing up a budget plan that wouldn't be needed for another two months, trying to keep myself focused and hungry, but knowing that the real drive wasn't there. It didn't need to be today. There were meetings for the rest of the week, but there was nothing I could have done about them then. I didn't know how much time the other guys spent doing this kind of thing, sitting at their desks drifting. Usually when you walked into anybody's office they would close whatever screen was open and try and look simultaneously relaxed and busy. I had just done a month's work in a week and all it had taken was early nights and enthusiasm. I was sure that the others were not working to their potential. It was something to think about. What could we be if everybody cared and did their utmost? Always the same story. Everybody fluting around, coming in looking like they'd slept in a doorway, stinking of booze, spending an hour in the jacks. Receptionists who had three-hour conversations with their friends, barely interrupted by answering calls. '. . . So I says to him well I'm disgusted now really disgusted, it's not on, you know, and he says I don't care what you think, I did the best possible . . . Hang on, Carmel, good morning Talisman, can I help you? No sorry, Ted's not in the office today would you like his voicemail, thank you now, yeah he says I don't give a fuck what you think, the old bollix . . .'

To think what we, the company, could be achieving if everybody actually worked year round rather than messing about for ten months and pulling it together with a lot of Red Bull and fourteen-hour days at the last minute. I could do something about it. I could get them motivated. Start with not the most important or senior people but with the AEs, the guys who made eighteen grand. Get those guys moving, get them stirred up, start off all slaggy and sarcastic, ha ha let's work a bit harder, cop on, let's only get pissed on Friday but I'll pay for it, best of friends. Such a thin line. The thought of getting it wrong, standing in front of them, with their open happy faces and turning away, missing the lips curling, the little sneers. What? This fucker gets his act together, gives up going on the piss and suddenly he's seen the light and we're supposed to be thankful that we're going to get to do a fifty-hour week for the same cash? Arsehole. Dream on.

Jesus. But they wouldn't. I was cooler than that. They knew too well that I could be sharp and nasty for them to take the piss. If I was nineteen and barely shaving I'd want to be like me. If I was a nineteen-year-old girl, I would want to be with someone like me. I knew that was true. Only a week previously, in a different world, I'd proved it. It was the old me but still me. I took out my wallet. Folded up was a piece of paper taken from a notepad. She'd written her name in a girl's writing all curls and soft edges. Even her writing said, Love me please. It was the number of a payphone in a hall in a house in Phibsborough. I'd made those calls before, years ago, waiting ages for someone to answer and then some foreign guy saying speak to who and thinking I don't know if I can be bothered with this. I shivered. I thought about Róisín. Me doing things to her. That's what it had been. Nice girl, but another life. A different path and one that couldn't be as happy as this. I crumpled up the paper and put it in the bin and got to thinking about how I was going to make this company capable of taking over the world.

I went for lunch with Gerry. I had to be careful. I didn't want to sound like I was criticizing his organizational skills.

'I think I can get more out of some of these guys,' I said out of nowhere. 'I think we can be a lot bigger than we are now.' He looked at me a second and then burst out laughing.

'What?' I asked him.

'I'm sorry,' he said. 'I shouldn't laugh.' He got himself together. 'You're a good worker, Rory. You know, I've no complaints about you, I think you've always been fairly solid and dogged about getting clients and the like, but I wouldn't have thought you'd be likely to start becoming a group leader or anything. I mean the work you do is important and I think you're very valuable but someone in your position really just needs to do the job and do it well. What's happened to you? Making the company a better entity. Where's this coming from?'

'I don't know. I think maybe I might be able to push some of them, make them feel more involved, you know. I'm surprised you seem unsettled by my suggesting it. I would have thought you'd want me to do stuff like this.'

'Absolutely, yeah sure. I'm not unsettled. It's just that you never have before. This is out of the blue. I don't know, maybe you're turning out to be different to the person I thought you were . . .'

'And is that not good?' I could hear the edge in my voice. I smiled to soften the impact.

'Yeah sure. Why don't you put what you're suggesting in writing and I'll have a look at it and talk it over with you?'

The conversation was stilted for five minutes after that but by the time we went back it was all grand, he'd got back to his normal self, joking and fucking around. I went back to my office and closed the door.

When he was leaving that night he came in to say goodbye. I wanted to see what he'd say.

'I'll have that stuff for you by Friday,' I said.

'What stuff is that?' he asked.

'What we were talking about at lunchtime. My ideas for getting more from the staff.'

'Oh right, yeah. Well, whenever.'

I laughed and shook my head.

'OK. Whenever,' I said.

'What's funny? I don't get it.'

'Nothing. Nothing,' and I laughed again. He kind of laughed back but he didn't know what was going on, or maybe he did but he wouldn't let it show.

'See you later,' he said and he was gone.

I told Niamh about it that night.

'He's probably getting used to the idea that you're interested in your job again.'

'Well, what do I have to do to convince him? I mean I've told him, you know.'

'I suppose it'll take time. You can't just decide suddenly, hey, I'm a new person and expect people to accept it straight away. They have to wait and see if you stick to it, if it's actually true. It's like trust. When it's broken, it takes time to rebuild.'

'But why wouldn't he trust me? I've never done anything . . .'

'That's not what I'm saying.' She smiled. 'Why is this getting to you so much?'

'Because I started thinking maybe it doesn't suit him if I start coming up with good ideas, big ideas that could change the company. Maybe it was easier for him when I was coming in all hungover and not getting anything done. At least I wasn't a challenge.'

'You weren't getting anything done before?' she asked.

'No. I was. I mean effectively or more or less or whatever. But you know what I mean. You can see the point, surely?'

'I can but I don't know. By the sounds of it he's always been very supportive of you, he likes you, you get on well. I'm sure he's just getting used to it.'

'It seems weird to me,' I said.

'OK, well, wait and see what he does, don't get paranoid.'

'Paranoid?' I shouted it and she jumped. I had to calm down. 'I'm not paranoid. Really. I'm just wondering if I need to look out for myself a bit more.'

'Maybe. I don't know,' she said and I could feel her drifting away from me. She was freaked out. I was getting too annoyed. I left it at that.

I didn't think about it again until we were in bed with the lights out, going to sleep. It was hard to keep this kind of enthusiasm going. I realized now that I felt great and relaxed and was getting loads done, but it didn't come naturally to block out all the shit. It was all still there and it was hard to ignore. You had to accentuate the positive. I laughed to myself. Not my style, but I had to try.

# 7

I didn't sleep well that night. Dreaming about things I had to do but never could. Waking up and counting down to the alarm. 3:51. 5:40. 6:21 and then suddenly it was 8:15 and I'd slept through.

'What's wrong?' Niamh asked me when I started shouting.

'Late. I'm too fucking late.'

'Don't worry.'

'You don't have to worry,' I said as I got dressed. 'You just have to get up for lunch.'

'OK. I will.' She was still asleep. Afterwards I was glad she hadn't heard me.

I got in at half-nine and went straight to my desk. Gerry came in. He was smiling.

'Back to the old ways already.'

'What?' I'd heard him.

'The new you didn't last too long, did it?'

'I couldn't sleep. I was worried about how much I had to get done. For fuck's sake. I can't sleep because of this place and still I get shit from you.'

He put his hands up.

'Jesus, will you relax. I'm only messing with you. It's no big deal.'

'Well, there's something there.' I said it without thinking. He was on to it straight away.

'What? What do you mean?'

'I don't know.'

He stood there in silence for about thirty seconds. I was holding a pen in my hand and was pressing my arm against my desk to stop it shaking.

'What's wrong, Rory?' he asked.

'Nothing. I just didn't sleep well.'

'Yeah, OK. Well, you will tonight. Come on, mate, you're doing well here. One bad day isn't going to fuck you up unless you let it. Keep yourself busy and tomorrow will be better.'

'Yeah, OK. Sorry.'

'It's nothing. Don't worry about it,' he said and he walked out smiling.

How had it happened? He gave me shit and I ended up apologizing. Everything was consistent with him having an agenda. I didn't want to think of him like that but it was all there. Keeping me in my place, undermining and manipulating. How do you know who your friends are? It's a bastard. A bastard. Cop on. Wake up.

I drank a load of coffee which got me going but I was jumpy and I couldn't concentrate. I made a few phone calls, chased up a few people to meet the next week and then lost interest. Gerry was right. It was better to write off the day and not get stressed when there was nothing I could do. I was flicking around the internet, looking for anything at all, thinking about nothing, wasting time.

Maybe it was the lack of sleep. Whatever. It was just something to do to get my mind off work. It wasn't like I planned it. At the time I didn't even think about it. I didn't let myself. I looked under my desk. They didn't empty the bin every day. I didn't know what I was hoping, but I could feel my heart skip when I saw that they hadn't. A sick excitement. Would I or wouldn't I? Would I or wouldn't I? I bent down and took the number out. I'll just have a look. I'll just ring and hang up. I'll just ask for her and hang up then. I'll just wait until I hear her voice and then there she was, speaking in a voice that I knew too well for someone I had barely met.

'Hello,' she said.

I couldn't just say nothing.

'Hi. How are you?' I said.

'Oh hi.' She knew who I was straight away. 'I didn't know if you were going to ring.'

I laughed. 'Neither did I, actually.'

'I'd given up on you,' she said. She sounded happy.

'Ah no. I was just, I was very busy this past week. I kept meaning to but there was never a good time. I'm sorry.'

'Oh it's OK. Don't worry. How are you anyway?'

'I'm fine. Grand, yeah. And yourself?'

'Ah yeah. I'm well.'

There was a silence. I should have told her. I should have just said it. I'm really sorry. I have a girlfriend. It was stupid of me and I'm sorry.

'I wanted to talk to you,' I said.

'Did you? What about?'

Tell her now. 'I don't know. How's college?'

She laughed. 'What's wrong with you? You sound really nervous.'

'Well it's been a while since I made a phone call like this.'

'And what? Are you nervous? That's kind of cute.'

'I'm glad you're enjoying it,' I said and we both laughed. I found myself warming to her, remembering what it was that I liked about her.

'Can we meet up? I'd like to see you,' I said.

'When?'

'I don't know. How's this evening for you?'

'Yeah. That's OK. In town?'

We made an arrangement. I picked an old man's place on the quays that nobody ever went to. I hung up and could see a mark on the phone from my sweaty hand. It was like I was a stammering nineteen-year-old and she was in control. I put my head on the desk, sitting there having done precisely the opposite of what I had wanted. I could feel nervousness in my stomach at the thought of meeting her, overshadowed by a huge potential threat. This could all go wrong. This would bring no good to anyone, this was not a part of my new plan for successful living.

But then what if what if what if? I was in charge of myself. I was capable of self-control. I could go along and meet her. We could have a drink, I could talk to her for a while, make her feel good, let her know that I really liked her but that it wouldn't work, it just couldn't happen and leave her feeling OK about herself and OK about me. An unexpected act of kindness. She was getting more out of me than she would out of guys who would matter more to her in the future. And if it didn't work, if I couldn't handle it, I could walk out at any time mid-sentence. My legs could stand and carry me and I would disappear from her life. I'd got to this point no problem. I could go along just to see.

I rang Niamh and told her I was going for a drink after work. She wasn't even listening, distracted with her own concerns.

'I won't be late,' I told her.

'Don't worry about it. I may be out myself.'

I put it out of my mind until people started going home and I saw it was after six. Without thinking I went into Gerry and told him I was off.

'Half day, yeah?'

'Yeah right. See you in the morning.'

I walked out of the office, down onto the quays and crossed the river. I walked quickly against the crowd that were moving towards the DART station, heads down, knackered and silent in office clothes. Nobody looked up. Nobody caught my eye. Nobody was interested or cared. I could have done anything and they would just keep going, heading home to dinner and telly and bed. I had no idea what I was doing or where I was going, if I would keep my arrangement or back out at the end.

But I knew well where I was going. My feet were carrying me there and I knew why, if not in my head, then somewhere in my stomach where a guilty thrill was lurking. You love this shit, it said to me, but I ignored it. I played dumb.

When I arrived I was ten minutes early so I got a pint and sat in the corner and waited, watching the door. It was a kip, a whole load of old lads lined up at the counter, balanced on stools, smoking and staring straight ahead in silence. I was chewing my finger when she walked in. I stood up and smiled and she came over and hesitated before leaning in to kiss me on the cheek.

'This is nice,' she said, looking around laughing.

'I kind of like it,' I said, embarrassed. It was such a dump.

'It's authentic,' she said. 'You can smell the river.'

I bought her a drink and we sat at a table opposite each other and talked about crap. She was in good form. I thought she'd be nervous or pissed off or something but she was cool. She made me relax. I asked her about college and she said it was fine and that she'd met a couple of people in tutorials who seemed OK but she couldn't believe people were studying already, the library was full.

'It wasn't like that in my day,' I said. 'Nobody went near the place until after Easter.'

'When was that?' she asked.

'You would hardly have been born,' I said.

'Why? How old are you?'

I thought about asking how old she thought I was because I wanted to know, but it seemed coy so I told her. Her face dropped.

'You're thirty?' she said looking shocked.

'Yeah. Why? I am.'

'My God.'

'What?'

She laughed.

'I thought you were joking. Jesus.'

'What did you think I was? How old?' I could ask her now.

'I don't know. Twenty-four maybe?'

'OK, I can live with that.'

'Yeah but . . . you're not.'

'I know I'm not.'

She shook her head.

'You're thirty.'

'Does it matter?' I asked.

'No. Not at all, no.'

'You'll get here someday.'

'Yeah. In eleven years,' she said and then we both laughed and I went up and bought another drink. There was no way I could tell her anything else after that.

When I got back, she was on the phone. She was giving someone directions. She said goodbye and hung up.

'Someone coming?' I asked.

'Yeah, a friend of mine is coming in.'

'Oh right,' I said, trying to sound upbeat.

'I'd arranged to meet her already, is it OK?'

'It's cool, yeah, no problem. I'll probably head off when she arrives. I'm meeting someone later on as well.'

'Oh right,' she said. And then she went quiet before speaking again. 'Get him to come here. I'd like to see a bit more of you tonight.' She looked straight at me and I knew I was going to kiss her. I had to so I did.

'I'll give him a call,' I said after.

I waited for her friend to arrive who was nice enough, blondy young one called Anna in a tracksuit thing. I said hello. I was trying to see if she knew anything about me, if Róisín had told her anything but I couldn't tell. She was friendly but neutral. They started talking about going out that night, what was on where and they fixed on a club I'd never heard of.

'Are you on for it?' Róisín asked me.

'I'm not sure. Let me talk to my friend.'

I went and phoned Patrick.

'Where are you?' I asked him.

'I'm at home. What's up?'

'I'm in a pub with two girls I don't even know, but I got talking to them and they want to go to a club or something.'

'Are you drunk?'

'No I'm not. I'm sober. Will you come in? They're nice girls. I don't really know what I'm at but they're a bit of a laugh. I thought you might be into it.'

'What are they like?' he asked.

'They're nice. Very. Both.'

'"Nice" nice or nice?'

'You'd like them.'

'They can't be that nice so.'

'So?' I said.

'OK. Where are you?' I told him.

'What the fuck are you doing in there?'

'I don't know. I just came in for a pint.'

'On your own?' He sounded doubtful.

'I'll see you later,' I said and hung up.

He was great when he arrived. All charm and kissing hands and totally over the top, but they got it so it was OK. He asked questions and kept the conversation going while I tried to work out what I was going to do. It was easier with him there. I acted as if everything was as I had told him. A bit dodgy and that but nothing much, just casual flirting with nobody important. We drank until closing and then went to the place they'd been talking about which was hardcore trance. I was in a suit and Patrick and myself were the oldest by about ten years. We sat against a wall in a corridor at the back. Róisín was sitting so close to me I could feel her breathing. She kept asking me questions, anything to keep me looking at her, talking just to her. Patrick was getting on OK with her friend and looked like he was moving in. It wasn't making my life any easier.

'Are you all right?' she asked after a while, drunk and with nothing else left to say.

'I'm fine. Are you?'

'No I'm not,' she said.

'Why?' I asked.

'I don't know why you're being so horrible.'

'I didn't know I was,' I said but I knew what she meant. Then she leaned in and kissed me. I was sure Patrick was watching. I pushed her back gently and stroked her face and whispered to her, told her I'd talk to her properly later, which to Patrick looking on could have been anything. She was getting messy. When I looked back over Patrick was kissing her pal.

I went to the toilet. He was at the bar when I came back.

'She seems keen,' he said.

'Yeah. How are you getting on?'

'She's nice.'

'I told you. They both are.'

'Pity for you,' he said.

'How's that?' I asked.

'You can't.' He didn't say anything more. He didn't mention Niamh. I shrugged.

'I don't know,' I said smiling.

'No. Not a good idea. Are you mad? They're just children, you know, they're fucking kids.'

'That's why I rang you. I thought it might be your thing.'

He laughed.

'It might be. But it's not yours.'

'Yeah I know,' I said. 'It's hard though.'

'You'll be glad in the morning.'

'It's all right for you.'

'That's the difference. Occasionally being single has its upside.'

We went back over. The two girls were sitting beside each other holding hands and Róisín's head was resting on the other one's shoulder. I sat down beside her.

'I want to go,' she said to me.

'Will we all go?' I asked. Patrick shrugged.

'I want to stay,' Anna said and Patrick smiled and put his arm around her and they started kissing like a couple of kids at a school disco. I went and got our jackets and when I came back five minutes later she stood up. She went over to Anna and they hugged saying goodbye. Patrick stood beside me and spoke into my ear.

'What's the story? Your one's after saying that you know this Róisín. You knew her before.'

'Yeah I met her.' I tried to sound casual.

'I thought you said you just met them in the pub tonight,' he said.

'I did. I'd met her before once – not Anna – and then I met the two of them tonight totally by chance.'

'What? When you went into that dump on your own? Anna's saying she thought you two had something going on.'

'Well, I don't know why she'd think that,' I said.

'Well, maybe because it fucking looks like it. You're going home with her . . .'

'I'm bringing her home, that's all. She's drunk. I'm not going to do anything.'

'Yeah, well I don't know. Why did you say you'd just met them? What's going on, Rory? Are you fucking around or what?'

I looked at him and shook my head. I didn't say anything.

'Something's up with you,' he said and then she came over and I had to go.

'I'll talk to you tomorrow,' I said to him.

'Yeah, whatever,' he said and he turned and walked off.

'Is he OK?' Róisín asked as we were going out and I said, 'Yeah, he's fine.'

We got a taxi back to her place. She was quiet on the way holding my hand and yawning. When we got there we went inside and up the stairs without speaking. She put on the kettle and we sat on the couch. She was flicking through a pile of CDs on the coffee table.

'Your friend seems fun,' I said.

'She is, yeah. She's great. A lot of fun. That's why guys like her.'

'Yeah. Patrick certainly did.' She looked at me. I smiled. She tried to smile back but couldn't. She waited a second before speaking.

'Were you embarrassed in there tonight?' she asked.

'How do you mean? Of what?'

'You didn't seem very interested in talking with me.'

'No. That wasn't it at all. I don't know. I was tired, I've been working a lot, it wasn't really the kind of place I'd normally go and I was in a suit, you know.'

'Do you like me, Rory?' she asked and I melted.

'Yeah. Of course I do. Why would you think that I don't?'

'Because you seemed really distant tonight.'

'Well, I'm sorry. I didn't mean to. I do like you. I think you're great, really I do.'

It would have been a good time to explain. I could have been done with it before I got more involved. I had no idea what Patrick knew or thought he knew and what impact that could have. He wouldn't tell Niamh or anything but it could get very complicated. There were plenty of reasons why I should have told her as quickly and painlessly as I could and be gone, finished in five minutes' time. But I wasn't thinking of any of them. They didn't enter my head because I meant what I said to her. I did like her, I really did, and sitting there looking at her, moving in to hold her and tell her that I was sorry, I knew I couldn't hurt her and whatever might happen afterwards, that was what was most important right then. Patrick and Niamh and work in four hours' time didn't even cross my mind.

I rang Patrick from work in the morning.

'Can you meet me for lunch?' I asked him.

'Yeah. I don't know. What time is it now?'

'Eleven.'

'Where am I?' He was still asleep.

'We were out,' I said.

'In that club?'

'Yeah.'

'Where are you?' he asked.

'At work.'

'You must be in bits.'

'I've been better.'

'Oh yeah. I remember now. What happened to you?' He was waking up. I didn't answer his question.

'Do you want to meet for lunch?'

I met him at two outside the office. We didn't speak, just nodded at each other. We started walking along the quays away from town. He was looking rough.

'So?' he said after a while. He was in bad form.

'What?' I asked.

'What were you fucking playing at last night?'

'I wasn't playing at anything. I wasn't doing anything.'

'Yeah, well it didn't look like that. You'd met that girl before.'

'Yeah, so? So what?'

'So. So. Your one, her mate was saying she was calling you her boyfriend. What's that about?'

I laughed, sarcastic.

'I don't bloody know. It's nothing to do with me what some girl tells some other girl I don't even know.'

'Which one?' he asked.

'What?'

'Which one don't you know?'

'Your one,' I said. 'The one you were with. Anna.'

'So you did know the other?'

I didn't look at him. I waited a second to let him calm down. I wanted to tell him. I really wanted to.

'I met her before, yeah,' I said. He turned away, looking off into the distance. I could hear my voice, plaintive when I spoke. 'You don't know what it's been like, Patrick. I swear to Christ, you've no fucking idea.'

'What what's been like?' he asked impatiently.

'Myself and Niamh. My work and everything. It's been doing my head in. It's too much. I can handle bits of it, but everything. It's too much.' I hoped he wouldn't ask what I meant. I hadn't thought it through.

'So? Everybody has problems.'

'Yeah. Well you don't have to deal with a girl who's hardly speaking to you across the table at breakfast every day.'

'Niamh?' he asked.

'Yeah. Well she wasn't before. So what am I supposed to do? I didn't want to go home after work. That's what it was like. I felt I was going mad, I'd do anything to avoid it, to avoid her. So I went to a pub and got chatting with this Róisín one, what a couple of weeks ago, and then she rang me up so what could I do? It's only a laugh.'

He was calmer when he spoke again.

'I'm not getting involved in your problems with Niamh, that's between you and her and I'm not going to say anything to her. If you've got problems or hassles, ring me and go for a drink with me, not the first girl you see who smiles at you. You can't play around, Rory. It's out of order. It's just stupid.'

'Jesus, man, I remember the days when you'd have three or four on the go—'

He interrupted me.

'Yeah, when we were twenty or whatever. And that was a bit of fun, but not now. You know? You live with Niamh. Your life is with her. I don't know how you can keep it going if there are lies all over the place. I'm presuming you haven't told her.'

'Who? Niamh?'

'Yeah.'

I looked at him.

'Are you mad?' I said. 'Why would I? No. Of course I haven't.'

'I don't know. I couldn't do it. I don't know how you can.'

'But I'm not doing anything,' I said. I'd had enough. 'What, one casual night with some student is suddenly a great deception? I don't need you to tell me how to live my life. When did you become so fucking sanctimonious?'

'I'm not. Sanctimonious? Really?' He couldn't help himself. He smiled and then laughed and I smiled too. The tension was broken.

'I'm not being sanctimonious. I'm not giving you shit. I'm a friend. I'm on your side. I mean Niamh is a friend as well. I like her, but you're more important to me. Obviously or whatever.'

'Oh stop.'

'Yeah, but if you ask me I think this could fuck you up. I'd say get out now. Don't start into that kind of stuff because it'll get ugly. I mean, how old is she, twelve?'

'Nineteen,' I said. 'It's old enough.'

'It's legal. But that doesn't make it a good idea. She's nineteen. She could do anything. You're risking a lot. Plus you're putting me in an awkward position. I'm not going to lie to Niamh. I'm not going to hang you or anything but I'm not going to cover for you either.'

'I didn't ask you to. I'm not looking for you to lie for me. I'm not doing anything. I've no intention of seeing her again. But there were good reasons for it, that's all. I'm not a complete idiot. I mean I had reasons that you know fuck all about . . .'

'I don't want to know,' he said.

'Yeah, well that's fine but don't judge me if you don't have all the facts.'

'I'm not judging you.'

'I'm just saying don't.'

'Well I didn't.'

'I think you did actually.'

'Actually I didn't.' It was getting silly.

'OK, fair enough,' I said.

'Fair enough.'

We had lunch and didn't discuss it any more. He was talking about another guy he knew from Holland coming in at the weekend and we arranged to do something. He walked back to the office with me and just as we got there he said, 'Don't ring her again. Don't talk to her or anything.'

I was getting pissed off.

'Jesus. I said I'm not going to. Why do you keep going on about it?'

He smiled, almost embarrassed. 'Because you look like you're thinking about it,' he said.

'Don't be stupid. I know. It's OK. You've done your bit.' I looked away but he bent over to look into my eyes and I turned to stare at him.

'What?'

He shrugged and said, "OK," see you, and he went off.

Before he would have listened to everything, understood everything and we'd have had a laugh about it. Now he was telling me what was right and wrong like a bloody priest in confession. I didn't want advice or his opinion. I just wanted him to listen. I couldn't tell him that I liked this girl. It was all about Niamh for him. He couldn't get beyond that.

# 8

I had a good day in work later on. I shouldn't have but I did. I started putting together a training plan for motivating staff. I wrote it all down and then read it back and it was great. It was inspirational. I don't know where it came from. I remembered then that when I worked in New York, I was good at what I did. With everything else going on it was easy to forget that. I should expect this from myself. I should be working at a higher level than all these other pricks. I stayed in the office until half-eight polishing it until it was perfect. Gerry had gone by the time I was leaving but I would show it to him as soon as I arrived in the morning. I wanted to see what he would say.

When I got home Niamh was on the couch. She was in good form.

'What happened to you last night, you bad boy?'

'I was out with that guy. You know I told you. Guy from school.' I went and got some juice from the fridge.

'What was he like?'

'A bit of an arsehole, but you know he was on for a drink.'

'So of course you had to find the latest-serving place in Dublin. Never go home when somebody somewhere might be having a good time.'

I flopped down beside her.

'I don't want to miss out if anything interesting happens,' I said.

'And did it?'

I was about to say something and then stopped.

'Not really.'

'Does it ever?' she asked.

I smiled.

'It might.'

'I don't know. You boys and your booze.'

She was joking. She didn't care.

'Well, despite it I had good day today,' I said, moving the conversation forward. 'I got a load done without even noticing. I'm going to give Gerry something to think about tomorrow.'

'I'm glad to hear it. I thought you'd be all hungover today.'

'I know. I'm knackered now though.'

I slumped over and lay my head in her lap. She ran her hands through my hair.

It was as if the guy who was seeing the other girl was somebody else altogether. But then everybody is like that. How many people are we in a day? With our friends, our parents, girlfriend, colleagues, the guy in the petrol station, the waitress at lunch. Each of them gets a version that is subtly different. Such huge importance is assigned to the truth but the only thing that is absolute about it is that it changes constantly, it exists in a liquid state, forever shaped by what surrounds it. I knew how shallow and dishonest the current situation made me seem, but who knew what would happen in the next month, week, day, moment. I could do this. I could work and come home to this girl and be normal and happy and think about someone else. If I couldn't have done it, then I wouldn't. Patrick obviously couldn't. He could say whatever he thought but he wasn't there at that precise moment to see the two of us together. Everything that had happened the previous night was irrelevant. Niamh was happy and so was I. In a different world maybe neither of us would be, but that wasn't real and this was. The two of us together happy.

The next day I was in early. I printed off the stuff I'd done the previous day and waited until half-eight before going in to Gerry.

'This is the stuff I was talking about, do you remember? Team building and that. I told you I'd have it for you this week.'

He didn't say anything, just stared at me.

'Do you remember?' I asked again.

He was hesitant when he answered.

'Yeah. I do. Yeah.'

'What's the problem?' I asked.

'No problem. Just I'd prefer if you concentrated on the work that we're paying you to do.'

I laughed.

'But you told me to write it down. And anyway I did most of it in the mornings before I started and after hours.'

'Was that why you came in at ten the other morning then?' he said. 'Staying up all night on your special project?'

I knew he was joking but I couldn't help the expression on my face.

'I told you why that was,' I said slowly.

'I know. Jesus, you're sensitive these days.'

These days. These days. What the fuck was that? I said nothing.

'I'll have a look later,' he said. 'I do appreciate what you're trying to do, but concentrate on your own area, yeah?'

'Yeah.'

I went back in and rang Róisín. I didn't think about it. I had her mobile now. She was having coffee between lectures. I arranged to meet her at half-twelve. I went out to the kitchen to get tea. There was a gang of about six of them standing around yapping. Young guys, one girl. I hardly knew their names. Trainees and account executives. They didn't even look up when I came through. They were talking about some DJ playing the Kitchen on Friday. It was like they were in a pub, totally chilled out. I might as well not have been there. As I was walking back through them, they stopped talking for a sec.

'All right, Rory?' one of them said.

I looked at him. I'd never even seen him before.

'Working hard?' I asked.

'It's a break, man. We're on a break.'

'Ah sure, I know,' I said. I walked out. They were quiet as I was going and then I heard them laughing.

At lunch I went and met Róisín in the place she'd arranged, some sandwich place in a basement that I'd never heard of. She was there when I arrived. She looked great.

'Twice in one week,' she said when I arrived. 'This is becoming normal.'

'I wouldn't go that far,' I said. She asked about my work. What I did. Where it was. I kept it vague. On the quays. Advertising. It could have been anywhere. I told her that usually it was fine but recently I was beginning to wonder if it was for me. She asked me why and I told her that I felt I lacked support. She didn't know what to say. I asked her had she ever worked and she smiled and said summer work on a farm and in a bar in Clones. She was thinking of getting a job in Dublin.

'Avoid suits,' I said to her.

'I try to but I made an exception for you,' she replied, which was kind of funny.

She wasn't scared of me, she wasn't intimidated at all. She was young, but it didn't matter. It made her different from all the jaded old fuckers I was used to, who had seen everything and were impressed by nothing. Enthusiasm was the opposite of cool and you just had to be cool. It was a quick hour. I walked back over to Trinity with her and kissed her in a doorway outside the arts block. She didn't suggest meeting again so I said it.

'We should do this again. It was fun.'

'You have my number,' she said, nonchalant.

'I might ring you,' I said.

'OK. That's OK.'

'You're very relaxed,' I said after her as she was walking away and she turned around and shook her head. I liked that. I stood there for a second and then ran after her.

'What do you have on this afternoon?' I said when I caught up with her.

'I've a tutorial at three.'

'Can you miss it?'

'Why?' she asked.

'Can you? I mean is it absolutely vital that you're there?'

'Not really. I should go to it though.'

'But they're not going to kick you out if you don't?'

Her smile was unsure.

'No.'

I took her to a hotel in Temple Bar. A boutique hotel. It couldn't be sleazy. We walked into the lobby and I went up to the counter and put my card down.

'I'd like a room for one night.'

The guy gave me a form and I started to fill it in. The first time I looked at her was when he gave me the key. She was holding her folder in front of her.

'You're joking,' she said.

'No. Come on. Let's get room service.' I walked to the lift. I looked back at her as I was waiting. She was still standing in front of the desk rocking gently back and forth, biting her lip. The lift dinged and opened behind me. I nodded her over. She walked over.

'I don't believe this,' she whispered.

'Why not?'

She laughed. I knew it would be OK. I kissed the back of her neck and hugged her and I could feel her relax. When we got into the room I turned off my phone. I started taking her clothes off. She helped me but her hands were shaking.

'It's OK,' I said and I lay on the bed with her and just held her for a while.

'I haven't done this before,' she said.

I laughed.

'Neither have I. Let's get a drink.'

I rang down and ordered a bottle of wine. We turned on the TV and started watching some kids' programme. When the drink came I turned it off and we sat on the bed and drank. She got up and went to the window and looked out. She could see the North Quays across the river, buses and taxis, people going about their business.

'This is mad,' she said. 'I should be in college.'

'I should be in work.'

'Why are we here then?'

'Because when you were going earlier on, I felt this pull, this wrench, and I just wanted to spend the day with you and nobody else. I had to. So. That's why. We can deal with everything else later.'

She put her glass down on the table and came over and pushed me back on the bed and started kissing me.

I let her take control. I only did anything when her confidence faltered, when she seemed to need encouragement. She stayed on top of me. At first she wouldn't look at me, just watching the walls or closing her eyes, and then as she leant forward and put her hands on either side of my head, she opened them and I was staring straight at her.

'Hello,' I said and she smiled. The words I love you stopped in my throat, but they were there, ready to come out, unthought, but if I'd said it I would have meant it.

We had a bath after.

'Are we going to stay the night?' she asked.

'Do you want to?' I hoped she wouldn't. It would have been difficult. I couldn't see her face.

'I don't know,' she said.

'Maybe not. If you're not sure.' I said it gently.

'It's not that. I've just got stuff in the morning.'

'We'll do it again,' I said. 'Next time.'

We didn't speak as we were getting dressed. In the lift on the way down I asked her was she OK. She said she was fine, but she didn't seem right. She walked out and waited outside while I paid.

'All right?' I said when I came out.

She nodded.

'What is it? What's wrong?'

She came over and hugged me.

'I'm fine,' she said. 'I have to go.' She left.

I turned my phone back on. There was one call from Carol wondering where I was and a couple of work-related things but nothing major. It was half-seven. I went home.

I was in good form the following day. I was busy, flat out, so when Gerry came in at five I didn't know what he wanted.

'I had a look at that,' he said. I had forgotten.

'At what?'

He smiled.

'At the ideas you gave me yesterday morning.'

'Oh yeah. What did you think?'

His face gave nothing away. Nor did his voice when he spoke.

'I thought it was great. A lot of it was very good. But I don't think we should use it now. I don't think we can. I will keep it though, and maybe at some stage later . . .' I held up my hand and he stopped. 'What?' he asked.

'You don't have to do this,' I said. 'I know the story. You'll keep it on file and should the need in the future arise. I've had those letters, Gerry. It's OK.'

'No, hold on. I'm serious,' he said sitting down opposite me. 'We may well use it but not right now.'

'Really?' I said. 'Why's that then?'

'It's quite political.'

'Ha!' I couldn't help myself.

'I'm serious,' he said. 'Come on. You understand how it works. These things come from different departments, this one should be coming out of training or HR or somewhere. Not from you. If I start implementing this stuff and it's like, you know, "Rory's had a brainwave so this is what you all have to do," there'll be resentment. It will do exactly the opposite of what it was intended to do. You know what it's like.'

'Yeah,' I said, my voice dead. 'So how are you going to use it?'

'I don't know. I could meet with the HR department. We could meet them together and suggest some of your ideas and let them take the credit. Let them put the plan in place. Get it implemented. Things improve. Everybody is happy.'

'Apart from me.'

He was getting frustrated.

'Jesus, Rory. You know what it's like. That's how it has to be. If you're doing this extra-curricular stuff for the good of the company then great, but I did warn you. I told you to concentrate on your own job. I know what you've done. I appreciate it but you hardly want to present it yourself to the entire company. "My manifesto for better living by Rory Brennan."' He was laughing.

'Why not? They need something to get them moving and if it's HR's responsibility then they're failing. Have you seen these guys? They're taking the piss. They come in at all hours and stand around chatting half the day. It's like a fucking social club. If you need them to actually do anything it's a major chore. I'm telling you, it's incredible that this place manages to keep going with so much dead weight.'

'But that's it,' he said. 'It does keep going. And just because you've had some sort of road to Damascus experience of late doesn't mean you have to change the way everything is done. Concentrate on yourself. Do your work well, as you always have, and just relax a bit. Don't worry about anybody else.'

'I was trying to look out for the company's interests,' I said, 'which ultimately are your interests.'

'Not your job,' he said smiling. 'My job. Don't worry. Relax. Have a good weekend and I'll see you on Monday,' and he was gone before I could say anything else.

Niamh wasn't there when I got home. It was a Friday night so she would probably have gone straight to the pub after college. She didn't normally stay out for long so I made some food and waited watching telly. She came in after nine. She was almost drunk, a controlled breeziness about her.

'How's my boy?'

'Fine. Yourself?'

'Yep. I'd a lecture until six and then I went for a drink with Léan and Aisling.'

'They're well?'

'Everybody is well. What about you?'

'Still fine.'

She collapsed down beside me.

'I'm knackered,' she said.

'So am I.'

'Is there anything to eat?'

'There's rice.'

She forced herself to stand.

'Do you want anything?' she asked.

'No.'

I shouted in to the kitchen after her. 'Do you remember what I was saying to you about Gerry? About the stuff I was going to give him and he didn't seem too keen?'

She came back through carrying a plate.

'Sorry. No.' She was shovelling rice into her mouth.

'It was only a couple of days ago. You said that he probably needed time to get used to the idea and that . . .'

'Oh yeah.'

'Well, he came to me today and said he wasn't going to use any of the things I gave him. He said it wouldn't be appropriate for it to be coming from me. Some sort of office politics issue.'

'That's a pain,' she said.

'I mean I spent so much time on this stuff and he just dismissed it out of hand. There's something going on there. It was good stuff I gave him. Well thought out and practical and everything. I said it already but I wonder if he's feeling under threat, if he's holding me back. He said he might pass on some of my ideas to the relevant people and let them take credit for them.'

She looked confused.

'Is this Gerry?'

'Of course it's Gerry. Who else would it be?'

'I don't know,' she said. 'I don't work there.'

'Well it's Gerry. Yes.'

'It sounds very annoying,' she said and carried on eating. I wasn't sure if she'd heard me.

'It's not annoying,' I said. 'It's a lot worse than that. I think I'm being seriously undermined here. I don't know if I can keep working in this atmosphere.'

'Oh come on.'

'What?'

'A a couple of weeks ago you were all fired up and enthusiastic and now you want to quit. You're good at what you do. You're an account director. Concentrate on that. Don't worry about this other stuff.'

I couldn't believe it. She said this.

'You sound exactly like him,' I said. 'Exactly the same story.'

Without saying anything she walked out to the kitchen.

'What?' I called after her but she didn't answer. She came back with more food and sat on the couch, her feet folded under her, watching the TV. I was sitting beside her staring at her. She wouldn't look at me. I picked up the remote and switched the telly off. She turned and faced me.

'What?' she said.

'What's wrong? What did I do?' I asked.

She said nothing for a minute. I was going to ask her again when she spoke.

'I don't know what's wrong with you. You're all over the place. One day everything's great and I'm the best girlfriend in the world and the next everything is shit and I'm conspiring against you. You told me that all the bad stuff was behind us . . .'

'This isn't about us. This is about my work.'

'It is about us. Of course it is. When you come home all wound up ready to jump down my throat if I say the wrong thing, that has an effect on us, on our relationship . . .'

'Relationship,' I said mocking. I regretted it immediately. 'I'm sorry. I just hate that . . .'

'No. No, you're right,' she said. 'Maybe we don't have a relationship. I don't know what you'd call it. We've tried so hard. I know you try but I can't handle this. Every time it's the same. A problem comes up and then you promise that it's going to get better and it does and then another problem arises and then more promises and it's exhausting. I'm tired of it. Up and down all the bloody time.' She looked exhausted.

'Just believe me when I tell you that this is real. I'm not imagining it. I want to do well but I think he's sabotaging me.'

'Why? It just doesn't sound like Gerry.'

'I know it doesn't. That's what makes it hard to convince you. I swear I feel like I'm losing it when I tell you about this, but when he's there in front of me there's no confusion. None at all. He smiles and it's all Rory me old flower and that but it's all complete bollocks and I'm not going to get anywhere as long as he's holding me back.'

'OK. But just ignore it as much as you can and get on with your work. It's just a job. It's not worth worrying about.'

'OK,' I said and I reached out to her. She took my hand but what she had said before was there with us. We sat hand in hand but it didn't feel right.

We went out with Patrick and his Dutch friend the following night. A lot of the old crowd were there, Ciaran and Jane and Phil and Catherine and some others. We arrived late. They'd all had dinner together but we came along to the club after. I'd spent the day in bed and she'd been out in her parents' place so we hadn't really spoken. She came back at seven and she seemed fine. Patrick was already out of his mind when we got there. I don't know what they were doing but the Dutch guy and him were all over the place. When we arrived he hugged us both and brought us over to his friend.

'This is Eddie,' he said. 'Eddie, this is Rory. One of my oldest best friends and a bad bad man.'

My heart stopped but I laughed.

'Why are you a bad man?' the Dutch guy asked me.

'Because I hang around with this arsehole,' I said.

'And this is Niamh his girlfriend. Isn't she beautiful? The poor girl stuck with this fucker.' We were all laughing. She was playing along but I could see she wanted to get away and talk to the others.

'Why don't you go on over?' I said to her.

'He wants rid of you now,' Patrick said. 'You better not let him out of your sight.'

'It's OK. I'll leave you guys to it,' she said.

After she went I spoke to Patrick with a smile on my face in case she was looking.

'What are you doing?' I asked him.

He laughed, his big gurning face split in half with a smile that wasn't natural.

'I'm messing with you. That's all. Don't worry. It's all completely innocent.'

'What do you mean innocent? Seriously. Do you want to break us up or something? I've done what I said I would. I'm not seeing your one any more. What more can I do? I can't undo what's happened. All I'm trying to do is forget about it and I can't do that when you're fucking me around like this.' I wasn't smiling any more.

He put his arm around me.

'Jesus, will you relax. I'm only having a laugh. You can't expect me not to rattle your cage a bit. You'd do the same to me. She didn't notice anything. She probably just thinks I'm off my head.'

'You are off your head. What's going on?'

He smiled.

'Eddie is a very bad man,' he said. I couldn't help laughing. We didn't talk about the other thing any more.

It was an OK night. I talked to all the boys, danced a bit. Niamh spent most of the night with the girls on the dance floor. I let her do her own thing. At the end when she came over and said she wanted to go, I was ready. We were saying goodbye to everyone, when Léan hugged me. She was drunk.

'Is everything OK with you?' she asked me.

'I'm OK,' I said. 'Yeah. I'm fine.'

'You'll be grand,' she said, all pissed and serious. 'Both of you. The two of you. You will be absolutely fine.'

I laughed.

'Thanks,' I said. 'I'm sure we will.'

'You will. I know you will,' she said and wobbled off somewhere.

We didn't talk in the taxi. We got back to the apartment and were getting ready for bed.

'What was Patrick on about?' she asked me out of nowhere. 'Saying you're a bad guy or whatever?'

It wasn't like her to notice.

'He was off his face. He didn't know what he was saying.'

'There was something going on there,' she said. 'It was like some sort of in-joke. Did you tell him we were fighting or something?'

'No. God no. Of course not. It wasn't anything. Really. I don't know. He was just on something.'

She looked at me. She was waiting for me to say something.

'I never talk about you and me with my friends. I never tell them anything. You know that, don't you?'

She didn't say anything. Then when she was standing with her back to me she said, 'I'm going to go to London with Aoife next week.'

'OK,' I said. 'What for?' I asked after a minute.

'Stay with Fiona. Neither of us has anything on so we may as well. Do a bit of shopping. Go to galleries.'

'OK,' I said. I wanted to say something else, to see if she was all right but I let it go.

# 9

Gerry was in a fouler on the Monday morning. I could feel the tension as soon as I walked in. Carol warned me but I went in to him anyway. He was normally OK with me.

'How are you? Good weekend?' I asked him.

'Yeah. Great.' Totally sarcastic. Then out of nowhere he said, 'When are we going to see something about H & H? They were supposed to be using us. Weren't you trying to get that account?'

I could barely speak. I wasn't ready for this.

'Yeah. I was, yeah.'

'So what's the story? What's going on?'

'It's fine,' I said. 'I spoke to them a while ago and they're still on board.' I tried to clear my throat.

'When's a while ago?' he asked.

'Are you serious?'

'Yes,' he shouted. 'I'm completely fucking serious.'

'I don't know, three weeks ago maybe.'

'Three weeks ago. Well maybe you should get on to them again.' I just stood there. I couldn't believe him.

'Now, Rory,' he said. 'From your own office.'

'Is something wrong, Gerry?' I asked him. 'You're in shit form.'

'I'm fine. I just feel things are beginning to slide.'

I couldn't help myself. I had to say it.

'That's what I was telling you. That's what I was trying to deal with.'

'Yes, well that's great but what about you? Are you leaving a three-week gap in communicating with potential clients or are you wasting your fucking time drawing up staff-training manuals that can't be

117

used?' He wasn't joking. He could be a scary bastard when he wanted. I didn't know what to say.

'You're still here,' he said. I turned and left without speaking.

I went to the kitchen and made a cup of tea. My hands were shaking. There was a guy there who'd started the previous week. I'd never spoken to him.

'How are you, Rory?' he said.

'Hi,' I said. I didn't know his name.

'Mark. I'm Mark.' He held his hand out and I shook it.

'Yeah. Mark. Sorry. You're new,' I said. I was still thinking about what had just happened. He nodded.

'He's in some mood today,' he said.

'Who?'

'Gerry.'

'He is,' I said. I left it at that. I didn't know this guy.

'Are you busy at the moment?' he asked then. I looked at him. He was just making conversation.

'I didn't think so,' I said. 'Fuck it. I'll live.'

'Of course you will. It's not like any of this stuff matters,' he said. I smiled at that.

'I'll see you later,' he said and I went back to work.

I rang Niamh. I needed to talk to someone, but her phone went straight to voicemail and I remembered that she was on her way to London. I called Róisín. She was fine. After a couple of minutes she asked why I hadn't called her over the weekend. I told her that I'd been really busy with work and that I'd meant to but I'd buy her lunch to make it up to her. She was OK with that.

We met in this place in Temple Bar that smelt of patchouli and rollies, making small talk, and she went quiet.

'What's wrong?' I asked her.

'What are we doing? I'd really like to know. I don't know what we're doing with each other. I mean, it's nice and that but I've only seen you a couple of times and I don't know what you want. I don't know if this is enough for you but I don't think it is for me. I'm not even sure. I mean, are we going out with each other?'

I didn't know what to say.

'I don't know. You have to understand that at the moment my life really isn't my own. So even if it seems like you're not getting much time, it's quite a lot of what I have to spare.'

'Yeah, I understand that,' she said. 'I'd just like to see more of you. I've never been in your flat. I've only met one of your friends.'

'It's a very small flat and all my friends are arseholes,' I said. 'You wouldn't like them.'

She kind of laughed and then said, 'You know what I mean.'

'I do. I will try and make more time. But it is difficult. If it's going to be a problem for you, I don't know, maybe you'd be better off – we'd be better off – not seeing each other.'

'But I don't want that.'

'Neither do I.'

'Well it seems a bit stupid to stop then,' she said, smiling.

When we came out of the café we walked down towards the bridge. She was talking about the tutorial she had that afternoon, when Ciaran and Jane walked out of a shoe shop right in front of us. I stopped and they started walking on ahead. Róisín didn't notice, she just kept talking. I thought they weren't going to see us when they turned straight around and there we all were face to face.

'Jesus. Rory,' Ciaran said.

'Hiya,' I said. 'How are you? Jane?' I was struggling to keep my voice under control. The only thing I wanted to do was start running. I almost passed out. Róisín said hi and they both said hi to her and we all stood there waiting. I had to do it so I said, 'Ciaran and Jane. This is Róisín,' and they all said hi again.

'How come you're not working?' I asked them.

'We both took the day off. Felt like dossing around town,' Jane said.

'Excellent,' I said. 'Excellent. Yeah, we're just on lunch. From work.'

'Oh right.'

'Do you work with Rory?' Ciaran asked Róisín and before she could say anything I said, 'Yeah she does.' Róisín looked at me really quickly and then just nodded.

'How's Niamh?' Jane asked.

'She's fine. She's in London for the week.'

'We'll have to all get together again soon,' she said.

'Yeah. I'm working my arse off at the moment. But, yeah, definitely we'll do something soon.'

'Definitely.'

'OK,' I said. 'Well, we better go.'

'Yeah. It was nice meeting you.'

'Nice to meet you both,' Róisín said.

'Nice meeting you.'

'Yeah. Bye.'

'Bye bye.'

'Bye.'

I could have fucking died. I needed to lie down and have a cigarette but before I could even think about it she was on to me.

'OK, that was weird,' she said. 'Why did you say we work together?'

'Yeah, I'm sorry. It's just. Embarrassing. I'm sorry.'

'What?' she asked.

I was flustered. I did the best I could.

'Well, it's just that if I'd actually told them that you were a friend they'd have built it up and they'd be telling everyone and just making a fuss and I don't know. You know. They're like an old married couple. They've nothing to do with their time. They're always trying to set me up with people, so it was just easier. Do you understand me? It's nothing to do with you. You don't mind?'

She shook her head.

'Not really. I suppose. I was just totally confused.'

'Yeah, I'm sorry.'

'Who's Niamh?' she asked then.

'She's my sister,' I said without thinking. 'Herself and Jane were in school together.'

'I didn't know you had a sister.'

'Yeah, well I don't see her very often. We don't get on that well.'

'See that's what I was saying to you earlier. I didn't even know that about you. Do you have any brothers?'

And that was it. She was fine. We arrived at the bridge and I said I'd ring her later in the week. When she was going, we kissed but I kept it as quick as possible and I was looking over her shoulder the whole time just in case.

I rang Dave at H & H that afternoon. Gerry was wrong to be worried. I knew this guy. I knew he needed a bit of space to make his decision but we had pitched better than anyone else could have and he liked me. The last day I'd seen him we'd gone for dinner with him and a few of his crowd and we wound up in Leeson Street. He'd told me then that we had the contract but he needed a couple of weeks to make it look like he was contemplating the others and to get everybody on side, so I'd left him to it.

His voice was friendly when I got him.

'Rory.'

'Dave,' I said, breezy. 'How's it going?'

'Grand. Yeah, fine. Yourself?'

'Ah yeah. Long time.'

'Yeah. I'm sorry,' he said. 'I've been meaning to get back to you.'

'Ah sure, I know. No problem. So what's the story?'

'With?'

I laughed.

'You know why I'm ringing you, Dave. It's not a social call.'

'Oh yeah, right,' he said. 'Look, Rory . . .' and I began to feel sick. I wasn't even listening. '. . . so there wasn't much I could do about it. I did try and get you but I never heard back from you, so it's gone to Delaney's now.'

'Jesus.'

'I'm sorry but you know, that's how it goes.'

'But Christ, Dave, you told me. You actually said it was a done deal.' I could hear how desperate I sounded but I didn't care.

'As far as I was concerned it was,' he said. 'Or as close to it as it possibly could be. But when this guy came in he took over on all these decisions and he wanted to go with them instead and I said we should give you guys a chance to pitch again so he said, "Well get them in today," and I couldn't get you so in the end Delaney's got it.'

'When? When did you try and get me?'

'I don't know. A week ago, last week sometime. Look they've shaken it up totally here. They've brought in this axe-man and we've lost about a third of our staff. I'm glad to have a job, so I'm not rocking the boat. What this guy says goes and I can't do anything about it. I'm sorry but I just can't.'

'Have they signed contracts?' I asked. 'I mean, is it absolutely water-tight?'

'It's gone, Rory,' he said. 'Forget about it.'

'That's what you said the last time. I don't fucking believe this. What's this guy's name?'

'There's nothing you can do.'

I hung up.

I went through to Carol.

'Can you get me phone records from the last week.'

She sighed.

'I'd rather not but I can.'

'I want to find out did David McGovern at H & H leave a message for me to call him at any stage in the past week.'

She came in to me five minutes later.

'Here you go.'

It was there in front of me. 'Thurs. 21st. 3.30 p.m. D. McGovern asks you to call him' and then his direct line number and his mobile.

'When was this?' I asked her.

She pointed.

'It says it there. Thursday the twenty-first.'

'I know. I know what it says but when was that?'

'Last Thursday.'

'And where was I?' I asked her.

'I don't know, Rory. Check your diary.'

I put my head on the desk.

'Are you all right?' she asked.

'No,' I said. 'I'm fucked.' Then I copped on and lifted my head and smiled and said, 'I'm fine. Thank you. Goodbye,' and she left.

I looked in the diary. I had had nothing on that day at all. It was the day we'd gone to the hotel.

Dave had told me we had it. He actually told me to give them a bit of space. It was worth forty thousand and it was gone now but it wasn't my fault. I could go and tell Gerry now, let him know that this guy had come in and given it to Delaney's. Explain what Dave had said to me. Be honest and up front. It was in the bag and this guy had come along and fucked us over. It was a pain in the arse and we could have really used the account, but there was nothing we could do. I couldn't tell him that day though, with the mood he was in. He'd get on to them and somebody would say something that could make me look shit. I'd have to wait.

He was leaving at half-six and he put his head round my door.

'So what's the story?'

'I couldn't get my guy today. He was out in a meeting all day. I'll get him tomorrow.'

'I presume we're still going to get it.'

I shrugged.

'That's where we left it,' I said. 'He just had to confirm.'

'Well he's taking his time,' he said. He stood there looking at me, waiting for me to say something. I couldn't think.

'I'm sure it's fine,' I said eventually.

I was still there an hour later trying to find anything that I could use to make up for losing H & H. There was a knock on my door and the Mark guy came in.

'We're going for a drink with Kate, it's her birthday, if you're interested,' he said.

'Which one is Kate?'

'Works in creative. Small girl, long hair. Kiwi.'

'Actually I don't care who she is. I want a drink. Give me a second and I'll go down with you.'

He waited in the hall outside. When we got to the pub a gang of people from the office had a table. I knew a couple of them from nights like this. I said happy birthday to Kate and bought a round. I sat in a group of guys and we talked about rugby for a while. They all knew a lot more than I did. I finished my first drink in a couple of minutes and went and got myself two more. When I sat down Mark watched me line them up.

'Bad day?' he asked me.

'Not the best.'

'Work stuff?'

I shrugged.

'A bit, yeah. Tomorrow will be better though. It has to be better.'

'What was up with Gerry today?' he said.

'I don't know,' I said. 'It's not like him.'

'Maybe not with you but then you're the golden boy.'

I just looked at him. He didn't know me well enough to be saying things like that. He could see me react.

'Sorry, I didn't mean that in a bad way, it's just what I'm told, that you've done really well since joining.'

'Nice recovery. Pamper my ego and I'll forgive you anything.'

'I've a degree in tactical arse-kissing.'

'Honours I'd say.'

'Masters.'

I got talking to him then. I asked him where he'd been before and he said he was with a crowd in Sydney. I told him I'd been in New York.

'What brought you back?' I asked him.

'Right time. It felt like it anyway. I just thought I could get places here now. Got the experience and that.'

'Yeah. A good time to be here,' I said.

'You glad to be back?' he asked me then.

I shrugged.

'I don't know, yeah. I suppose. It's OK. Normally.'

As the drink warmed me up I talked to the office people, told them they were all great and was a bit flirty with the girl whose birthday it was. She got off on it. It was fun. After the pub a few of them wanted to go to a club. I was going to go home. I wasn't too drunk, I could have saved the morning. I was weighing it up and then

I remembered that Niamh was away so I thought, Fuck it. I can't do anything about H & H now, a few more hours won't hurt. So I went and it was a laugh. I danced like an arsehole with the girls for a while and I began to feel sober so I went and found the boys. It was Mark and a couple of the young dudes. I sat beside Mark and we got into a shouty conversation most of which I don't remember. He was asking what I wanted to do, really like with the rest of my life and I remember saying not fucking advertising anyway and we clinked glasses. And there was something about Sydney and New York and girls and then he shook hands with me and passed me a wrap so I went to the jacks and had a little toot and when I gave it back to him, I wanted to hug him.

I don't remember what happened to the others but we ended up in a pool hall at five o'clock drinking cans of 7UP and doing the rest of the gear. I was kicking his arse at pool. I don't know if he was really shit but I kept on winning. Every jammy shot going down. I was slagging him and then putting my arm around him to let him know I was joking and then out of nowhere he started getting all grandiose saying he was going to be a star, that he'd have his own company by the time he was thirty. I laughed.

'I'm thirty,' I said.

'Well I'm twenty-five and I'll be running the show by the time I'm your age.' I could have got annoyed but I knew he was just wired so I said good luck to you and we kept on playing. We got taxis home and I lay there for ages chewing my jaw and wishing Niamh was with me.

# 10

It was eleven before I got in. Gerry was out of the office all day. I couldn't remember if I knew that before or not but I was happy. I made a cup of tea and was heading for my desk when Mark came in. He laughed when he saw me.

'State of you.'

'Whose fault is that?' I said.

'I didn't make you do anything.'

'Fair enough. When did you get in?'

'I don't know. Eight. Half-eight.'

'How did you manage?'

'That was my body,' he said. 'I'm expecting my brain later.'

'It can share a cab with mine.'

I rang a load of people around town, trying to find out what was going on, anything I could go after, and came up with one guy who had heard that OBS had dropped Mercury after the boss fell out with them over their creative. I spoke to a guy in our office who knew somebody there and got him to check and he found out that they hadn't settled on anybody else yet and then I talked to a few other people and heard that there were two companies pitching. I rang them and asked for the main man to call me back and spent the rest of the day waiting.

Gerry came in at three. He walked into my office with his coat on.

'You're here,' I said to him, 'obviously.'

'I'm going out again. How are things?'

'Grand, yeah. I think I may have something new for you by the end of the week.'

'Good. Any word from H & H?'

'No,' I said. 'Because he's out sick today.'

'Who?' he asked.

'My guy.'

'Who is he?'

'David McGovern.'

'McGovern,' he said, thinking. 'Is there nobody else there that can help us?'

'Look, there's no problem. He'll be back tomorrow they said. He's who I've been dealing with so I think I should stick with him.'

'Yeah, well I don't know,' he said. 'Maybe I should give them a call.'

'One day isn't going to make a difference. If I start pushing it when he's not there it may just piss him off. He specifically asked that I give him a bit of space to sort it out last time we talked.'

'That's nearly a month ago. I hope he's still on side.'

'He's a good guy,' I said. I really needed this conversation to be over.

'Well, we'll see tomorrow.'

After he left I rang Dave.

'Yeah, Rory?' he said when he came on the line.

'I just wanted to clear something up.'

'Yeah?' He wasn't so friendly this time.

'When your man, this new guy, came in he just wanted to go with the others, yeah? I mean there was nothing we could have done, his mind was made up, right?'

He hesitated.

'Well, he might have been open to some sort of negotiation. He did want to talk to you, but he only left that open for, I don't know, a day.'

'So he wasn't really serious. It sounds like that anyway. We had a deal and he came in and broke it.'

'Hang on now, we never officially had anything . . .' he said.

'Officially, yeah, but I remember that conversation—'

'So do I,' he interrupted me, 'and I was drunk and I was trying to do you a favour because I think of you as a friend so if you're planning some sort of legal thing . . .'

'I'm not. Jesus, Dave. Of course I'm not. I just wanted to make sure that there wasn't anything else we could have done.'

'Well, returning my call might have helped.'

I sighed.

'Yeah but seriously. It wouldn't have made any difference, would it? Really?'

'Probably not. If it salves your conscience.'

'Hey, my conscience is clean.'

'Well so is mine so everything's cool.'

'Except we've lost out on forty grand, and I'll probably miss my bonus.'

'Well if I'm still working at Christmas I'll consider myself to be doing well,' he said. 'We've turned a corner.'

The guy from the OBS crowd rang me in the afternoon. I had to schmooze him but I got an appointment for the following afternoon. He didn't seem too keen but he agreed to give me fifteen minutes. It wasn't much but it was something and it would get me out of Gerry's way for a while longer. When I was walking out to go that evening I saw Mark at his desk. He looked up and nodded me over.

'All right?' I said.

'Pint?'

I laughed.

'You are joking.'

'No, come on. A cure. Just a couple.'

'No, I'm in bits,' I said. 'I've a big day tomorrow, I want to get home.'

'One. A swifty.'

'Are you ready to go? Right now?'

He picked up his jacket and turned his computer off.

'What were you doing, waiting for me?'

'Don't flatter yourself.'

I felt like shit in the pub. I shouldn't have been there. He started yabbering away doing a post-mortem on the previous night. I wasn't listening. He ordered a second drink before I could stop him.

'You're very quiet,' he said after a bit. 'What's wrong with you?'

'What's wrong with me is I'm in bits. I've had about four hours sleep.'

'More than me.'

'Yeah well, congratulations. That's what age will do to you.'

'Is the drink not working?'

'I don't think it's going to.'

'Don't say that,' he said. 'Don't ever say that. One more will do you.'

'I don't think so.'

He changed tack.

'How was your day?' he asked.

'Shite. Painful.'

'What was going on? At least the big man wasn't around.'

'He was there,' I said.

'Yeah, but not for long.'

'Long enough.'

'Don't you and him get on great?'

I hesitated before speaking and then I thought, Fuck it.

'When everything's going well, then we're the best of pals.'

'What's the problem then?'

'What's with all the questions?' I said to him. 'You're just making conversation to keep me here and drink with you, you sad fucker.'

'No. I'm interested. Seriously. I'm new to all this, how these places work. The politics and all that. Anyway you should be glad. This is therapy, man, you should be paying me.'

I laughed.

'You're full of shit.'

'So what's the story?'

The alcohol was working its way through into my bloodstream, well-being and comfort flowed through my joints and eased the pressure in my head. I was emotional, close to tears but happy in a sad way. I knew all this was just chemicals topping up, moving around, swapping places in my brain, down my spine, endorphins coming and going. All I wanted to do was talk to someone who would listen. My house was empty and this guy was sitting beside me and he wanted to hear it so I talked.

I told him a lot. How I'd had problems with Niamh and sorted them out and as a part of starting over had decided to put more effort into my work but felt Gerry wasn't happy with my efforts, that I wondered why.

'And now I think we've lost an account because of some fucker coming in and rattling his sabre and I'm going to have to bear the brunt.'

'What's it to do with you?' he asked.

'Nothing. Or you know, it was my job to try and get the account but what can I do? They brought in this guy and he just decides to give it to someone else.'

'What could you do?'

'Nothing,' I said.

'So what's the problem?'

'All Gerry's going to see is us forty thousand down. That's it. The rights and wrongs aren't going to matter. He'll just think I've cost him forty grand.'

'What's he said about it?'

'He doesn't know yet. I'll tell him tomorrow or the next day, whenever.'

'But surely you can explain to him, I mean it's not your fault.'

'That's all I can do. I'm trying to get another account opened so I can give him good news with the bad but I don't know.'

'I can't believe they just changed agencies like that. No consultation.'

'I know. They did . . .' I stopped.

'What?'

'He did ring apparently, asked me to call them back and then about an hour later called the other crowd to give it to them.'

'Did you ring?' he asked me.

'I never got the message.'

'Well fuck it,' he said. 'It sounds like it wouldn't have made a difference anyway.'

'That's what I thought,' I said. 'It wouldn't have. Fuck it anyway.' I ordered a drink. 'Last one,' I said.

'Yeah, I know. Absolutely.'

We sat in silence for a second.

'How are you feeling?' he asked.

'Better actually.'

'See I told you. Therapy.'

There was pain in my smile.

'Two pints of therapy more like.'

'Whatever. You felt crap. Now you're better.'

We drank the last one quickly. As he was putting on his coat I said to him, 'This is all between you and me. Seriously, yeah?'

'I know.'

'Nobody knows this stuff.'

He sat back down on the stool.

'I don't talk to people in work. I come in, do the job and go home. Few pints occasionally that's it. I don't talk to those people. Anyway you've got worse shit on me.'

'I suppose.'

'It's only a fucking job. Don't worry about it.'

'I know,' I said. 'I don't.'

It was only ten o'clock. I got a taxi home and fell asleep on the couch with the television on. I didn't know where I was when I woke at half-two. I got undressed and went to bed.


I was in work putting together the proposal for my meeting that afternoon when Ciaran rang.

'Is Niamh still away?' he asked me.

'Yeah. Why?'

'We thought we'd have you around and feed you, couldn't have you starving to death. Her coming home to a corpse.'

'It's not been easy,' I said. 'I can see my ribs.'

He laughed.

'It's been a while since you could say that. Would you like to bring your friend?'

I knew he'd bring it up.

'Who's that?'

'That little girlie you were with the other day. You made a lovely couple.'

'Oh fuck off. She's a nice girl. There were a few of us out at lunch and the rest were just ahead.'

'Hey. I'm not saying anything. Your secret's safe with me.'

'There is no secret.'

'Of course there's not.'

'You're such an arsehole,' I said.

I knew the thought hadn't even crossed his mind. If it had he wouldn't have said anything.

At two o'clock I got my stuff together and was walking out to get a taxi to the meeting. Gerry was coming back in after lunch.

'Where are you off to?' he asked.

'I'm talking to this OBS crowd in East Wall.'

'How are you fixed?'

'I don't know. I'm ready for it but we may not get anything out of it. We came in on it late.' Straight away I regretted saying it.

'Why's that?' he asked.

'Well, we don't know anybody there. I just got a tip from somebody that they were looking for a new agency, but they'd already started into the process when I heard.'

'Right,' was all he said, leaving a silent accusation hanging there.

'I can't cover everything, Gerry,' I said. 'You know that.'

'Yeah, I know. I know you can't,' he said.

They left me waiting in the lobby for fifteen minutes before bringing me up. I was sitting there trying not to let it get to me and the thought crossed my mind, Is this part of the test?

It was just me and him. He was sitting behind a desk with two empty chairs on either side of him. He was such a prick. One of these guys who's got fat and stupid because nobody ever says no to him. I did what I could but it was hard to keep the enthusiasm going, telling him how we were just what OBS needed, when he kept looking out the window and yawning. All I wanted to do was smack him. I was surprised when he interrupted me.

'You're going through the motions, aren't you?'

'I'm sorry?'

'You know what I mean,' he said. 'You look like you've done this a thousand times before and you'll do it a thousand more.'

I stood there for a second saying nothing.

'Not at all. No. I . . .' I waited for a second and then let it come. 'I just found it hard to keep going when you're so obviously not interested. I don't want to waste your time any more than I have to, and I certainly don't want to waste my own.'

A flash went through his eyes. I had his attention now.

'We told you before you came in that no final decision had been made about this contract,' he said. 'That remains the position and it's your job to pitch as well as you can. If I'm standing on my head or asleep or drunk that's what you do. Whatever you may think of yourself, you're a salesman. Nothing more or less. I'd heard you were good at what you do, I've heard your name before, but if this is Talisman's concept of professionalism I would say I've been misinformed.'

We stared at each other in silence. I thought about doing something, letting myself go, but I needed him more than he needed me.

'I'm sorry,' I said. 'Let's carry on.' My voice stayed clear and I managed to keep my hands steady. He sat there impassive and completely still but his eyes were watching. They were taking it all in. At the end when I finished he didn't stand. He picked up a pile of papers and started flicking through them.

'Thank you, Mr Brennan. We'll be in touch.'

'Thank you,' I said. I gathered my bits together and left.

I scabbed a cigarette off the taxi driver and the two of us sat in solid traffic, filling the car with smoke.

'You're enjoying that,' he said to me in the mirror.

'I earned it,' I said.

It was nearly four by the time I got back. I went straight over to Carol.

'Did anyone call for me?' I asked her.

'I don't think so.'

'No messages?'

'No.'

'Where's Gerry?'

'He's gone.'

'For the day?'

'I don't know? What time is it now? Yeah, I suppose.'

'He wasn't looking for me?'

'He knew where you were,' she said. 'You were with OBS, yeah?'

'Yeah yeah.'

I went into the office. I thought that they would have already called. I expected the message. Thanks but no thanks. Tough shit fuck you. I thought I'd blown it. I would have to wait. The phone went. I answered.

'Who is it?' I asked Carol.

'Rory?' It was a girl's voice.

'Who's that?' I said.

'Jesus, who do you think it is?'

'Niamh. OK.'

'You don't even recognize my voice?' she said. 'I've only been gone a couple of days.'

'Well, you know. I wasn't expecting you. When are you coming back?' I asked.

'Tomorrow.'

'How has it been?'

'Fine. Eating loads, drinking too much, spending too much. I don't know why you hate London.'

'I don't hate London. I just couldn't live there, that's all.'

'I don't know,' she said. 'I think it's great.'

'So you're back tomorrow?'

'Yeah. What have you been up to?'

'Nothing,' I said. 'Just working really.'

'Busy?'

'Yeah. It's been too much. I don't know.'

'Have you seen anybody else?'

'No. Nobody,' I said. 'Or yeah. Well I'm seeing Ciaran and Jane tonight.'

'That'll be nice.'

'Yeah, he just rang this morning and asked me over.'

'And me?'

'Well they knew you were in London.'

'How did they know that?' she asked.

'I don't know. What time tomorrow?'

'Early evening.'

'Well I should be at home,' I said. 'You don't want me to come out?'

'No. Sure I'll be with Aoife. I'll see you at home.'

'I miss you,' I said.

'No you don't. You're too busy to miss me,' she said.

'No, I wrote it in my diary, "must miss Niamh", so I'm doing it.'

'Miss Niamh. Very nice.'

She seemed OK.

I went home and had a shower. I bought a bottle of wine and walked to Ciaran's place. He answered the door and took my coat. The house smelled of garlic and perfume. When I walked into the living-room Léan and her boyfriend Johnny were sitting on the couch and Patrick was lying on the floor.

'Howaya?' I said.

'How's the boy?'

'All right.'

I stood above Patrick.

'All right?' I said looking down at him.

'Not bad.' He smiled up at me.

I sat in an armchair and Ciaran gave me a beer. We talked for a while. The mild buzz off the beer, laughing about stupid things. People I knew so well we didn't finish our sentences. It was like being in the womb. Completely natural. The shit of my life beyond the door didn't matter.

We were sitting around the table after dinner when Léan asked about Niamh.

'She's fine,' I said. 'I spoke to her today.'

'What's she planning on doing next year?' she asked.

'I don't know,' I said. 'She was talking about doing a doctorate at one stage, but probably not next year.'

'Rory may have moved on by then anyway,' Ciaran said. I looked at him. His face was red and he was swaying in his chair with a grin from ear to ear. Hammered. I ignored him and kept talking.

'So I don't know for sure. Has she said anything to you?' I asked her.

'He's got himself a bit on the side,' Ciaran said.

'What are you rambling on about?' I asked, smiling though I could have killed him. The risk, how drunk he was, the stupid antiquated expression.

'Shut up, Ciaran. You're pissed,' Jane said.

'What's this?' Léan asked. 'Is Rory being bold?'

'I'm not,' I said. My smile was wearing thin. I flashed a quick look at Patrick and he was just staring at Ciaran, his arms folded across his chest.

'Well, he says he just works with her but I don't know. They looked very cosy. A lovely young one.'

'Shut up, Ciaran,' Jane said again. 'You're embarrassing him.'

'That's why he's doing it,' I said and Ciaran laughed.

I looked at Léan.

'I was at lunch with a load of work people,' I said to explain, 'and we were going back to the office and I was at the back with this secretary when I met Ciaran and Jane and because he's so fucking bored and has nothing better to do, he's decided I'm having an affair.'

'I didn't see anyone else,' Ciaran said.

'Well, you see what you want to see,' I said and I thought that was it, but then Patrick spoke.

'What was her name?' he asked. I looked at him. He was staring at Jane. She was thrown, his tone out of place in the atmosphere.

'I don't know,' she said. 'I don't remember. What was it, Rory?'

I didn't know what to say and then before I could speak Ciaran said, 'It was Rosaleen or something. What was it? Something Irish. What was it, Rory?' And he looked at me.

'Róisín?' Patrick said.

'That was it,' Jane said. 'Roísín.'

I couldn't look at him.

'How did you know?' Léan asked him.

'Just a guess,' he said.

I sat there and the conversation continued. I couldn't hear it any more. I just lifted my glass to my mouth, lifted the bottle to my glass and drank and it all went on around me. I didn't even know if he was telling them about it, telling them what a wretched bastard I was, lying to my girlfriend and to my friends, even to them. I didn't know. When I started listening again their voices came back to me like I was coming out of a tunnel and they were laughing. I chanced a quick look at Patrick. He was smiling at the conversation and then he turned to me and his expression changed, the smile melted off his face and left a cold blank absence. It was horrible. I kept smiling and turned back to follow the conversation.

'I'm going to go,' he said and he stood.

'What?' said Ciaran. 'Sit down, you fucker. I was just about to get the grappa.'

'That's a good reason to go,' Patrick said and Jane went to get his coat. I sat with my smile fixed and when he was going I said goodbye with the others.

'What's wrong with him?' Ciaran said when he'd left.

'It's getting late,' Léan said. Nobody said anything for a second and I nearly spoke. I felt I should explain something. That they all were wondering and waiting for me to tell them why Patrick had been so weird but I knew there was no point. These silences and awkward moments become loaded when you're stoned or guilty, you think it's all about you but it's not. Ciaran went and got the grappa and after a couple of minutes we were back to normal, pouring that fucking poison into us in shots, drinking coffee in between to get rid of the burning foulness. Then I could feel myself drifting and I knew I should go. When I tried to stand to get out, to go and get a taxi, I took a step sideways and grabbed onto the table and the bottle fell and I watched the drink glug across the tablecloth.

'Fucking hell, you big ox,' Ciaran said.

'Don't worry, it's fine,' Jane said, wanting me gone but it was time anyway so it was fair enough.

'I'm going to go,' I said and they all said goodbye.

I was talking to myself outside as I walked to find a taxi, trying to remember what was worrying me and I knew it was something bad and then I knew it was Patrick, I remembered, the bastard, looking at me like that. That's not what a friend would do, all that fucking stupid mate stuff just gone out the window. I wanted to ring him and say it. Say, Yeah, I'm not perfect but are you? Who is? Because it's not about being perfect. It's about sticking with the people who matter. I wanted to ask him. Is anything worth losing that? Because surely without it we're all fucked, we're on our own and that's not how it's supposed to be. I tried to ring but it went straight to his message and then I couldn't remember what it was I wanted to say anyway so I hung up. I got a taxi but the driver put me out because I was giving him shit about the radio programme and he wouldn't turn it off so the bastard put me out and I had to walk the rest of the way.

# 11

I puked in the morning when I woke up. The alarm got me just in time. The grappa came up the same as it went down. I had a shower and walked to work. I was sweating when I got there.

'You look like shit,' Carol said when she saw me.

'I'm not feeling the best,' I said.

'Why did you come in?'

'I had to. I've too much on.'

'Yeah, but it's not worth killing yourself for.'

'I'll be all right.'

I sat at my desk with a cup of tea. I was shivering. I started reading the media pages on the Internet. Gerry came in.

'Jesus,' he said when he saw me. 'What happened to you?'

'I'm all right. I'll be all right.'

'What were you at?'

'Nothing. It's just a bit of flu or something.'

'You look like you've got the plague.'

'I'll be all right,' I said. 'If people stop going on about it.'

He shrugged.

'How did you get on yesterday?'

'OK. I don't know. It was OK.'

'So?' he said.

'So I'm waiting to hear back from them,' I said. 'If they haven't rung by lunch, I'll ring them at two.'

'OK. Who was it anyway?'

'It was O'Brien himself.'

'The son?' he asked.

'No, the old lad.'

'Robert?'

'Yeah, I think so, yeah.'

'I know him,' he said, smiling to himself.

'What's he like?' I asked.

'He's all right. He's sharp enough, you know. Not as stupid as he looks.'

'Yeah,' I said. 'I thought that.'

He was walking out and then he stopped at the door.

'What are you doing today?' he asked.

'I don't know. Catching up on a few things.'

'You're not leaving the office?'

'No,' I said.

'OK. Because you look . . .'

'What?'

He smiled.

'Contagious.'

I couldn't help laughing.

I tried to ignore it. I tried to focus on anything else but it built and built in my mind until I just had to deal with it. I rang Patrick.

'Hello.'

'How are you?' I said.

'OK.'

'I'm fine,' I said but he hadn't asked. 'I tried to ring you last night.'

'Yeah?'

'What's the story?'

'How do you mean?' he asked, playing thick.

'What's going to happen?'

'You tell me.'

'Oh for Christ's sake. What's wrong with you?'

There was nothing for about ten seconds. I thought he was gone and then he spoke.

'It's so stupid. You don't even see that I'm pissed off because I care. That's all. You can do what you want. Have an affair with a little kid if it makes you feel good about yourself, but it's wrong. It's just wrong and you don't see that you're compromising me by continuing with it.'

'That's bollocks. Absolute shite. It's nothing to do with you.'

'No. You're right,' he said. 'It has nothing to do with me now. When I thought you were listening to me, when I was giving you advice and it looked like you were going to take it, then, then it had something to do with me, but now it doesn't because you've decided to behave like a fucking moron. You're about fifteen years too early for a midlife crisis but there's nothing I can do about it.'

'Hold on a second. You have no idea what kind of shit I've had to deal with—'

'So that entitles you to do what you want? To lie to your girlfriend and mess around with this other girl's mind and to sit there so fucking blasé and talk complete bollocks to your friends and watch them smile and lap it up because they know you and they know you would never lie to them of all people. That you'd tell them if something was wrong.'

'Well, considering the first person I tried to tell jumped straight up on his high horse are you surprised?' I said.

'Don't try that. You know full well the reason you didn't tell them is because you were fucking shitting it. You can try to convince yourself that it's OK. You think what you're doing is cool, fucking jack-the-lad. But whatever you say, whatever may or may not have happened, whatever reasons you think you have, all you're doing is having your cake and eating it and people will get hurt and more than likely, and this is what is so fucking laughable, you'll end up hurt worst of all.'

'Well, you'll be happy then. What's happened to you?'

'To me? Oh for Christ's sake. You should be asking yourself. You used to be all right. Not this prick that you're becoming.'

'I'm on my own. I've got fucking nobody here. I'm trying so hard and I can't make it work.'

'What are you talking about? I don't understand you. You know what you're doing is wrong. You know it's going to end badly but you're going to keep on doing it and you expect me to be supportive and to be there like a fucking idiot believing whatever spiel comes out of you, patting you on the back telling you you're a great guy. Well I won't do it. Cop onto yourself, for fuck's sake.' He was gone. I dialled his number straight away but I hung up before it started ringing. I'd lost momentum.

When he used to get into trouble I always took his side. When he was mad getting into fights and hassle all the time, I'd always pull him away, shut him up, sort him out. When we were sixteen and he was too fucked to go home, he would crash on the floor of my room. When the others were saying he'd lost it, I always argued with them. I'd never let him down. And now he'd got himself together, he was bollocking me? He wasn't standing by me when I needed him and I didn't know why.

Carol rang me half an hour later.

'Gerry wants you.'

'Can he not come in himself?'

'I don't know,' she said. 'You better get in there.'

I walked into his office and he told me to close the door.

'I just spoke to Rob O'Brien,' he said as I was sitting down.

'So?' I asked. 'What's the story? Did we get it?'

He laughed, short.

'No, Rory. We didn't get it.'

'Shite.' He was looking at me, almost smiling. I had to say something.

'So did he say why?'

'He did.'

These stupid pregnant pauses.

'So? What? Am I supposed to guess?'

'Well, maybe. How did you think it went?' he asked.

'I told you, Gerry, I thought it was OK. I did what I always do and he didn't seem too interested—'

I jumped when he shouted.

'So you bollocked him. You fucking sorted him out, did you?'

'No. No.'

'Because that's how he tells it. Except he said you were half-asleep while you were giving the presentation. He said you looked like you'd spent the night under a fucking hedge.'

'Oh come on, Gerry,' I said. 'You know this guy. He's an arsehole.'

'No he's not an arsehole. He is the boss of a company who could have paid two of our people's salaries for the whole of next year, if you'd swallowed your fucking pride and just done the job properly.'

'They were never going to let us pitch anyway. I swear to God.'

'That's not how he tells it. But anyway, what is the point of going in with that attitude? You may as well stay here and scratch your arse. If you get a chance of work you do whatever you can to get it.'

I tried to calm him down.

'OK. OK. But I swear it wasn't me, Gerry. I went in there and did everything I could. I know how to do the job. You know that. I mean, Jesus, FitzPatrick's?'

'That was two months ago,' he said. 'You've done fuck all since then. What's the story with H & H? I still don't know.'

'It's getting sorted,' I said. 'They've had a bit of a shake-up and they're all over the place but I'm meeting Dave next week.'

'When next week?'

'Monday,' I said off the top of my head.

'Why do you have to meet him?'

'I don't know. When I rang he couldn't talk and he asked could I come in and see him. It could be good.'

Anything to get him off my back, anything.

'OK, well listen to me. I've never had a client ring to complain about the complete lack of professionalism of one of my people. Never. I know he's a bit of a wanker, but it's not good enough. I mean, look at the state of you.'

'I'm sick. I'm sick and I'm here.'

'Sort yourself out for fuck's sake, Rory. What happened to this new and improved you? You've been walking around like a fucking zombie for the past two weeks. Get your act together or we're going to have a serious problem.'

It was better that I didn't say anything. I left and went back to my office.

When my phone rang I hoped it would be Niamh. I needed to talk.

'Rory?'

'Yeah. Who's this?'

'It's Róisín.'

'Róisín. Hi. How are you?' She'd never rung me at work before. She was talking. I interrupted. 'How did you get my number?'

'You rang me last week. The number was still in my phone. Is it OK?'

'It's fine. How are you?'

She started chatting away. I couldn't handle it. I cut in again.

'I'm really sorry, but it's not a great time.'

'Oh right. I just wondered if you were free for lunch?'

'Yeah, OK. When and where?'

The restaurant she had chosen was packed by the time we arrived so we had to find somewhere else. We were walking along the street and we passed a place that Niamh and her crowd were in all the time.

'Let's go in here,' she said. I knew she would.

'I don't know.'

'What's wrong?' We stood outside and looked in. It was a really nice place, the smell of coffee and baking wafting out of it, a free table for two in the window. It was stupid. It was my head. I couldn't think of anything to say. I couldn't see anyone I recognized.

'OK. Fuck it. OK.'

We sat in the window like animals in a cage at the zoo. My head was pounding. I wasn't well.

'Why didn't you want to come in here?' she asked. 'It's lovely.' I was looking over at a girl that I thought I recognized. She was standing with her back to me paying. The same hair as a friend of Niamh's. I looked down as she turned to walk out and then I saw it wasn't her. When I looked up Róisín was still staring at me.

'What?' I said.

'This is a nice place. Why did you not want to come in?'

She just wanted to know.

'I'm not well. My head's in bits. I don't know. I don't feel like being seen. It's too exposed. But it's fine. It's all right.'

There was a guy walking by on the street outside who caught my eye and held it. He slowed for a second and then walked on. I felt like screaming.

'What is it? What's wrong?' she asked.

I took a deep breath and I was OK.

'I'm sorry,' I said and I smiled.

'What do you think it is?'

'What?'

'Are you getting flu or something?' she asked.

'Yeah, maybe. Something. I don't know.' I rubbed my head. It felt like it was going to blow apart. 'I'm really sorry,' I said. 'I'm not great company today.'

'It's OK,' she said and she held my hand. I smiled at her and looked her in the eye and then took my hand away and flashed a quick glance to the street outside. We didn't talk as we ate. Afterwards when we were having coffee she asked could I meet her that night.

'I can't. I'm not. I've got,' and the words didn't come. Funeral. Party. Work deadline. Anything would have done, but all I could think was, Niamh is coming back tonight. 'Something to do,' I said after too long.

'Oh,' she said, disappointed.

'Yeah. I'd love to but . . .'

'Right. It's just that it's my birthday tomorrow and I'm going out tonight and I'd like it if you could be there.'

'Oh Christ.'

'If it doesn't suit.' She sounded hurt. I couldn't leave her. I knew with every word that it was going to be a problem.

'No, I want to. I might be able to get free a bit later on.'

'Could you? Do you think you could? I'll be out with a few people and I'd love if you could meet them.'

I couldn't back out. It was her birthday.

'OK,' I said. 'I'll give you a ring later and find out where you are.'

'That's great.'

We left and I said goodbye to her on the street.

'I'm sorry,' I said. 'I'm not normally like this.'

'I know. It's OK.' And she went off.

I went to get her something. What do you buy a nineteen-year-old? I didn't know if she read or what kind of music she was into. I wandered around Grafton Street, totally lost, and in the end I went to Brown Thomas and bought perfume. I just didn't know. I got something light and expensive that the girl sprayed on her wrist to let me see. It smelt young to me. I thought she'd like it.

I went back to the office. My mind wasn't working. I was sick. I fucked around on the internet all day. I left at five without saying anything to anyone.

I made food when I got home. Niamh came in from the airport at eight. Aoife was helping her carry her stuff.

'You're here,' she said when she saw me.

'I said I would be.'

'I'm going to go,' Aoife said. 'See you, Rory.'

They stood in the hall talking and then they both laughed.

'Are you all right?' she asked when she came back through.

'I don't know. I'm feeling pretty rough.'

'Was it late at Ciaran and Jane's?'

'Yeah. But it's not that. I don't know. I think I'm getting something.'

'Don't go to work tomorrow,' she said, 'if you're sick.'

'I am sick. Or something. I don't know. I have to work tomorrow anyway.' She didn't ask why so I continued. 'I had a bad day today. Gerry went through me because some guy I was trying to get to pitch to—' She breathed in as if she was going to speak. I stopped and waited, looking at her.

'What?' she asked. 'What happened?'

'I thought you were going to say something.'

She sat back in the couch and closed her eyes as she spoke.

'I'm sorry, Rory. I don't need to hear it right now. I'm tired. I had a long day and I just can't handle another story about Gerry the bastard.' She sounded exhausted.

'OK,' I said. 'Fair enough.' I went and put her dinner on a plate and brought it in to her.

'Thanks,' she said. She turned on the TV. We didn't talk for the next fifteen minutes.

'I may go out later,' I said.

'OK.' Nothing else. Then she looked at me. 'You shouldn't go out if you're sick. You don't seem to be up to it.'

'It's just that I said I would.'

'OK. Whatever.'

I went into the jacks and rang Róisín's message minder direct. It was a cop-out but I couldn't handle a conversation. I said I wasn't going to be able to make it, but I'd ring her the next day. I said I was sorry. I turned off the phone and went back and sat beside Niamh.

'Are you off?' she asked.

'No. I'm not going.' She nodded. I went to bed after an hour and I was asleep before she came in.

Anto called to see did I want to go out that Friday. I hadn't seen him since the conversation about Rachel in the sushi place and I felt bad. I thought it might be good to get out and just talk shite for a while.

It was packed wherever it was. Some new place that still had queues. When we got in we stood at the bar and drank. He was in good form. He didn't mention the Rachel thing and I didn't ask. He'd been trying to save which is why he hadn't been around, he said, and I felt bad that I hadn't called him. He wanted to go to Brazil and fuck around for a couple of months. He asked me how everything was, Niamh and work and all. I said it was all fine. There was no point. We were out.

It kept getting more and more crowded. People were pushing by moving through the bar, stepping in between us to get to the counter. The music got louder. Anto didn't seem to notice, shouting around people, leaning backwards and forwards to let them through, all the time describing a route up the Brazilian coast and talking about all the drugs and girls he was going to do. I couldn't hear half of what he was saying. The crowd was doing my head in.

'Why are we here?' I asked him when I could stand beside him.

'What? Where? In general?'

'Here. In this bar.'

'I just thought it would be fun. For the pose.'

'There's a lot of them. Whoever they are.'

'We can go,' he said.

'Where?'

'There's a salsa club thing in the Gaiety. I thought we might for a laugh.'

I shook my head.

'What?' he asked. 'What's wrong with that?'

'Salsa. I mean for fuck's sake.'

'What?'

'I don't know. And this place. The whole thing. All these pricks. It's all bollocks.'

'I'm not with you,' he said. He was getting pissed off.

'This is what you're supposed to do on a Friday night,' I said. 'Come to a place like this or to a salsa club or to whatever Norwegian ambient fucking jazz DJ is playing in the POD. It's so contrived, you know. Nobody says it but everybody is thinking, We are just the dogs' bollocks. We'll queue up in the rain and pay too much for everything and move on to the next über-trendy bar in five minutes because Dublin's just like Paris or Barcelona or London, except it's not. It's like fucking Sheffield except Sheffield isn't so completely up it's own arse.'

Anto looked at me.

'I'm going to the salsa place,' he said. 'I'm sorry. I didn't know you had a philosophical problem with it,' and he went. I waited a second and then followed him out.

He was walking fast up towards the Green. I caught up with him and pulled on his arm.

'Hold on a sec,' I said.

He shook my hand off.

'What is wrong with you? You come out with a face like death and then piss all over my idea of a good time.'

'I'm sorry. I wasn't. Just that place.'

'What's wrong with it? Too hip for you? Look at yourself. You're wearing the same clothes as the guys in there, you've got the same haircut. The only difference is they're having fun and you . . .' He hesitated. 'You're just not.'

'My head's not right. I'm having a bad time at work. It's like everything is closing in on me and it's driving me mad—'

He cut across me.

'It's Friday night. I don't care.'

'I know. But that's all it was.'

'I don't care. I don't want to know. I rang you and asked did you want to go for a drink and you said yes. If you have a problem with work or with Sheffield or Dublin or the general public, that's OK, but deal with it when I'm not around. I don't know what you're on about and I'm not interested in your sociopathic ranting. That's not what I want on a Friday night. So I am going to this club. Do you want to come?'

I felt stupid.

'Yes. Yes I do.'

'Are you going to be normal?'

'Yes.'

'OK.'

We walked in silence for a minute or two.

'I'm sorry,' I said again.

'Don't start,' he said.

We went and danced for four hours. It was full of Spanish girls and sweaty uncoordinated drunks like us. It was fun.

I hugged him when he was getting a taxi.

'I'm sorry,' I said again.

'Are you all right now?' he asked.

'I'm great,' I said. 'Salsa is good.'

'I told you,' he said, 'or whatever.'

I woke Niamh when I got to bed.

'Guess what I was doing?' I said.

'Drinking?' she said without opening her eyes.

'No. Well, yeah, but no. I was dancing. Me and Anto. It was brilliant.'

'You and Anto dancing?'

'Yeah. Salsa.'

'That's nice.'

'It was great. A really good night.'

'You're obviously hammered.'

'I'm not too bad.'

'You were dancing with Anto?'

'I wasn't dancing with him. I was with him and we were dancing.'

I was still laughing when I went to sleep.

On the Monday I knew I had to leave the office to go to my meeting with H & H. There was no meeting. Of course there wasn't but I was glad to have a reason to get out of there. I didn't know what I would do. Go to a film or something and then ring Gerry with the news. It wouldn't be good but it was time. I'd put it off too long and it was time to confront it.

I was reading a report in the paper, starting over and over, and after half an hour I was still on the first page. It wouldn't go in. It wouldn't gel together, each sentence standing independent from the one that preceded it, making sense word by word but you can't read like that. Carol came in and said, 'Gerry wants you,' and she was gone when I looked. I stood up and went out to the corridor. Mark was walking by.

'All right, Rory?' he said.

'How are you, Mark? Talk to you later.'

'Yeah, see you.'

I opened the door without knocking and walked in. He was behind his desk and sitting to the side on a chair was some guy from the HR department, Mike or Mick or someone.

'Sorry,' I said. 'Carol said you wanted to see me.'

'I do, yeah,' he said. 'Sit down.' I sat.

'What's up?'

'OK,' Gerry said. 'I'm going to talk and you just listen. You'll get your chance later.'

He breathed in and started.

'Last week I spoke to you about OBS and your attitude that Rob O'Brien was complaining about. Our reputation was damaged by your behaviour. I've tried to convince him that this wasn't typical, but I don't know if they'll ever seriously consider using us again. Next thing. I've been on at you for I don't know how long about the H & H account and you said you'd have an answer today after your meeting. I was thinking about this after you left and for various reasons, which I may go into presently, I decided to ask Mark if he could find out what the position was.'

I was thinking about his use of the word presently, his formality, and when he mentioned Mark I had to think back and replay what he'd said. I looked at the other guy. He was staring down at the desk in front of him. Gerry had stopped. I looked at him. He continued.

'It's not good, Rory. I know what the story is. There was no meeting arranged for today. The contract was gone and Mark has told me subsequently that you knew this last week. He says you told him about it in the pub and that he had intended to tell me about it, but held off out of some sort of loyalty to you which I think was unnecessary, but I understand his motivation. David McGovern tried to contact you on the Thursday before last to give you a chance to pitch again and he couldn't get you. I know that at that stage it mightn't have made a difference but what I don't know is where you were that afternoon, why you didn't get back to him, and why when I asked you what was going on you didn't tell me. Rory? I don't understand. I have tried at all stages to be approachable and I have treated you at all stages with respect and quite a bit of indulgence and you've taken advantage of that. You've called in sick I don't know how many times . . .'

'Three,' I said. 'Three times.'

'You've been consistently late,' he continued without reacting.

'Your appearance has been dreadful. Your attitude to the junior staff has been superior and I believe occasionally quite offensive. I don't know what's been going on with you for the past few weeks, but since your announcement that you were going to be working harder and giving it your all, you seem to have fallen apart completely. Looking back now I wonder what really happened with Anne, but there's nothing I can do about that at this stage. Professionally I've lost confidence in your abilities, but what upsets me, really upsets me, is that on a personal level I feel betrayed.' He stopped to let the impact of that sink in and then continued. 'I am hereby terminating your contract. You'll be paid until the end of this month. You will return your company credit card and swipe card. Whatever outstanding charges you have incurred will be deducted from your last pay cheque. After this meeting you can clear your desk and go. Is there anything you want to say?'

I was quite cool.

'Can I talk to you alone?' I said. 'Without this guy here?'

Gerry stood up.

'No, you can't. If you've anything you'd like to say, you can say it to both of us.'

I stayed sitting.

'OK,' I said. 'You're not alone. Do you know that? You're not the only one feeling betrayed. Can I say that? I mean that fucking weasel Mark is obviously incapable of loyalty and you should bear that in mind if you're going to keep him on, but can I ask you, do you have any idea of the extent that I've lost faith in you? I mean, think of how you've held me back, I tried as hard as I could to keep in control and when it became too much for me and I lost it a bit, who could I go to? You? That's a laugh. I got the FitzPatrick's contract which will continue to bring in serious amounts of money for a long time. I tried to develop staff motivation and you just dismissed me. I played the H & H thing as well as I could. Nobody else could have got past the door and we would have had the contract if they hadn't brought in this other guy. And I don't know where I was that day that they rang. Probably out scouting around for something, looking for something new rather than all these fucking desk jockeys sitting around talking about who's their favourite Spice Girl.'

I could see the HR guy try not to smile.

'What are you laughing at? Who is this guy anyway? Why is he here?'

'OK, Rory, that's it. That's enough. Let's go,' Gerry said. I hadn't even got to my main point. He opened the door. I stood up and walked out. There was a security guard, arms folded, waiting.

'You are fucking joking me. You're winding me up,' I said to Gerry. He shook his head and closed the door behind me. I banged on the door. The guard put an arm around me, gently, not really pushing, and just said, 'Come on, leave it.' Nobody was looking. All heads down. I went to my office and got my coat. I left everything else and walked out. Carol was waiting for me. She smiled.

'See you, Rory,' she said. 'Sorry.'

'Thanks,' I said. 'See you sometime.'

I looked across the open plan. He was there somewhere.

'Get the charlie out, Mark. Do a few lines to celebrate, you fucker,' I shouted and then we walked off.

Myself and the security guy walked to the lift. He came down with me.

'It's a nice day,' he said in the lobby. 'It could be worse.' I walked out into the sunshine. It was eleven o'clock.

# 12

I didn't know what to do. I rang Róisín first but her phone was off. I walked across to the Southside and went to a café and sat at a table outside. There was something illicit about being in town during the day. It was quieter, sure, but who were all these people wandering around shopping and yapping and posing at noon on a Monday? I didn't know what to do. My phone rang. It was Niamh.

'Where are you?' she asked.

'In town. On lunch.' I wasn't going to tell her until I sorted it out.

'Listen. I was just talking with Jane. Herself and Ciaran are going to come over tonight. I've got loads to catch up with in here. Can you sort out food? I'm sorry. Anything at all, I'm not going to have time.'

'I saw them last week,' I said.

'Yeah, I know but I didn't. It's only them. Anything at all.'

'Yeah, OK. When will you be home?'

'I don't know. About seven.'

'OK. I'll see you then.'

'See you.'

I thought about what I was going to do.

I bought wine on Harry Street and cheese on Anne Street and went to a French shop for bread. I'd got stuff before there which I liked, really heavy stuff. There were two French guys inside standing in the window as I went in. They were having a conversation which seemed quite involved. I walked straight in over to where the bread was, picked it up out of the basket and walked up to the counter and stood there with the exact money in my hand ready to go. I stood there. Where I was standing was out of view of one of them but in full view of the other. I mean he was practically facing me. The conversation continued, involved, fluent, impenetrable. I stood there. It made it worse that it was French somehow, that if I had understood what they were saying I would have known how trivial it was. It was probably less than a minute but the guy was fucking looking at me, looking through me. I put the bread on the counter and made a move to the door and stopped right behind the other guy. He turned around and I waved my hand in his face.

'Bye bye,' I said.

Their loss. I didn't look back as I left. You can ponce around in a uniform and apron and sell the best wine and pastry in the world but if I want to buy something and you won't let me, then you're not going to last too long.

I went around the corner to another deli. They had competition a hundred yards away. I picked up rye bread and chorizo.

'Anything else?' the girl asked.

'That's it.'

'Nine fifty.'

Nine pounds fifty for five little sausages and a loaf of bread.

'How much is the chorizo?' I asked her.

'It's done by weight . . .' she said.

'I know that. How much is it?'

She stopped a second.

'It's fifteen pounds a kilo, it's about one fifty a sausage.'

'And what, two quid for the bread?'

'About that, yeah.'

I handed her a tenner, shaking my head. She gave me fifty pence back.

'Sorry about that,' she said, smiling.

'Yeah, OK. No problem. Not your fault anyway.'

'It's hardly coming out of your dole cheque, is it?'

I looked at her a second. She smiled and shrugged and turned away. She was trying to be nice. I left.

In a café on Suffolk Street a girl too cool to open her mouth when she spoke sold me a takeaway coffee. Their coffee was always good. It was made by a machine. As I was going back to the flat I stopped and turned around, then turned again and went back into the French shop. The two guys were behind the counter now. One was serving a blonde girl in a big anorak and the other was labelling stuff.

'Hello,' I said, loud. The girl jumped. 'Remember me?' The two guys just stared at me.

'Do. You. Remember. Me?' The second guy whose back had been turned to me spoke.

'No.'

'I was here ten minutes ago. I came in and wanted to buy some stuff. Do you remember? You were very busy. You were having a conversation and I interrupted you.'

He looked at his friend. They both shrugged and then he looked back at me.

'I don't know. Maybe it's you are busy. You have a hurry.'

'Well it's OK. I went to the place around the corner. They speak English.' I knew I sounded like a prick but I didn't care. 'I spent a tenner there. Doesn't bother me, but next time you should think about serving the people who come in, when they come in. Maybe.' I turned and as I walked away he called after me.

'Bye bye. See you,' and then something in French.

I turned and walked back and stood with my face in his.

'Sorry didn't hear that. What you say?'

He spoke quietly in French, cool, showing nothing, but straight back at me. I moved off but then turned and threw the coffee cup into his face. I wasn't thinking. It was just too much. He shouted and went for me. I dropped my bag and pulled back my arm, ready to go. In that moment I saw him, his hair wet, holding his face, his composure shattered and I didn't want to be there any more. The other guy came out and pulled him back. I dropped my arm and stood looking at him and then picked up my bag and left. In the café across the street the customers were all staring out at me. I looked back and the two of them were standing in the doorway shouting after me. I turned the corner and went back into the park at the Castle and sat there waiting for my heart to stop pounding.

She came home at seven.

'What a day,' she said. I wasn't in the mood.

'I've been here since five o'clock picking up your shit and cooking.'

'I was in college, Rory. What was I supposed to do?'

'Well next time I invite people over, I'll try the same approach. I'll swan in an hour before they arrive.'

'Jesus, Rory, will you chill out. It'll be fine. They're your friends too. They won't care what the place is like or what we eat. It's Jane and Ciaran.'

I tried not to shout.

'Do you have any idea—'

'What? What, Rory? Do I have any idea what?'

There was nothing to say. She went and had a shower. I hoovered the living-room.

In the middle of the meal they started talking about cameras. Auto focus, shutter speeds, lenses that cost five hundred quid. I just drifted off. I wanted to be anywhere else, on the moon, on an island, in a pub. I was lonely and I wanted to be on my own. When I looked up they were watching me in silence.

'Hello,' said Ciaran.

'We lost you there for a sec,' Jane said, smiling.

'Space cadet,' said Niamh.

'I've never really got what the point of photos is exactly,' I said. 'I mean yeah OK if they're art then that's one thing, but why do we need to capture every memory on film? It interferes with the actual moment, you know, you go to the Grand Canyon and look out across this vast space and it's like, Oh hold on I've got to get the fucking camera, you know.'

'Rory refuses to smile in photos. Every shot we have his mouth is somewhere through saying "Take the fucking shot."'

'We were at the Grand Canyon last year,' said Jane.

'How was it?' Niamh asked.

'Big,' said Ciaran, smiling and looking at me. 'You should see the photos.'

'What were you doing zoning out like that?' she said when they were gone. 'You freaked them out. Staring into space and then attacking them because they like cameras. It was so rude. It was just embarrassing.'

'I didn't attack them. I was making a point. I'm allowed to have opinions. Surely. Anyway they didn't care, they didn't think it was rude.'

'No,' she said. 'They thought it was weird. What's wrong with you? You're so quick to get angry.'

I lay back on the couch, half pissed, and sighed. I couldn't tell her.

'I don't know. Work is a pain in the arse and it's getting me down.'

'Everybody's work is a pain in the arse, Rory. That's why they pay you. You have to be able to separate your work life and your life. Eighteen-year-olds can do it. I can do it.'

I wanted to tell her everything. Everything and be done with it, and hope there was enough still in her, love or interest or concern, to hear it and stay and work it out. I wasn't sure. I was too tired. She went to bed and I stayed up until two watching shite on telly.

In the morning Niamh left at nine. She tried to get me up but I told her I didn't have to be in until later. I was going to tell her about it that evening.

I rang Róisín. She was cold.

'I'm sorry I missed it,' I said straight away.

'It's OK,' she said in a voice that said it wasn't.

'Can you meet me today? I'll buy you lunch.'

'I've got a lot on.'

'I have a present for you,' I said.

We met at one at a pizza place. She wouldn't look at me.

'I'm sorry,' I said. 'I really am.'

She nodded, her eyes darting around anywhere but at me.

'How have you been?' I asked.

'Fine. Grand.'

'I got you this,' I said and handed her the bag. She put it on the table and left it there, without looking at it.

'Open it,' I said.

'I can't do this,' she said so quietly I could hardly hear her. I leant forward.

'I know, I'm sorry,' I said.

'That's fine. You're sorry, but what good is that to me? It's easy to be sorry. It's changing that's harder. I don't want somebody who isn't there and then apologizes. It's not enough.'

I didn't know what to say. I'd never seen her angry.

'I don't want to do this any more,' she went on. 'I know you've got a lot happening and all that but it's not enough for me. I'd like to know you better, I'd like to feel that I'm a part of your life and not just . . .'

'What?' I asked.

'I don't know. Somebody you kind of like, who you can meet when it suits you and have a nice time with and then forget about until the next time. I don't want to be the girl leaving messages on your phone. Chasing you. I'm not like that. I'm not some stupid girl, whatever you think.'

'I don't think that at all. At all.'

'I want somebody I can know, who rings me and who involves me in their life and doesn't keep a distance like it's some sort of power game or something. I'm not interested in that. I just want to relax, and I'm not relaxed with you. I'm not myself.'

We'd been there ten minutes and nobody had come near us to take an order or anything. It was pissing me off.

'I know,' I said. 'But I can see what you're like. I know the kind of person you are. I can see that you're funny and bright and you're a good person and very beautiful and I like everything about you. I really do and you do deserve more.'

She was looking down. She sounded bitter when she spoke.

'So what? That's great. But what difference does it make? When my friends are asking me when are they going to meet you and I don't know what to say. Soon. Never. Whenever it suits him. I don't even know if I should say you're my boyfriend. What am I supposed to say?'

'That I work all the time. That I've got a lot going on and if it was up to me, I'd be spending all my time with you and giving you what you want and deserve but I can't. Not at the moment.'

'That's what I thought. And fair enough, you know. I understand that. But it doesn't make it any easier. So I think we should just stop. Just forget about it. Seeing each other.'

I waited a second.

'OK,' I said. 'I'm sorry but I understand.'

We sat in silence.

'Should we just go?' I said.

She didn't say anything.

'Do you want to? Or we can stay. I'm easy.'

'For someone who—' She stopped and then started again. 'You say that you like me and think all these things, that I'm great or whatever, but it doesn't seem to bother you very much. If I'm so great then why is it so easy? Do you feel anything at all?'

'Of course I do. I'm human, you know, I'm not happy.' I could hear myself, calm and reasonable. I sounded like I was talking about shutter speeds. I leant forward and spoke faster.

'I don't want to stop seeing you. I really like you. A lot. But I don't want to keep on doing this if it upsets you. I can't give you what you need or whatever so I can leave it and I'm trying to make it as easy as possible for you. For you. That's all.'

'Why can't you? Don't tell me it's about work, because that's not it. You could be working a ninety-hour week and see me when you could manage it and it would be enough. It could be. Easily. It's not about time. It's about you. What am I, this casual little thing you have? This young one? You can say I'm great and you really like me but you don't really care. I know it's not about time. It's about you. You don't think I know but there's something else. You don't feel it or something. What is it?'

I didn't know what the question was.

'What do you mean?' I asked.

She shook her head and laughed even though she looked like she was going to cry.

'For God's sake. Just. Don't.'

I only said it because I thought it's what she wanted, that it would make it easier for her or better.

'OK,' I said. 'I have a girlfriend. She lives with me but for all the difference it makes—'

She stood and picked up her coat and walked out. She was quite calm. She just went. She didn't look at me or throw a glass in my face. There wasn't anything to throw apart from the Brown Thomas bag. I let her go and then picked it up and walked out. The waiter tried to say something but it didn't matter. It would be easier for her to hate me. I went to Burger King and had some lunch.

It was OK. It could be worse. She wasn't pregnant and she hadn't ever met Niamh. I had answered the question which had been worrying her in a way that didn't reflect badly on her. Easy for her to move on when I was just a bad bastard. That's all it was. It wasn't her. How long does it take to get over someone at that age anyway? Fifteen minutes? The colleges were full of sensitive, goateed little fucks who knew how to treat women. Big rugby-playing oxes all physicality if that's what she wanted. Junior intellectuals. Fun drunks. Cool druggies. Bearded weirdos. All of them had more of a future for her than I would ever have had.

It was a shame. She was fun and easy and beautiful. The easy life where nothing was real. It was better but it wasn't real.

Everybody was in work. I thought about ringing Patrick. He'd be eating pot-noodles and watching Jerry Springer, but a hardness cut through me and I wouldn't. He'd let me down. I went home.

I thought Niamh would be happy about the work thing. I was getting out and all those problems would be gone. All those distractions. She wouldn't know it, but now there was nothing interfering. She had my attention. It was just me and her. I could make it better. I was watching telly when she came in. I turned it off. She sat down on the chair across from me.

'How are you?' I asked.

'I'm fine,' she said. 'And you?'

'OK. I didn't have a great day.'

'Right.'

She wasn't interested. I laughed.

'No, but seriously. Wait. I really didn't.'

'Why?' she asked, totally bored.

'I lost my job. I got fired today.'

She kind of smiled.

'I did,' I said again.

'You're serious? Why?'

'I don't know. You know the whole thing with Gerry that I've been going on about. It's been boring for you I know but, seriously, he's not an easy guy to work with. It wasn't working out and there were things which he thought I should have done that I didn't and a couple of deals that went against me, just bad luck and stuff that I said totally off the record to some little prick which came back to haunt me, but that's it. Nothing really. I'm out of a job.'

'My God.'

'Yeah.'

She was shocked. She had gone pale.

'So what happens now?' she asked. 'What are you going to do?'

'I don't know. It's not that bad. I'll take it easy for a while. Despite what Gerry thought, I have been pushing myself pretty hard recently, so I'll chill out for a week or two and then start looking again.'

'Wow. It's a pity though. Are you all right?'

'I'm fine,' I said. 'I'll be fine.'

She was sitting with her elbows on her knees looking at me.

'And this just came out of the blue.'

'It had kind of been building but I didn't expect it. I was pretty shocked. They had a fucking security guard escort me out. Like I was going to stab someone or something.'

'I think that's standard enough. That they'd have one.'

'If it's some malcontent maybe,' I said, 'but, you know, me? I could have done without it. He was very nice about it though.'

'Who? Gerry?'

'No, the guard.' I laughed. 'Gerry wasn't so nice.' I tried to think of something to say. 'We could go on a holiday maybe. A long weekend or a week or something. I feel like I haven't seen you in ages.'

'I don't know,' she said. 'I've got a lot of work to get done. I've just been away. You could go with Patrick or someone,' she said.

'No. I don't know.'

'It's not a good time for me.'

'It was just an idea.' I didn't mean to sound hurt.

'Poor old you,' she said and she smiled. She stood up.

'It's fine,' I said. 'I'll get something else. Just relax the head for a bit.'

'Are you going out tonight?' she asked after a second.

'No.'

'Oh right.'

'Are you?' I asked her.

'No.'

'We're getting old,' I said. She kind of nodded. 'It'll be nice. What's on telly?'

She made dinner and I just zonked with the remote in my hand flicking. It was after we'd eaten when I was just beginning to relax that she told me to turn the telly off.

'What's up?' I asked.

'I'm going to go,' she said.

'Where?' I asked. I hadn't a clue.

'Home. To my parents.'

'What? Why?'

'I don't want to be here any more. I meant to say it to you before and I'm sorry but it's not working for me.'

'You're going home?' I still didn't understand. 'What's not working for you?'

'This. You and me. I've tried and I know there's all sorts of pressures on you but I can't do it any more. I'm sorry. I know it's bad timing for you but it's better that I tell you when I'm thinking of it. I couldn't be sitting here pretending everything is OK when it's not.'

I couldn't believe it.

'Twice in one day,' I said. 'This is hilarious.'

'I know, I'm sorry. I'm sorry but I didn't know it was going to happen like this.'

'But everything that's been happening, everything bad, is because of the pressure I've been under. You know that.'

'It's not, Rory. It's just not. That may be the reason but you've changed so much and I don't like it. I don't.'

'Can you not just give it a week?' I asked her. 'Give me a week and see what a difference it will make. It will be huge. I know what the problems have been and they've been there because I haven't been able to deal with them. I've had to just let them go. But now I can sort them out. I can sort it all out and I will. I just will, Niamh. Please. I'm sorry.'

'I can't. I'm sorry.' She was crying now, which was a bit much. She stood up and went into the bedroom. I sat there and called after her.

'Are you going to come back?'

She walked back in with a plastic bag full of clothes and bits.

'I don't know. No. I'm not. I'll come back for my stuff and I'll leave my keys and a cheque for the bills.'

'I don't give a fuck about the bills,' I shouted.

'OK,' she said. 'Well I will anyway. I'm going to go.'

I stood up.

'Hold on. That's it? You're just gone?'

She shrugged.

'When did you decide this?' I asked.

'I don't know. I mean, what difference does it make?'

'When? When?'

'This week. In London. Before that.'

'So what am I supposed to do?'

'I don't know, Rory. Sort yourself out. You're a mess.'

'Why do you think that is?'

'I don't know. I don't care. Whatever it is, look after yourself. Just unwind a bit. You're hard work, you know. You're not easy to be around at the moment.'

'Do you know what's been going on?' I asked her.

'Of course I know.' She was shouting now. 'Of course I know. You tell me every night what's been going on and I tried to help you but it makes no difference because you don't listen. You never just stop and think that people are on your side. The whole world is not against you. It's not all about you. Why do you think I'm going? I want my own life. I've got my own problems. I don't need to be constantly dealing with yours. The same thing over and over and it never gets better. It always ends up worse than before.'

She stood there, her face swollen with tears. She wiped her nose on her sleeve.

'So if I'd been out tonight, would you have just gone?' I asked.

'I don't know. Who cares anyway?'

I turned and walked off.

'The world's not against me? That's a laugh. I'm having a great week. Jesus Christ.'

I sat on the couch. She opened the door and left without saying anything else. I listened to the door close and then silence. I could hear the sound of the floorboards in the hall creaking quietly as they got back into place where she had been standing. The hum of the central heating. The clock in the kitchen pulsing. The bass of the voices on the television in the flat below. I picked up the phone and rang Anto.

He was out with his work crowd in town. I got a taxi and found him, sitting at a table with a whole load of drunk suits. I bought a pint and sat beside him. He introduced me. They all had English names, Dave and Nigel and Steve. He started talking to me, pissed.

'So how are you?' he asked me.

I breathed in and then I started.

'Shite,' I said. He laughed at first and then when he saw I wasn't joking he listened.

# 13

I didn't stay long with Anto. He was too pissed and I was bringing him down. It wasn't fair. I left them after the pub. I went home and slept for fifteen hours. I just slept and slept. I spent the next three days in the apartment sleeping, watching TV, eating what food there was. I didn't want to talk to anyone. It was Friday before I got dressed. I was in the living-room with a couple of unopened bank statements and a piece of paper working it out.

I needed a job. Looking at the bank statements, I could see that I cost about three grand a month to run, which was fine when you had it but scary when you didn't. I had four grand in a savings account and I had thought that would do me for a couple of months. Not likely. I looked through the paper. There were loads of jobs. Loads of shit-paying jobs in call-centres and IT stuff. There was nothing in advertising, nothing for me. I'd ring people on Monday and get something by word of mouth.

I wasn't in the mood to go out. I went and got some beer and a video. The kind of crap Niamh wouldn't watch. I went back to the apartment and ordered a pizza. I was there when Róisín rang at about eleven.

'I need to talk to you,' she said.

I couldn't tell if she was drunk.

'I can't,' I said.

'Are you with your girlfriend?' she asked, her tone mocking. It wasn't like her.

'No, I'm not.'

'So what are you doing?' she asked.

'I just can't. What's the point? What do you want?'

'I want to talk to you. We didn't talk about this at all.'

'You were the one who ran off. You were the one who was finishing with me, so what's the point now?'

'The point is that I don't understand how you could do this.'

'I'm sorry,' I said. 'Maybe I shouldn't have told you.'

'Maybe you shouldn't. I'd have been better off not knowing but you did tell me. And I can't understand. I thought you liked me. I really believed you did and then this. Do you not know? Do you not know how horrible that is? To find out. It's so easy for you to just say it like it's nothing.'

'I thought it would help,' I said. She laughed. 'I did. I thought it might explain to you why I was the way I was. That it wasn't anything to do with you. It's my problem.'

'Are you completely stupid? What you've done is take everything I thought and was feeling and just turned it upside down. I don't know what to think. Everything you said to me was a lie. And everything you did to me was . . .' She stopped and waited. I really wanted to hold her and tell her that it was OK and my other life was over and she was so wrong but it wasn't right. 'It was wrong and horrible and I can hardly live with myself, that I did that with you. That I thought I might love you. Nearly. Did you know that?' I didn't know what to say. 'Did you?' she asked again.

'I don't want you to feel that you were used,' I said, ignoring her question. 'I really don't want you to feel bad and I understand that I was in the wrong. Completely. But I'm human, and all of this, it's all about me and my weaknesses and what I wanted and nothing more. I promise you I wouldn't have started into this if I'd known how hurt you were going to get.' I was trying to be as honest as I could. 'I'm sorry,' I said again.

'No,' she said. 'Not good enough. You walk away with your conscience clear and go home to your wife or girlfriend or whatever and tell her some lie like you lied to me and go to bed smiling at your happy life and who cares what I'm doing here. Don't tell me that you care about me, or how I feel or that you're sorry it turned out the way it did. I'm not stupid. I know exactly what you thought.

You thought you could get to have fun with someone else and that if it went wrong you could get out of it and walk away because you're so reasonable. But you're not so reasonable. You're a horrible bad man.'

'OK. Fair enough.' What else could I say? I didn't want to tell her about Niamh. There was no point. Let her think what she wanted. Put an end to it all.

'And I'm not going to let you just walk away and go back to your happy little life. Does your girlfriend know? Does your great sense of conscience mean you've told her? Because I bet it doesn't. Have you?'

'No, I haven't told her,' I said. 'But that's my problem, not yours.'

'It is your problem. Because if somebody found who she was and told her, it wouldn't be good, would it? You wouldn't like that.'

I couldn't help smiling.

'What good would that do you?' I asked her.

'I don't know. To see you have to deal with it. You're not going to be so reasonable when it's your life that's messed up, when you have to deal with what you've done when it's there in front of you made real. To know that you had to do that might make me feel better.'

'Is this who you are, Róisín? Is this what you're like, the bitter ex trying to screw me up for no reason other than to enjoy it, to enjoy making a mess of my life? You couldn't do a better job of it than I've managed on my own.'

'What else can I do? What can I do?'

She was crying now.

'Nothing. I'm sorry but there's nothing either of us can do. It didn't work out and it's my fault. I know that. But it happens every day. I'm sorry,' I said again.

'I thought I loved you,' she said. Melodramatic. She might just as easily have said, I hate you.

'I did love you. I did but I can't,' I said as I hung up. It didn't even make sense.

The phone woke me in the morning. It was Phil. I hadn't heard from him in ages.

'What's the story?' I asked him.

'Ah you know yourself. Same as ever.'

'How's Catherine?'

'She's fine,' he said. 'Everything's fine. I heard your news though.'

'What's that?' I asked, playing dumb.

He hesitated.

'About Niamh?'

'Oh right. Yeah. It didn't take long for that to get out.'

'Are you all right?' he asked me.

I was still waking up.

'I'm great. I'm fine. Did you hear the other thing? About the job?'

'Yeah. Well, you're not the first,' he said.

'I'll get something else,' I said.

'Yeah of course. Of course you will.'

It was a pointless conversation.

'Did you want something?' I asked him.

'No, I just wanted to see if you're OK. We're going for brunch in town and I thought you might want to come. Get out of the house or whatever.'

'Who's we?' I asked.

'Me and Catherine.'

I tried to shake my head awake.

'Why not,' I said.

I met them in a restaurant off Grafton Street. They never came into town.

'I'm surprised you knew about this place,' I said when I arrived. 'I thought you guys never crossed the canal.'

'We make the odd exception,' he said. 'Into the big smoke.'

'Hi, Catherine.'

She smiled like I was Mummy's brave soldier. 'Are you all right, Rory?' she asked.

'I'm fine.' She wore middle age like a fur coat. It kept her warm. She was only twenty-eight. It was nice when she hugged me.

'I could do with a drink,' I said. Myself and Phil ordered mojitos. She was driving.

We talked about nothing. When the drinks came I lit a fag and toasted them. I could see them trying not to look at each other.

'So what happened with your job?' he asked.

'Do you know Gerry McIntyre?' I asked him. He shook his head. 'He'd be known around town. I thought you might. I got on great with him at first, but he has a reputation as a bit of a hard bastard and a couple of things didn't work out and that was it. He just wanted rid of me.'

'Would you have a case?' he asked.

'What's the point? I don't want to work there any more and it could be years before anything came of it. You don't want to get known as the guy who sued his ex-employer anyway. It's fine. I'll get something else.'

The waitress arrived and we ordered food.

'Can we get another couple of these,' I asked her, holding up my glass. Phil made some sort of noise. He'd barely started his.

'Get it into you,' I said. 'They go down easy.'

'Too easy,' Catherine said, smiling.

'What else am I going to do?' I said and she laughed. Phil knocked his back in one.

They asked about Niamh. There wasn't a lot I could tell them. I didn't know what they'd heard. Presumably her version of events was knocking around out there. I talked about work pressures and the hours I'd put in and how I understood. It was her decision and I couldn't do anything about it and I was sorry. I was very reasonable.

'It's fine. I'll get someone else. There's a lot of girls around,' I said and it took a second before they laughed.

There's white rum and lime and fresh mint and sugar syrup and crushed ice in a mojito. You drink it with a straw and it tastes like it's good for you. The waitress looked like Penelope Cruz. The place was dark, there were no windows and I just wanted to drink and talk. I didn't care. I asked them about everything. They went to the Caribbean on holidays. She had left her job and was doing nothing. Just taking a break.

'We should get together in your place for coffee one of these mornings,' I said. 'I've nothing on. I'll bring something in Tupper-ware.' She looked nervous.

After two hours, Phil paid the bill. He wouldn't let me contribute. When he went to the jacks I asked her.

'So did you hear Niamh's version of why we broke up?'

'No. I haven't heard anything.'

'You must have heard from someone.'

'Phil heard from Anto, I think. I didn't know until he told me.'

'I see. I see. Well if you are talking to her, tell her . . .' I stopped. 'Nothing. I'm sorry. I'm a bit drunk. I'm not used to drinking in the day.'

'You're all right, Rory,' she smiled. 'You probably need it.'

'You're very nice,' I said. I stopped the waitress.

'Excuse me.'

She smiled a professional smile.

'I've recently become unattached and I have singled you out for special attention. You're very beautiful. Do you know who you look like?'

'Penelope Cruz,' she said while she was walking away.

'I don't think she's for me,' I said to Catherine, whose face was rigid. 'I was only joking. It was only a joke.' She tried to smile. Phil came back and we left.

On the street outside I did my best to talk them into going for a pint. Phil looked at her so quickly I hardly noticed and then said no they better go on. I hugged him and I hugged her and it was still nice. She wasn't bad. I'd say they had an interesting conversation on the way back to deepest suburbia. We hate it when our friends become successful. Oh, but it's so much worse than that. We're happy when they fail.

I started ringing the following week. I had my diary with all my contacts and I started working my way through, asking if they knew of any work going. It was the third call that I made when somebody said something before I'd even started. It was a guy in one of the recording places. I'd only met him once.

'I heard about you,' he said.

'Really? What did you hear?'

He laughed.

'You know yourself.' I laughed too to get him to talk.

'Go on,' I said. 'Tell me.'

'Jesus, I don't know.'

'Oh come on. I'm entitled to know what lies they're telling about me.'

'I suppose you are. If they are lies.'

'Of course they're lies. You tell me what you've heard and I'll give you my version.' I kept it light, like I was joking, like it didn't matter.

'Ah no. Jesus, this is hard.'

'It's grand. Go on.'

'No, they're saying that you were stringing the lot of them along for months. That you were pretending to be going out to meetings and talking about all the great stuff that you were going to get and—'

He stopped.

'And there was nothing there?' I said.

'Something like that. I shouldn't really be saying this, Rory. You know. I'm sorry. I'm sure it's just talk.'

'No, it's good to know,' I said. 'Can you remember where you heard it?'

He was getting worried.

'I can't. I'm sorry. It was just talk, you know, around the place.'

'Well it's bollocks. It's shite.'

'I'm sure it is,' he said. 'I'm sorry, man.'

'No. Seriously thanks a lot. It's good to know what's going on. Fuck them.'

'It's only talk. I wouldn't worry about it. Nobody pays any attention to that kind of shit.'

'Well you did,' I said and waited a second before laughing.

We both laughed and then he said, 'Ah no.'

'So have you any work going?' I asked and we both laughed again and he started saying how there wasn't much going on but to send in a CV. He gave me a name of somebody in HR. I didn't write it down.

It was such a small town. I knew what it was like. So much of the time nothing was going on and everybody spent their days on the phone. People meeting for lunch and on Friday nights for drinks in the pubs around Leeson Street. Just talking and talking. Every day that went by my story would get worse and worse. I'd never been to New York. I'd never been to college. I'd put fake expenses through. I was schizophrenic. I'd been fucking Gerry's wife. I'd been fucking Gerry. Christ knows. All the time this shit just festering away in space growing exponentially and I could do nothing about it. Nobody would admit it, but everybody listened to that kind of shit. That's all they listened to. They didn't care about awards and trade journals and cold hard figures, they wanted flesh and blood and weakness because they all went home to their semis in Rathfarnham and Clontarf and Lucan and they prayed that someone somewhere was doing something scandalous because the alternative was that life was too dull to contemplate. Reality, truth had nothing to do with it. This was my life.

I rang a recruitment consultancy to make an appointment. I told the guy on the phone what I'd been at in New York and he was impressed. He said they had loads of stuff that would be just right for me. It felt like he was licking my ear.

I went in the following morning. They gave me an espresso while the guy looked at my CV. He came out after a couple of minutes.

'Rory!' he said like he knew me, like he was surprised to see me. He looked me in the eye and shook my hand. 'Do you want to come in?'

'This looks fantastic, Rory,' he said after we'd sat down. 'It shouldn't be any problem at all. We'll get you sorted out in no time.'

'That's great,' I said. 'Because I'd heard things were slowing down a bit.'

He shrugged.

'A bit, yeah, for some people, but six years in New York, Rory, with a company like this should put you at a level where that wouldn't affect you. It's more the . . .' He paused.

'Lower?' I suggested.

He smiled.

'Well you know yourself,' he said and we had a laugh about that.

'So, Rory. I don't know if it's a mistake but there's a gap of eight months between here and here.' He showed me. My mouth was dry. I coughed and then went for it.

'No, I was working for Talisman from October until recently.'

'Right?' He waited.

'I didn't put it on because I wasn't happy with the way I left. I didn't know if I should put it on or not. I mean, I was there over six months and that, so I do have experience of working in the area in Dublin but I just didn't know.'

'OK. OK. So can I ask?' He smiled. 'How can I ask? Why did you leave? The circumstances were . . . ?'

'Not great. I had done good work for them, I'd got a couple of big contracts and then my relationship with the MD deteriorated and in the end, it wasn't sustainable. So I left.'

'You left?' he said.

I smiled this time.

'There wasn't much option. But you know it really was just a communication problem where his expectations and mine didn't match. Initially I have to say we got on very well and I was very happy there, but after time it became quite strained. I'm sure he'd tell it one way and I another.'

'How would you tell it?' he asked.

'Well, like that. I thought I was behaving in the company's best interests, by not overly aggressively pursuing a particular client and he thought different. That's all really. I would say.'

'Yes?'

'Do you know him at all? Gerry McIntyre?'

'I know the name.'

I smiled.

'What have you heard?'

'Nothing really. Why?'

'He would have a reputation for being somewhat difficult. I wouldn't be the first person to have left in questionable circumstances,' I said.

'Right. Right. Well obviously I can't say anything about that, but I'll talk to a few people and we'll see what the best way of dealing with your particular situation would be. I'll give you a ring this afternoon but I would be hopeful that we could get you something quite soon.'

'Great,' I said. 'That sounds great.'

'Depending. Obviously,' he said as he was giving me his card and shaking my hand in one movement.

'Of course. Obviously.'

'Thanks for coming in, Rory.'

He didn't call that day. He didn't call the next day. It was fine. I didn't leave the house. I watched TV and played video games and slept. I was totally relaxed. On the third day I rang and he wasn't in the office. I left a message on his mobile and then I rang again at five.

'James, it's Rory Brennan,' I said when he answered. 'I saw you earlier in the week.'

'Rory. How's it going? Sorry, I meant to get back to you.'

'No problem.'

'Yeah. We don't have anything right at the minute, Rory. I'm sorry. I meant to ring you but it's been mad.'

'But there's nothing?' I asked.

'Not right now, no.'

'OK. That's a bit disappointing.' I waited but he didn't say anything. 'Because you said that you thought you'd have something for me more or less straight away. You know?'

'Yeah. It's not a great time, you know, Rory. It's just not. But we might in a couple of weeks. I'll give you a ring if we get anything at all. I'll give you a shout. OK?'

There was no point.

'OK,' I said.

'OK thanks, Rory. Bye now.'

# 14

After that all I wanted was to get hammered. I rang Ciaran but he was tired and he was staying in. I rang Anto but he was in Cork on a stag. I rang Phil and he was knackered but he said he might do a few out in Blackrock later. I wasn't going to Blackrock on a Friday. All I could think was that Patrick would be doing something outrageous, something big that would keep me out until Sunday but I just couldn't ring him. I had a shower and got dressed and went out on my own.

All I wanted was to be drunk anyway. I didn't want to talk or meet anyone. I wanted to be alone but I knew I couldn't stay in the house. All I would do would be think about Niamh and everything I'd done and I didn't need that. What good would it do? I needed to stop thinking. I had to get out. I went to a pub off Dame Street, a dump where you could always get a seat but they'd changed it. They'd put in a PA and they were playing dance music to a load of displaced students down the back as the same old lads held the counter. I got in among them and ordered a drink. A Scottish stag party came in, already locked, and stood behind me shouting at each other. I could see a few of the old lads looking over, bridling. The Scottish guys started jostling me, knocking off me as they ordered Guinness and vodka and Red Bull. They were spoiling for something, talking about the fuckers in Temple Bar who wouldn't let them in. It wouldn't have taken much to set them off. I got out and went to a place down the lane but there was a guy singing rebel songs to a load of scary bastards so I only had a couple there and then went over towards Parliament Street and went into a place that was packed but had a nice vibe. I bought a pint and wandered around thinking I might find someone I knew but there was nobody so I stood at the bar and moved onto large whiskeys. Staring into middle distance, stepping to one side and then the other letting people in to the bar. It was too busy. I was trying to order but the barman wasn't coming anywhere near our end at all. I started talking to the guy next to me, the two of us bitching about the service. Then a girl at the far end who'd arrived way after us got served and we started flapping. She spoke to the barman and sent down two tequilas to us, which was fair enough. She lifted her glass at the far end and me and the guy downed them, clinking glasses.

'Will we go over?' I said to him.

'I would, but I'm with my missus.'

'Well I'm not,' I said.

'Go for it, man. Good luck to you.'

I walked over. Halfway there I saw she was with a crowd of about ten. All girls. I was going to turn back and then just thought, Fuck it. I don't know them. How bad can it be? They were English from somewhere up North. She greeted me like we'd known each other for years.

'How are you?' she said when I arrived. Her smile was crooked. The others were looking at her, a couple of them talking into each other's ears, assessing me. I knew I was OK.

'I'm great,' I said. 'And you.'

I stood close to her and we started talking. I wasn't doing anything, just being a bit flirty and that. I bought a round for them all which cost thirty quid. Two of them put their arms around me when I came back.

'We like you,' they said. 'We've decided we like you.'

'I really like all of you,' I said.

'No no no. You like Karen,' they said and they pushed me towards Karen who was the first one. It was like I was thirteen. I hugged her and they cheered.

'You'll have to do better than that,' one of them said and I laughed. All I could do was laugh. I didn't know what else but it seemed to be enough.

At the end they asked me where they should go and I said there was a place across the street. I was pissed. The guys on the door stopped me but the girls all started giving them grief and they laughed and let me go ahead. Not like bouncers at all.

'You're a brave man,' one of them said to me as I was going down. 'Must have a lot of stamina,' the other said and I just said no.

They were all standing around in a circle dancing. There were guys trying to get in among them and after a while I couldn't handle it and went and sat down and looked after their bags and jackets. They kept coming over and giving me drinks. I thought English didn't do rounds but they kept on buying and buying. I was drinking Smirnoff Ice because it made the round easier. It wasn't too bad. Then Karen came over and sat beside me. I was hammered. She started kissing me and it was OK. I got a bit turned on.

'Do you want to come home with me?' I asked her. I wasn't thinking any more.

'Where do you live?' she asked.

'Around the corner. It's like five minutes.'

'Wait there.' She went off. I thought she wouldn't. After a couple of minutes I put on my coat and was about to go when she came back.

'Are you coming?' I asked her. She kissed me again as I was standing there and then she got her jacket.

As we were walking along she pulled me into a doorway and pushed me back against a wall.

'You don't have a wife or a girlfriend, do you? Because I don't do that. I'm not like that.'

'No. I know. I know. No I don't. Not at all. I did,' I said, 'but I don't.'

'You must be loaded,' she said when we got in.

'Not really. Not any more,' I said and she smiled, waiting for me to tell her something but I didn't. I got a bottle of gin and started making drinks. She was looking around the living-room. There were photos of Niamh's family on the mirror, all nights out and of her when she was a kid and communions.

'Who are these?' Karen asked.

'My ex-girlfriend's family.'

She looked confused.

'She only moved out last week. She's coming back to get her stuff sometime. It's OK.'

'OK.' A look which was something like concern went across her face.

'It's not a problem. Seriously. I told you I don't have a girlfriend and I don't.' I laughed. It seemed stupid. What was it to her? She didn't know me. She didn't have to care. We sat there and drank for a while. I put on music and we talked for ages about her and what she did. It was nice. I didn't expect it. Then we went to bed.

I was drunk. I was OK but I was drunk. All I wanted was to make her come. I didn't want to be the drunk Irish disappointment. She was fine with it, let me do whatever I wanted for a while and then she said, 'Can we just fuck?' So we did. I liked that she said fuck. It made it easier.

Niamh arrived in the morning to get her things. I was out cold. I didn't wake up until she came into the room and said something. I sat up and the girl was beside me holding the duvet over her head.

'What are you doing?' Niamh said. It wasn't a question but I answered anyway.

'You're gone,' I said. 'You moved out.'

She looked pissed off more than hurt. She left the room. I thought she was going to come back in. I thought she was building up to it, but she didn't. The door banged and that was it. She didn't take anything with her.

'Should I go?' the girl asked me.

'If you want,' I said. 'You don't have to. She's gone. There's nobody else going to turn up.' I was lying with my head under the cover looking at her. She smiled and then we went back to sleep. I woke up I don't know when and she was still there trying to get me going. I felt like shit but I gave it a go. It only took about two minutes and then I fell asleep again. It was six when I woke up again and she was gone.

I felt terrible. I went out and got eggs and papers and went home and had breakfast watching the evening news. I had a shower and settled into the couch. I rang Niamh.

'I'm sorry,' I told her. 'I really am.'

'You can do what you like.'

'No but I'm sorry. I wasn't thinking. I was just pissed and it didn't even occur to me that you might come back.'

'I told you I was going to,' she said.

'I know but I wasn't thinking.'

'Do what you like, Rory.'

'I'm just really sorry.'

'Oh fuck yourself. It didn't take you long. I thought there might be some chance that we might have tried. But I move out and you don't even ring to see if I'm OK or talk or anything. You just get some girl in. Who was she anyway? Did you have her on the go before we broke up or what?'

'No. God no. I just met her and I was drunk. She was English. I don't know who she was. I'd never seen her before.'

'Didn't stop you sleeping with her.'

I couldn't say anything.

'Were you cheating on me while we were together?'

'No. No. Why would you think that?' I asked. I didn't know what somebody might have said to her.

'Because it took you no time before you found somebody else,' she said. 'It doesn't say much for you, you know. It's really cheap. I thought you'd all sorts of stuff wrong with you, but that you were just going through a bad patch. I thought you might get your act together. You might ring me or whatever. You might care enough but you're like, you're like an animal, a stupid fucking animal that doesn't know what it's doing.'

'I'm sorry,' I said. 'But look, you left me. You walked out. I lost my job and you left, so don't give me that. I'm sorry but I can do what I want because you're gone. You left.'

She had hung up. I put the phone down and took it off the hook.

I was shaking. The adrenalin buzzed through me, then gradually faded away and I felt exhausted. This was where I was. I'd got myself some of the way there and then everything else just conspired against me. That fucking Mark prick. And Patrick able to turn on me the way he had. A whole load of friends who were Niamh's friends as well who would think I was a shit because they didn't know what it was like. I fucked another girl in our bed a week after she had left. They wouldn't bother to think about it. They would just never ring me again. The only way to get over it was to start again. Monday was a new week and I could begin from there. It would be better. I could make it better. From Monday.

But it was Saturday and I wasn't going anywhere. I didn't want to go out to a world of drink and drunks, girls pissed enough to let their inhibitions down and grab you by the arse. I didn't want sex or drink or crowds or noise. I didn't want to stay where I was in the flat surrounded by her things. Her food in the fridge, her pictures on the wall, all her stuff in the bathroom. I didn't want to go to a bed that smelt of another girl.

So I sat on the couch with the phone beeping quietly in the background and I couldn't move. I wanted tea. I wanted somebody beside me. I wanted somebody to tell me that Monday was the new beginning and between now and then everything would be fine. We'd be OK. I wanted anyone, a girl in leggings and a T-shirt watching some crap. I wanted the boring suburban evening that Phil would be having with his comfortable girlfriend drinking red wine and letting his belt out as the Indian take-away expanded in his fat belly that he didn't care about, because she didn't mind and that's all he had to worry about. I wanted to go to a bed with clean sheets where everything was white and be held and have somebody talk me to sleep with long boring stories about when they were a kid and the toys they had. I wanted it to be Christmas morning. I wanted my mother. I wanted Niamh. I wanted the night we'd had three weeks ago. I wanted to stop and be happy and go to work on Monday and have two pints at lunch with Gerry as he bitched about his fucking kid puking in the back of his Merc station wagon. I wanted to come home and not have to think or worry. Just let kids and school and baldness and middle age find me. I'd be the fat one reading the paper and harrumphing in the big leather chair beside a fire. Starting to go to mass again as the end got nearer. Drinks in comfortable pubs with all the boys talking about how great we once were. I nearly had it. I nearly had it and I didn't want it so what was the point? There was no point.

I put the glasses in the dishwasher. I made the bed. I had a piss and made tea and got a spare duvet from the hotpress. I lay on the couch wrapped up and watched Cilla Black introduce three girls from Croydon or somewhere, one of whom looked a bit like the girl from last night.

There was no work for me. I rang everywhere during the week and got nothing. I thought about lying. It would have been easier, rather than having to breathe in and think how to explain it when they asked where I'd worked before. If anybody had been interested enough to give me a chance I could have told them. I could have made them understand, given the opportunity, that I'd been shafted. People knew what he was like. It wasn't my fault. Look at what I'd done, not what I hadn't done. But the same story can mean completely different things to different people, particularly when there was this low background hum of rumour. Every secretary that I spoke to trying to make an appointment would be on to her pal in the next place on my list talking, so that when I rang I was expected. They were ready and I felt like I had to go through a show of demonstrating my desperation for their entertainment. Give them a laugh before they sent me packing. The air crackled every time I walked into a lobby. Standing in front of a crowd of them in a suit with my track record saying this is who I am and I don't give a fuck what you think, I could turn this place upside down and sort it out, bring you more money than you've even thought of, if you're big enough to ignore whatever shite you've heard about me. I told them it was a difference of opinion. It was a gulf in communication. It was about unattainable targets. It was a personality clash. All real things that these guys would know about and have dealt with themselves. They could have chosen to believe me. But it's a different story when there was three of them facing one of me across a table, their view clouded by a fog of innuendo. I could see through the door as I walked out, see their faces as they turned and looked at each other and shook their heads. There was nothing I could do.

No. I could have begged. I could have confronted them. I could have asked them what they'd heard. I could have said, Try me free for one month and if you're not happy I'll go. Just try me because I'm better than this and I don't deserve it. But I wouldn't. I wasn't that low yet. I walked out tall every time, silencing the pool of headsetted yappers and went home waiting for the phone to ring, for the post to come but the phone never rang and the postman only brought bills.

The mortgage went out on Thursday. I had enough for one more payment and then I was finished. I would have nothing left. I needed money and I had nowhere to get it. It wasn't right.

I had nothing to lose. That was all it was. I'm not really like that, I couldn't handle that kind of shit. But he'd turned me over and I couldn't let him get away with it. It made no difference anyway.

I decided I would give it one day. That was all. If it didn't happen then I'd leave it. I sat with a paper and a coffee on a bench under a tree. It was half-five and almost dark. The light of the lobby showed the people as they left. I was near enough to see but not be seen. I could recognize some of the faces as they came out. All happy at the end of the day, the furthest distance possible between them and tomorrow. I might have missed him. I might have had to wait for hours, but I knew I wouldn't do that. It would be too weird to put so much effort into it and I wasn't weird. It was only worth doing if it was easy. If it so happened. One day, that was all.

At a quarter past six I decided I would leave at half and then he came out. He was on his own. I stayed where I was. He lifted his head in my direction as he came through the door and I felt my heart begin to pound, but he didn't see me. I let him walk off and then hopped up and followed him.

I didn't know what I would do. I might just talk to him and listen to his side and shake hands and walk away or go for a pint or I could feel it all kick in and barrel into the back of him and knock him over. I didn't know.

I walked about a hundred feet behind him as he went down onto the quays and turned to walk towards a side street where a lot of our people parked. When he went out of view I ran as quietly as I could and turned into the street after him. He was only fifteen feet away, still unlocking his car door, his papers on the roof of the car and his jacket folded over his arm. He looked up as I came around and I knew then, whatever happened, whatever came of this, that it had been worth it. His face just dropped. He didn't know what the fuck was going on. I stood there, panting slightly, and I smiled at him. He planked it.

'Hello, Mark,' I said. There was no way I could have said it that didn't seem like a threat.

'Rory,' he said. 'How are you?'

I walked over quite casually and stood away from him.

'I'm OK. And you?'

'I'm fine.' He hesitated. I could see him toying with his car keys. 'What are you doing here?'

'You know what I'm doing here,' I said. 'I want to talk to you, that's all. That's it.'

'Do you not think you could have called me in work rather than jumping out of the shadows trying to scare me to death?'

'I'm not trying to scare you, Mark.'

We stood there in orange street-light and I began to feel stupid.

'I can't get a job because of you,' I said. 'I don't understand why you fucking shafted me like that,' I said. 'It's sounds really funny now but I thought we were friends.'

He was calm when he spoke.

'First of all I didn't shaft you, you lost your job for lots of reasons none of which had anything to do with me. I was next in line and that's why it looked the way it did. I only told Gerry what I knew after he'd decided to let you go anyway. And if you don't understand the concept of workplace friendship and how it works then I don't know where you've been.'

He wasn't nervous any more. He opened the car door and that was enough to trigger it. I stepped forward and kicked it closed.

184

'Hold on a second. I'm not finished yet.' I was standing beside him now. I was about six inches taller than him. He looked up at me.

'What?' he said. 'What do you want?'

I couldn't think of anything to say.

'You think you're fucking clever,' I said and I knew at this stage that I just wanted to hit him and be done with it. I took a step closer and pushed him on the shoulder. 'Don't you?' I was just poking at him. He should have known that.

'Go away from me,' he said. 'Just leave me alone.'

It was too sad. I gave him another shove.

'You're pathetic,' I said. I turned away to walk off and then I couldn't believe it. I turned my back and he just threw himself into a punch to the back of my head. He clobbered me. It hurt. I went down onto my knees and he pushed me over. He kicked at me a couple of times, jumping back after each kick and I scrambled to my feet and ran off to get myself together. He was over at his car again trying to get in when I turned back. I ran at him. I just wanted one shot at him and I got it. I grabbed him by the tie and punched him straight in the nose and then once hard on the side of the head where it would bruise. That's all I wanted. I didn't want to damage him. I just wanted to mark him, for people to ask and he'd have to tell them that it was me, that I'd done it, or else lie and when he lied he'd know I'd be thinking of him and laughing. I let him go and he slumped down against the side of the car.

'Why did you do that?' I asked him. 'I wasn't going to do anything.'

He didn't speak, just sat holding his face in both hands, breathing heavily.

'You're a sneaky fucker,' I said to him and I walked off.

I just wanted to get away. My jeans were covered in mud and my hands were covered in cuts where I'd fallen. My head was aching. I walked quickly back onto the quays and stayed on the Northside until the new bridge. I crossed over and went back to the flat.

I had a bath and lay there soaking. It seemed funny now. Neither of us really knew how to have a fight. I hadn't known how to heighten my aggression with words, how to build up that rage by talking. It just seemed stupid. I was glad he'd thrown the first punch. I was glad I hadn't hurt him. It just made him seem ridiculous and small. I'd done what I wanted.

# 15

Shane rang me in the morning to say that Dad had fallen. He was in hospital. He'd broken a wrist but he was fine. He was going to be in overnight. I met them all there, him and Brian and Brian's wife Rebecca. He was in a private ward. It was great. It had a telly and his own bathroom and it looked out over a golf course.

'This is OK,' I said when I saw him. 'You won't want to go home.' He was fine. A bit pale but he was in good form. He'd been asleep at home and somebody had come to the door and he'd woken and stood up too quickly and his leg just went from under him. He said he felt really stupid. I said it could have happened to anyone. His arm was in a cast held up on a trolley. I asked did he need anything and he said he was grand, he'd be going home in the morning. He asked about Niamh and I told him she was in good form. It wasn't the time with all of them standing around. I talked to them a bit. I never knew what to say to them. After a couple of minutes Brian and the wife left and myself and Shane sat there with Dad. I went out and got a few papers and a load of chocolate and we sat there for a while reading and eating. We watched the news and then he said he was getting tired so we left. I told him I'd be back in the morning. Shane had a go at the nurse on the way out telling her that Dad was paying for this room, he wasn't getting it on VHI or whatever, and to make sure he was well looked after, which I'd say had them spitting in Dad's food. Shane loved bollocking people.

We went for a pint across the road. There were big gaping silences. What could I say to a forty-year-old whose only hobby I knew of was torturing his siblings? Then after a while he got going.

'I'm worried about him,' he said. 'We're going to have to keep a better eye on him. Somebody should go out at least every other day.'

'Yeah.'

'I mean you as well,' he said.

I looked at him.

'I don't have a car, Shane. How the fuck am I supposed to get out to Dun Laoghaire from town?'

'On the bus. Like a normal person. When's the last time you were out there?'

'I don't know,' I said. 'A couple of weeks.'

'You should do it a bit more than that. He's on his own.'

'Why, how often do you go?'

'Every Sunday for dinner. You should come out. He'd love to see you. For some reason.'

'I'm not fit to talk most Sundays,' I said.

'Well whenever. Just try a bit harder.'

He went to get another round. When he came back I had a thought.

'Maybe we should think about putting him in one of those care centre places. He'd be looked after all the time and there'd be other people around him. I hate the idea of him in the house on his own all the time.'

'What are you talking about?'

'You know, those residential care places.'

'What, a home? You want to put Dad in a home?'

'It's not a home,' I said. 'It's not for mad old fuckers. They have ones for normal people, who just want company. They get looked after. There are good ones.'

'How do you know all this?' he asked.

'I don't know. But there are.'

'We're not putting Dad in a home. He's too young for starters.'

'He's sixty-five now, isn't he?'

'He's sixty-two, Rory. For fuck's sake.'

'No, but think about it right,' I said. 'He uses, what, three rooms of that house? The rest is just rotting away. He's on his own. Even if there's people going out to him every other day, he could still fall or get sick or something. He'd be supervised all the time. There would be other people around him. You know, he's a sociable kind of guy and I don't think he's gone out once since she died.'

'Who's going to pay for it?' he asked.

'We could sell the house. What's the point of holding onto it when none of it's getting used? It's got to be worth seven hundred now. Pay his fees, bring him on holiday or down to Galway for fishing a couple of times a year. He'd love it. He'd be a lot better off. We'd know he'd always be being taken care of. Split the extra between us. You pay less tax that way, than if you wait until he's dead. He said it to me himself. He'd prefer it.'

He was looking at me.

'What?' I said, defensive. 'What?'

'He's not some decrepit old fucker. His mind's not gone yet. We can have this conversation in twenty years if we have to. The way you're going you'll have dementia before him.'

'No I'm serious, Shane. It makes sense. Think about it, will you? Think about what he'd want. Does he really want us turning up every couple of days making conversation like we're the Vincent de Paul? Like he's some charity case?'

He laughed at me.

'Where's this coming from? You see the guy once every six months or something and suddenly you know what he wants better than any of us. He would hate, absolutely hate, to go into a home. You can call it a five-star resort if you want, whatever, but you're talking about a home and he's going to know that in about two seconds. He might even go along with it, you know, because he doesn't want to be a burden, but it's just wrong. End of story.'

I waited a couple of seconds.

'Well we should at least think about selling the house. Get him into somewhere smaller. It's just stupid him rattling around in a six-bedroom house out in the middle of nowhere.'

'It's Glenageary, Rory, for Christ's sake. Not the fucking steppes of Siberia.'

'Well whatever. He'd be better off.'

He took a fag from my pack. I didn't know he smoked any more.

'We're not selling the house. We're not putting him in a home. We'll look after him, we all will, and if you don't want to, if it's too much hassle for you to get out once a week, then you don't have to. Someone else will do it.'

'Of course I'll do it,' I said. 'Of course I will. That's not the point. I'm just trying to think of what he'd want.'

'Enough, Rory. Enough. He'll decide what he wants. We're not going to decide for him. If he wants to sell the house fine but it's his house and it's his decision. He's sixty-two, for Christ's sake.'

I put my head in my hands. It was terrible. I didn't know what I was saying.

'What's wrong with you?'

'Can you lend me some money? A couple of grand?'

He laughed. 'Are you joking me? I've got Ingrid going on a ski trip next week. My card's at its limit. I'm up to my bollocks.'

He waited. I was totally miserable.

'I could do you a couple of hundred maybe,' he said after a minute. 'No, it's OK.'

'Why anyway?' he asked. 'I thought you were raking it in.'

'No. I lost my job a couple of weeks ago. It's just until I find something else.'

'How did you lose your job?'

He was getting ready to tell me what to do. I didn't need it.

'I didn't get on with the boss. It's no problem. Just with the mortgage and that.'

He got going about how times had changed and the whole thing was going down the toilet and we'd been kidding ourselves to ever think it could have lasted.

'They'll all pull out and ship off to India or Thailand or fuck knows where.'

'I'm in advertising, Shane. I don't think my crowd are going anywhere. I'm not putting microchips together at two in the morning in poxy Leixlip.' He smiled. I'd forgotten his wife was from out there.

'Well you know what I mean anyway,' I said. 'Forget what I said before, will you? About Dad and that. I was talking shit.'

He looked at me and didn't say anything for a second.

'You want the money. All that stuff about residential care and stuff was just about selling the house and getting your cut.'

'It was stupid. I wasn't thinking. I'm all over the place. I'm not having a good time. Just forget about it. It was fucking stupid.'

I couldn't tell if he was horrified or about to laugh. In the end he smiled with something like sympathy.

'Are you all right?'

'I will be.'

'We could just poison him and take the insurance if you like.' He was laughing now.

'Don't.'

'You poor sad bastard.'

He gave me a cheque for five hundred quid and drove me home. I told him I'd pay him back but he told me not to worry about it. He wasn't the worst.

When I got home Niamh had been in to get her stuff. It was all gone. She'd left three hundred in cash for bills. No note or anything. It was like she'd never been there. She must have rung first to make sure I wasn't there. Already I was missing her around the place. Another person. I didn't like being alone but I'd done it myself so there was no point in complaining.

I rang Phil.

'How are you doing?' I asked him.

'I'm great,' he said. 'Fine. How about you? How's single life suiting you?'

'Don't forget unemployed. It's fantastic. I'm loving it. If I'd known it was going to be like this I would have fucked my life up a bit earlier.'

'Your life's not fucked up,' he said. 'You're just going through a change.'

'Are you saying I'm menopausal?'

He laughed. I took my chance.

'This is embarrassing,' I said. 'Is there any chance at all, and say no straight away if you can't, but . . . ?'

'Can I lend you some money?' he said.

It was a bad idea. I was exposing myself.

'I'm really sorry to ask.'

'It's no problem,' he said. I felt the hope rising in me. 'It's no problem to ask. I'm a friend. I'd help you if I could. But I just can't. We're trying for a kid and we need every penny. I don't make the kind of money you make. Or made.'

'No problem.'

'I would if I could, you know that.'

'I know you would,' I said. 'And I hate having to ask.'

'Asking is no problem. Getting is more difficult. I'm sorry.'

'No, I'm sorry.'

I walked around the flat, squirming. I hated doing this, but they were my friends and I knew it was OK. I rang Ciaran that evening, when I felt up to it.

'How are you?' I said.

'The very man.'

'What's this?'

He laughed.

'Phil said you might call.'

I nearly died.

'What? Did he ring you?'

'No, I called him. We're going to go out later on. If you're around?'

'I don't know.' I didn't know whether to ask him or not. It was like he could hear me thinking.

'You need money,' he said.

'Yeah. I'm really embarrassed but it's just until I get something else. It's a bit scary with the mortgage and that.'

'You're all right. It's fine, but I can't help you, I'm broke myself. I'm just about keeping my head above water.'

'Right,' I said. 'Well, thanks anyway.'

'No. I'm sorry. You know I'd give it to you in a shot but I just don't have it.'

'I know. I know. It's not a problem. I'll get it somewhere.'

He gave me the number of a guy he said was good, a financial adviser, said he'd help me sort out everything. Then he asked again if I'd come for a drink.

'I've enough to buy you a pint,' he said.

'So have I just about. But I'll give it a miss.'

'Do you good. Get you out. Few scoops.'

'I'll give it a miss,' I said. 'I've some stuff to sort out.'

'Like avoiding the bailiffs?' I knew he was messing but I couldn't make myself laugh. 'I'm sorry,' he said. 'Bad joke.'

'It's OK,' I said. I hung up and walked around the flat shouting until I got it out of my system.

Two days later I went to the guy Ciaran had recommended. He added it all up, money going out and money coming in. It took a lot longer to do the first bit. He asked about work prospects and whether I'd thought about getting somebody into the flat to share the costs, but it was such a small space for two people who didn't know each other. One bathroom, one kitchen, one telly. There was nobody I knew. It wasn't an option. He said I could cover the mortgage by renting it out and get a smaller place for myself.

'What if I just sell it?' I asked him.

'You'd probably make a small profit, cover your costs and a bit more, but really if there's any way of avoiding selling, I'd recommend it. The market has more or less stagnated in that sector. Could you move into a family home?'

The thought of it. Out in the boondocks. Dad wouldn't say anything but he'd think I'd completely blown it.

'No,' I said. 'Not an option.'

'Well, you need to do something as soon as possible. Get someone in or rent it out or whatever. And start earning as soon as you can. You need to start bringing in a salary, any salary, or you're going to find yourself in serious trouble quite shortly.'

'And why shouldn't I sell the flat again?' I asked.

It made sense. I was sick of it anyway. Too big for one, too small for two unless it was a couple. All the time I was there I kept on thinking about Niamh, sleeping in our bed, trying to spread out on the couch to fill it. I spent the whole time thinking about how much I missed her and it didn't feel right. He was talking about small profits and I just thought, To hell with it. Start again.

I told him that's what I was thinking and he gave me the name of an auctioneer who worked in town and knew places like mine. He'd get the best deal possible for me. He gave me a card and told me that he was charging me a discounted rate because I was friend of Ciaran's.

'I'm guessing you're not selling your place any time soon,' I said as I wrote the cheque. He smiled like I was an idiot and asked did I have a good lawyer.

I got a phone call from Gerry. I was expecting it.

'How are you?' I asked him, totally neutral.

'What were you playing at, Rory?' he said. He sounded tired. Tired and fed up.

'What?' I asked.

'Do you not know what's going on? What were you thinking? What were you trying to achieve?'

'This is about Mark, is it?'

'Yeah, it's about Mark. You broke his nose.' I didn't say anything. 'Have you lost the run of yourself entirely?'

'It wasn't right, Gerry,' I said. 'It wasn't fair. The whole thing. Anyway I didn't start it. Ask him. Ask him who threw the first punch.'

'I don't give a damn who did what or any of that. Did he break your nose?'

'No, I'm fine,' I said. 'Sore hand a bit but nothing serious.' I enjoyed that. I couldn't help it.

'Hanging around street corners to beat up a guy who's half your size. Jesus, Rory. What's wrong with you?'

'I got shafted. I got shafted by him and by you. Do you know what's it been like for me? Nobody will go near me because of whatever poison is coming out from Talisman.'

194

'That's not true,' he said, 'but even if it was, I don't see how hitting someone is supposed to make things better. How could it?'

'I can't make it better,' I said. 'I can't do anything. I'm going to have to sell my apartment. Niamh's gone. I'm going to have to get some sort of shit job because of you lot, so actually yeah, hitting him did do something. It made me feel better. I'd do it again.'

'OK. Well you've got serious problems, Rory. You may be happy with yourself but you should think about this. What you did, you alone, led to your dismissal, not me or Mark or Rob O'Brien or anybody else. You lost your job through your own incompetence and laziness and dishonesty and I'll tell anybody who asks me exactly that because that's the truth.'

'Bollocks. That's such bollocks.'

'It's not bollocks,' he said. 'It's absolutely true and you'd want to get that into your head unless you want to add a criminal record to your list of woes. Try getting a job then. You'll be scraping chewing gum off the floor in Dublin Airport. Mark doesn't want to press charges. But I'm ringing you to say that if I see you within a hundred yards of here or if you go near any of my staff, I'll have you arrested. And I will press charges. I cannot believe that this is you, Rory. What is going on in your head?'

'You fucked me over. That's what. You're very clever and subtle and you wanted me out and you got it and I'm not going to do anything else. I'd a score to settle and I've done it, but tell that fucking scum that if I see him again I'll break more than his nose.'

'Is that a threat?' he said.

I made myself laugh.

'No, Gerry. It's just funny.'

I hung up. Big talk from me, the hard man. All I wanted to do was to rattle him. I was thinking of the nights out I'd had with him, the lunches in pubs where we didn't bother going back to the office, the mornings where he'd brought coffee into my office and he talked about how he'd disgraced himself pissed in his club at the weekend. I thought of the bonus he'd given me at Christmas, twice what I was due, out of his own pocket. It was so hard to believe that he'd turned on me, that he'd forced me into this, but at every stage, step by step, the evidence was there.

I sold the apartment. After the auctioneer and the lawyers and the duties were paid, I made a small profit like the financial guy had said I would. But it was worth it to get out and away from the past. A few grand in the bank. Enough to keep me going until I got something.

I looked at flats. Bedsits and studios. I didn't want to live with other people. I'd done it before. Getting up and walking into other people's detritus from the night before. Being the fucker coming in to complain about noise at four in the morning. Being the fucker coming in at four in the morning with a bunch of drunks playing Stone Roses records and partying like it was nineteen ninety. It was no good. I would be better on my own.

It didn't take long to realize that I'd have to go Northside. Damp stinking shitholes three hundred square feet in Rathmines were going for five hundred quid. There were dumps in Ringsend that were exactly the same as dumps in Phibsborough but in Phibsborough they cost a hundred a month less. I had to go over. I looked at a place off a main street near the Courts. I had to find it on a map when I went to view. It was fine. Nondescript modern, all white. Same place over and over two hundred times in one block, but fine for me. Disappear into anonymity, living the same life as everybody else. I took it.

I sold the fittings with the flat so I didn't have much stuff. Books, CDs, videos, clothes, some kitchen stuff and a television. That was it. When I was a kid I had a vision of myself when I was thirty. It was always a big house in an American suburb with a wife making breakfast and two kids getting ready for school and me saying goodbye and going to work in a flying car. As I crossed the river in a taxi with some criminal driver ranting on about some shite, with everything I owned in the world behind me in the boot, it seemed pretty funny.

# 16

I got set up. It was warm all the time and the noise that came through the floors and ceilings was a comfort. Other people talking and laughing and listening to music and fucking. It was nice. So close to others, only a few feet away at night. To feel the comfort of life without having to live it. It was enough for me. I didn't want to talk.

I spent the first few days wandering around. It wasn't my city. It was foreign, like being in Liverpool or Naples or some other kip abroad. I got lost in the streets around the markets and the courts. Skinny junkies in handcuffs joking with the guards as they were brought back to the Bridewell, guys on forklifts weaving in and out of traffic carrying pallets of turnips wrapped in plastic. Eastern European types all gold jewellery and teeth and black leather walking along, heads down, talking into mobiles. African women in robes with children wrapped on their backs wheeling prams full of shopping. Everybody in tracksuits, black, white, Chinese. Hatchet-faced old women telling French girls not to touch the fruit. Romanian newsagents, Chinese cafés with big pots of stock and grubby fat men ladling steaming liquid and noodles into white bowls for Hong Kong students. Dirt, rubbish and shit everywhere. Gangs of kids, none older than eight, smoking like their lives depended on it, just roaming, looking for anything to break or burn or steal or destroy. Graffiti. Darren loves Sharon loves Warren loves Karen. Families all dressed up on the steps of the Four Courts in tears, holding on to each other. Guys stumbling around the quays at nine o'clock in the morning after being put out of an early house. It was life, real, dirty, hard life, being lived up-close by all these people on top of each other and nobody looked too happy about it. Nobody smiled or laughed. I hadn't known it was there.

197

It was real and it was alive. I hated it. It was good to get lost in it, to be able to walk for hours and never meet anyone you knew. But it wasn't mine. People were rude in shops, everybody bumping and pushing, like it was all going to go off any second. It was better at night. It emptied until there was no one on the street. I was nervous at first but there really was no one there. All the muggers and handbag crowd and beggars went to the Southside where there was more business. No shops opened past nine o'clock. Even the Spar closed. Nowhere to get fags or milk at two in the morning. Corner shops that were like the places we had when I was a kid. Nothing had changed since 1980, not one new product line in twenty years and loads I thought were gone since then. Marrowfat peas and steak and kidney pies in tins. But then there was the friendly local community spirit that everybody talked about, how it was dead on the Southside but still alive on the Northside. My arse. These old ones knew what they were at. They had me rumbled in about two seconds when I walked in looking for the *Irish Times* and natural yogurt. Another displaced yuppie here out of need, like any other economic migrant. I'd never go to mass or send a kid to the local school or join the GAA club. I was doing my time until I got the money to get back to where I wanted to be. Back to trees and front gardens and schools where they talked like little English kids. This was purgatory for me and there was no point getting to know me or trying to like me because I'd get out as soon as my bank balance allowed. They were right. Why should they bother?

So I stood in line as the kids spent their Saturday pounds on a hundred sweets that they'd planned out all week, turning purple behind a six-year-old going through a list of stingers and flogs and blackjacks and fruit salads. How much is that? Seventy-six pence. How much have I left? The woman looked up at me and smirked. You may wait or you may go back to where you belong.

I went to the Southside for coffee, just to the edges of Temple Bar, to cafés full of tourists and Italian students. Never as far as Grafton Street. Close enough to feel comfort without exposing myself. My exile. I'd gone to ground.

# 17

I rang Anto after a week and arranged to meet him in a place near Christchurch. I told him I'd sold the flat. I told him where I was living.

'Where's that?' he asked.

'Near the markets.'

He looked at me blankly.

'On the Northside?' I said.

'Northside,' he said, like it was Hull. 'Why?'

'You get more for your money.'

'Wow,' he said. 'You're a Northsider. Who'd have ever thought.'

'If I live there a hundred years I'll never be a Northsider. For fuck's sake.'

'I better buy you a drink,' he said. 'Cider? I can check if they do flagons.'

'Hilarious.'

I asked him what was going on and he talked about his work and some girl he was seeing. She sounded nice. He was happy, full of hope.

'Have you seen Niamh?' I asked him.

'Yeah, I saw her last weekend,' he said.

He didn't say anything else. He looked like he was trying to think of a different direction so I asked him before he spoke.

'How's she doing?'

'She's fine.'

'What was she saying?'

'Nothing really,' he said. 'No news. She's back with her folks.'

'Yeah, I know.'

Another silence.

'Did she say anything about me?' I asked.

He smiled.

'Nothing you want to hear.'

'I do. I absolutely do.'

'I don't know. She was saying she'd gone back to get her stuff and she'd walked in on you in bed with some girl.' He looked embarrassed, like it was his fault. I was chewing my lip.

'I know,' I said. 'It was bad. I just wasn't thinking. I didn't think she'd be back. It was nothing at all, I was just out and I met some girl and it ended up that she came back. I didn't mean it to happen or anything. I was mortified. It must have been hard on her.'

He smiled sadly.

'She seemed pretty pissed off all right.'

'Pissed off I can deal with. She didn't seem down or depressed or anything?'

'No. Well everybody was . . .'

He stopped.

'What?' I asked.

'Everybody was very supportive, you know.'

'Right. Well that's good. I think.'

'Ah yeah. It was only because she was there in front of them. It's not like they were putting you down or anything.'

'Right.'

'You know it's none of their business what you get up to. Nobody's judging you.'

'I'm glad to hear it.' I didn't know what to think. 'Was Patrick there?' I asked.

'He was, yeah. He's in good form.'

'What was he saying?'

'I don't know. Nothing really. I don't remember.'

I looked at him.

'Seriously,' he said. 'I don't remember. If you want to know, why don't you ring him and ask him, don't be looking sideways at me.'

'Did he say something to you?' I asked.

'No.' I could see he wasn't lying. 'Why?'

'Me and him had a bit of a falling out,' I said.

'What about?'

'About nothing. About nothing at all, but he got my back up. He can be a judgemental bastard when he wants.'

He didn't say anything.

'I'm sorry,' I said. 'I'm not trying to get you involved. I'm just mouthing off.'

'That's OK,' he said. 'You should ring him.'

I shrugged.

He asked me about work, what I was going to do. I told him I'd taken the pressure off by selling the flat, but that there wasn't much work out there.

'Do something different,' he said. 'You should. Work for a charity or go back to college or anything. Don't go back into what you were doing before.'

'I don't have the option.'

'Well that's maybe not a bad thing. Make a change. That last job was no good for you.'

It was hard to know what he meant, what he knew that I hadn't told him. He was only looking out for me. I was sure of that.

'But do something,' he said. 'You can't be moping around the flat over there on your own all day. You'll go mad.'

'I've a very high boredom threshold,' I said.

'Well it's not good for you. Do something. Get out and meet people. Get a bit of social interaction going. Try not to screw them.'

I laughed at that.

At the end he offered to walk me home. It was a joke. Then I thought it would be nice, get him back and have a few drinks. Listen to music or whatever. But he couldn't. He'd to be up for work in the morning.

'It's well for some,' he said as he was walking off.

I headed down to the bridge.

\*

Here is the evidence in my favour. When I tried to establish myself as a serious, hardworking team-player in Talisman, Gerry knocked me down. When I tried to tell him about the problems that I had been having, which was reasonable enough given our friendship, he was suspicious and not at all supportive. When I put a lot of work into developing staff morale, he took it from me and said it was impossible that I could take any credit for it. My work could benefit others but not myself. I was friendly and receptive to Mark when he tried to involve himself in my life. I was open and honest with him, trusting that what I told him would remain confidential, and I got punished for that trust. The situation with H & H came about because of a situation entirely beyond my control and while I would admit that I should have told Gerry about it sooner, my relationship with him at that stage had deteriorated to such an extent that I was scared to tell him. Intimidated would not be too strong a word. Gerry knew what Robert O'Brien was like, he knew he was a nasty piece of work, a 'wanker' he'd said, and even if I was just a salesman there are things which nobody should have to tolerate. There are ways that you should not treat people and I was perfectly within my rights to make it clear that I expect a certain amount of respect. Yes, I was occasionally late and occasionally hungover and occasionally didn't go back to the office after lunch, but I was no worse than anyone else and better than most, I would say. In terms of how I dealt with the junior staff, I was friendly with Carol and polite to the others, but given the position I was in I couldn't be expected to spend my day pondering the romantic entanglements of an eighteen-year-old trainee or sending flowers to the women who sporadically cleaned my office. It was ridiculous. I make these points only to demonstrate that at the very least there were arguments in my favour. It wasn't a one-sided thing with me the guilty party and the company the offended. Incompetence, laziness and dishonesty? I had a strong case to put that none of these applied to me. More than could be said for most of the people on that office floor.

And Niamh. If she had been prepared to wait until I got myself sorted out, it would have been fine. It wouldn't have taken long.

I wasn't the best company in the weeks before she left, but if you need a reason for that, look at what I had to deal with. Look at how she reacted when I tried to tell her what was going on. She was dismissive and in the end she wasn't interested. She didn't want to have to deal with my problems, even to hear them. We lived together. That was supposed to mean something in itself, I thought. It should have meant that some sort of commitment existed between us. That she wouldn't just bale out as soon as things got a little rough, straight back to her parents. If I had to deal with things on my own, that would be OK. I could handle it. But I expected her support and it wasn't there. That made it much harder. If she had known about Róisín then it would have been fair enough, but she didn't. All she knew was that I was struggling at work, I was unhappy and just as it got really bad for me she left. If there was supposed to be a period of mourning where I wasn't allowed go near anyone else, she should have told me about it because to my way of thinking she was gone and my life was my own business. I owed her no apology.

The only person I had treated badly was Róisín. I hadn't been completely straight with her. But even then I hadn't really lied to her. There was just the time on the street with Ciaran and Jane and that obviously was not something that I had planned. It was a spur-of-the-moment thing where I didn't know what was going to come out of my mouth. I panicked. But that was the only lie. She had never asked did I have a girlfriend. Everything I said to her I meant. I liked her a lot. I was good to her. I treated her kindly. I was never cruel or in it just for sex. I listened to her when she talked and I laughed when she was funny and I had given her an experience which, if she chose to, she could learn from. In my defence I would say that although I had been cheating, the history of the world is a constant repetition of men and women from all ages, all cultures, all races, constantly fucking people they shouldn't for gain and power and a two-minute thrill. How is a man built? To propagate, to spread the seed, to find attractive what is different and new. Our society is built on the notion that the self is supreme. Look after number one. Take care of your own. Tell me I behaved badly but look at the characters in books and films, the films, the quiz shows that actively promote treating others badly for personal gain. TV ads that repeat over and over, It's mine, it's not yours, it's not for sharing, it's all mine. The stupidity of the weak being exploited by the cruelty of the strong. The greater good was a notion that crumbled with the Berlin Wall. Society was an idea that was struggling, slowly dying in the face of an ideology that sat more comfortably with the reality of how people were and are and ever will be. Selfish and fighting all the time to improve their station, their level of comfort, the esteem in which they are held. You could not describe our very nature, the programming that is inherent within us, as wrong. With Róisín I don't think I'd ever been calculating. I didn't do it for any of those cold, hard reasons. I wasn't trying to put one over on anyone. I was just having fun. I didn't talk about her like she was my latest toy. Listen to how men talk to each other in a pub on a Friday. Listen to the gap between the words they whisper in a girl's ear as they gently negotiate their way into her bed and then afterwards the laughter as they describe in tones of cruelty and domination how they bagged her. How she fell for it. The shite she'd believed out of desperation. I wasn't like that. I didn't think of Róisín in those terms and I would never have that kind of conversation with anyone. That's not who I was. She had been hurt and I regretted that. I really did. But to call it cheating made it seem worse than it was. It was like a joke that went wrong. The intent at the beginning could not be further from the pain at the end. It was supposed to just be a bit of fun. If she had felt the same, like I thought she had, there wouldn't have been a problem.

All of this was true. Thinking back and assessing everything that had happened this was at the very least an acceptable interpretation. I would be happy to stand up in court and argue my case. With an unprejudiced jury I could win.

But I wasn't in court. I wouldn't get the chance to put my point of view and the world in general would never be unprejudiced because the parties involved, who saw themselves as aggrieved, were out there spreading their message. And that was all the shit and poison that made everything I had done seem corrupt and cruel and wrong. I was on my own away from it all as their case built against me and I, unconsulted and unheard, had to rely on the benefit of the doubt. In a case like that there could only be one result. I would lose.

I thought about what Anto had said. He was right. I needed to get out of the flat. It was doing me no good staying in and avoiding the world. On the Monday I bought an evening paper and looked for a job. Money didn't matter. With the lower rent I didn't need anything professional. I wasn't looking to advance my CV. I just wanted to work in the world with other people who I didn't know, who would take me as they found me. It didn't matter what it was. I was ready.

There were jobs in kitchens. I'd worked there before and liked it. The antisocial hours, the enclosed world, the buzz and thrill of a busy Saturday night, the drinks with a crowd of wasters in after-hours underground dives. The escape from everything else. I rang a number and made an appointment. It was an Italian place fifteen minutes from the flat. Nothing clever or fancy, just popular and uncomplicated. I met the chef and filled in the application. I had one related job eight years previously. I didn't bother putting anything else down.

'Why do you want the job?' he asked me when I gave him the form.

'I want a change,' I said. 'I've been working in an office for too long and I want to do something different.'

He looked at me like I was mad.

'Do you know anything about food?' he asked.

'Well, I eat a lot,' I said as a joke and when he didn't laugh I explained that I ate out a lot and I knew the difference between good food and bad food. I knew what people would be expecting.

'How old are you?' he asked.

'I'm thirty.'

'Have you ever been in jail?'

'No.'

'Convicted? I'm not talking about traffic or GBH or drugs stuff. You know. Fraud or theft or anything?'

'No.'

'Any allergies?'

'No.'

'References?'

I gave him the name of the guy I'd worked for years ago and a college professor. He had a good laugh at that.

He rang me back that evening.

'I'll give you a trial on Wednesday night,' he said. 'I'll put you on starters and see how you go.'

It was fine. It was easy. I could keep up. I did the prep list and then stood beside another guy and helped him do service. The chef gave me another shift the following night.

I ran the section on my own that night and coped when it got busy. The head guy was a lunatic. He spent the night standing there, drinking tea and abusing everyone. Nobody seemed to mind. Nobody was who they claimed to be. There were Romanians who said they were Italian, Algerians who said they were French, Russians who said they were Finns. Everybody wanted to be European apart from the Irish guys who all wanted to be black. I did the weekend and on the Sunday he rang to say he'd put me down for the next week.

It was horrible, sweaty, dirty work. Everybody looked sick. Everybody bitched all the time about the money, the food, the conditions, each other. But I could do it. I just kept my head down and did the job and concentrated the whole time on what was next in line, what was to be done. For nine hours a night I could think about nothing but orders, preparation, organization. I kept beer in the fridge and rented videos at home and when I finished my shift I'd go back and have a shower and watch stupid comedies and drink and laugh on my own and it was fine. Phil rang me on the Friday after I started when I was just about to go in. He said he was meeting Ciaran and Anto in town and did I want to come. I said I couldn't.

'Why?' he asked.

I didn't want to tell him.

'I've something on,' I said.

'What? What's happening?'

'A thing. I don't know.'

'Jesus, you're very mysterious. Anto said we should get you out. Give you an airing. You've been cooped up on your own on the Northside too long. Come out. For fuck's sake. We worry.'

'You don't need to worry. I'm fine.'

'So what?' he asked. 'What is it?'

He only cared. It didn't matter.

'I'm working,' I said.

'At what?'

'In a restaurant.'

'A restaurant? Doing what?'

'I'm a chef.'

He laughed. And then he kept laughing.

'What's funny?' I asked.

'You're a chef,' he said.

'I'm quite good.'

'I'm sure you are. What's the name of the place? We could go there tonight.'

'Oh fuck you. No chance of that anyway. It's on the Northside.'

'How do you go from working in an office to a fucking kitchen?' he asked.

'I wanted a change.'

'Well Jesus, you're getting that all right. Southside ad exec becomes Northside kitchen boy.'

He was getting on my tits.

'I'm doing it because I want to,' I said.

He backed down.

'Sorry,' he said. 'Absolutely. Fair enough. Well what time do you get out? Maybe we can meet you later?'

'Around midnight. I'll give you a call.'

'Do. I'll talk to you then. Don't poison anyone.'

'I'll poison you, next time I see you,' I said. He was still laughing when he hung up.

When I turned my phone back on after work, they'd left a couple of messages. I turned it off and went home.

It gave a structure to the day. I didn't owe anything to anyone.

Nobody needed me so I didn't have to worry. Get up, have breakfast, watch a bit of telly and head in. Get the prep done, have dinner, do service and then home. It wasn't how I wanted to live the rest of my life, but for now it was mine. I was just some normal punter doing a normal job. I turned up on time. I never complained. I got on fine with the others. The chef liked me. With all the shit he had to deal with, I was easy. Reliable. He said in a couple of weeks he'd try me on mains.

I went out with them after a while. We went to some place off O'Connell Street, playing pretty serious music, with the smell of dope like a blanket when you walked in. It was scary. All standing around down the back just throwing drink into us. Kitchen in one group and the floor staff in another, until we started getting hammered and then it all merged. Some waitress started talking to me about what she was doing, what she wanted, why she was here. She was boring but I was getting a kind of kick out of her buzzing in my ear. She was talking about being in a bar in St Petersburg, Florida, for spring break and her and this guy were doing body shots.

'Doing what?' I asked. Lamb to the slaughter.

She talked to the barman and then she was licking salt off my neck and we were knocking back tequila.

'Now you do me,' she said so I bought the shots and licked her neck and when I looked up the lemon was between her teeth. All I could think as I went to kiss her was I'm thirty years old.

She tried to blow me in the taxi but the driver started coughing.

'I know here,' I said when we got to her place. It was directly across the road from my flat. The whole place was a mirror image of mine. It was all very confusing. She was a lot of fun in the end.

When I walked into the kitchen the following evening, scars on my neck, they gave me a round of applause.

'I take it I'm not the first,' I said and the chef just smiled and said no. I felt like I belonged.

I went out with them all the time after that. We were in a flat near Heuston with spliffs and Spar wine when we were pissed and beginning to fade. One of the Dublin guys said it to me.

'You're an educated guy. You have the accent.' He waited like he was trying to think of a nice way of saying it and then smiled. 'You're a posh cunt, what are you doing working in a kitchen?'

'I can do the job and I do it. I want to do it and that's it.' I looked at him, waiting for him to say anything, to escalate things but he didn't. 'I needed a change,' I said after a second.

'Whatever you're into. Fair enough. I'm not saying anything.' He didn't mean to be rude.

He didn't mean to be rude but afterwards, sometime the next week when I got home and had the shower and was about to start watching another bloody video, I was thinking about it. What he couldn't understand was why I would choose to work at this job. What he was thinking was that if he had what I had, he'd be doing something more than this. He would push himself harder, take advantage of the opportunities presented. I needed a break, I had said, and that was good enough for him, but the truth was that I was spent. I could do no more with what I'd been given than this. All those advantages and opportunities and I was here for the change, for the scenery? Bollocks to that. I was here because this was where I'd washed up and I could do nothing about it.

They were nice people. All of them. Of course there were agendas and power struggles and guys who didn't get on but it was all out in the open. Everybody said what they felt. People liked me because I never said a bad word about anyone and I'd cover for them when they needed it. I could drink with them, sit in the corner of an early house when we'd made it through and keep my shit together when they were falling apart. They respected me for that. I could drink with any of them.

At ten o'clock one morning we were leaving a place on the quays and I was going to go home. I started walking towards the flat and then changed my mind and crossed the river and headed up towards Grafton Street. I was drunk but I could walk straight. I walked along Dame Street passing by girls in suits from offices with trays of coffee, through guys in suits going to meetings, through the tourists. It had been weeks since I'd been over. It was faster and cleaner and I could feel the pulse of the day getting going. Nobody knew what I was doing, walking among them off my head. It was like a dream, seeing and thinking and laughing and forgetting. I went into a record shop on Grafton Street and listened to the students around me, so safe and unchallenged in this cocooned, unreal world. I knew what was going on. I was living. I was the only one who could see what they were like and it was tragic. They wouldn't last five minutes in my world. The security guard stared at me as I was walking out and I went back to him.

'What's your fucking problem?' I said and he took a step back, not ready for me. I walked away and when I looked around at him he was talking into his radio, his eyes following me down the street.

'It's me. Here I am,' I said to the guy outside a babies' clothes shop. 'Here I am,' I said to the next guy and they looked but didn't speak or react and the people on the street parted in front of me without ever seeing me. I was the invisible man. I was an inanimate obstacle, like a bin or a lamppost that you step around without thinking. I was just some drunk. But I wasn't. It was me and I could see them and understand. I was the same as them and this could happen to any one of them like it had to me. A couple of bad decisions, a run of bad luck and they would be exactly the same. They didn't know how close they were to me. I wandered down to the river and back over to the flat and slept and slept.

# 18

I had to go to the dentist. I broke a tooth eating a mussel that had a piece of barnacle in it. It was like biting a stone. There was a crack and I felt with my tongue and found two hard bits, one the barnacle and the other a bit of my tooth. I took a drink of cold water to see if it was going to hurt and it didn't but I thought I should go anyway. I went to the family guy because I thought he'd put it on the account, but he didn't so I ended up having to go out to the cash machine and get money for a filling which almost cleared me out. I got a bus to work. Even my own body was against me. I thought that was kind of funny. Evidence of conspiracy theory. Booby-trapped mussels, compliant teeth that followed orders and fell apart at the slightest provocation.

I was supposed to be in work at four but the traffic was a bastard. We were crawling down Clare Street at ten to and it was doing my head in. I probably would have been quicker walking but I thought once we got around the corner onto Westland Row it would be OK but it wasn't. It was just solid. I was going to ring but what was the point, I was going to be late, so what could I do about it? I was in the window seat upstairs, halfway to the back on the right, and as we were about to go under the rail bridge, the lights changed. I was sitting there watching people coming and going at the station and then I saw them standing there beside the newspaper guy, the pair of them. Patrick and Niamh. They were face to face, less than a foot between them, and they were both smiling and talking. Smiles and talk and ha ha. He reached out and put his hand on her arm and it looked like he was about to hold her. I said out loud, 'Fuck me,' and I could feel the guy beside me looking over but I said nothing to him. I got my mobile out and I rang Patrick. I wanted to talk to him more than to her. The lights changed and the bus didn't move and the two of them stayed there, chatting away. I watched him look around as his phone rang and then go through his jacket pockets until he found it. I was less then fifty feet away staring straight at him. He took it out and looked at it and said something to her and then held it up to her to show that it was me. He cancelled the call.

'You fucking wanker,' I shouted. 'You fucking coward.' I hung up without leaving a message. People were looking at me. The bus moved forward and I sat there. I needed to get off. I stood up and your man got out of the way and I went downstairs. We were around the corner and into a bus lane so the next stop wasn't until up near Trinity. I got out and ran back the length of Pearse Street. I didn't know what I was going to do. All I wanted was to stand in front of them and let them know I'd seen them. I didn't want to talk to them or beat them up or anything. There was no smart-arse comment to make. Just to stand in front of them and nod like I'd known all along that this would happen. But when I got to the station there was no sign of them. I bought a ticket for Lansdowne and went up onto the platform and walked along trying to look normal. I was sweating after running and I was wired up to fuck. I couldn't find them. There was no sign. I crossed under the track onto the Northside platform and still they weren't there. They could be anywhere. I crossed back over and walked out. The guy on the gate started giving me shit but I told him I had to go and he knew better than to argue with me. I needed to get my head together. There was a pub on the corner.

I rang work as I was walking up the street. I told them I'd been on my way in and I'd started getting sick and I'd tried to ring and I was sorry but I'd be in tomorrow. It was completely crap and he was pissed off but there wasn't anything he could do. I felt better after I'd called. I could just go and get wrecked in comfort. Get a taxi later and sleep. Fuck the money. I sat in the pub on the corner trying not to think about it. I didn't feel too bad. It showed I was right. That anybody could do the wrong thing, that it wasn't just me. But it also seemed to say that everything that could go wrong would. It just would. It was comical. Two months ago they were my best friend and my girlfriend. And him bollocking me about cheating and poor Niamh at home crying herself to sleep. Things changed pretty quick. I was off on the Northside working in a kitchen and they were doing whatever they were doing. Talking about me. Her saying that I was a head-case. How shit I was in bed. What would he say? How I'd been fucking around with a schoolkid? I never would have thought that he'd tell her. I thought he'd know that there are things you never do. But he didn't. If you make a move on a friend's girlfriend when he's off the scene, then you're the type of guy who doesn't respect any of those rules. You don't fuck your friends over for a girl. You never tell a girl anything about her boyfriend. All that stupid lads-together, mates' code-of-honour bollocks. But it meant something. It says something about somebody if they disregard it. There are things you don't do. It was too much. Too much of me exposed.

I drank and I thought. I thought as hard as I could, trying to decide what it meant before I started to get drunk. I would reach my conclusion sober and stick to it drunk. I didn't know if it really was anything. They could have just met by accident, her going in, him coming out. She could have asked to meet him to see if I was OK. He could have done the same. Maybe they were meeting everybody else to go to a film or something. There were plenty of innocent explanations but every time I began to believe, I saw his hand on her arm and him showing her his phone. My name on an inch-wide screen. Rory calling. Cancel. And from there it wasn't hard to see the two of them in a bed, him trying to fuck the memory of me from her head. It was no good. It was all wrong. I wanted to be away from it all and I wanted to be there right in the middle of it, standing beside them unseen, hearing what they were saying, watching what they did. Because even if I hated it, even if it made me sick, even if I could feel it as real as pain, I needed to know what the truth was because without that I didn't know where I was. And then I knew. I could ring the others and meet them the next day. Anto and Phil and those. I hadn't seen them in ages. Go for a pint, talk a bit and find out what was going on for definite. I could feel the drink across my forehead. I bought cigarettes and smoked one in two minutes. I stood up to go for a piss and nearly fell over with the buzz of it. When I came back I knew I didn't have to think any more.

I knew there was something wrong when I woke the following day. It was there before I felt the hangover and started putting the previous day together again. It was there and I remembered what it was. I knew what I had to do. I rang work and told them I was still sick but that I really expected to be back the next day and they couldn't say anything because I rang in time and people get sick all the time so why couldn't I.

I rang Anto to see was he on for a drink and he was. I rang Phil and I had to work him a bit because he wasn't too keen, bitching about having to get home after. The fucker had earned his taxi fare by the time the conversation was over. It was all ready. I went back to bed.

When I woke up again the last thing I wanted was more booze. My body was aching and I felt sick, but it had to be done. Take it easy. I didn't have to get hammered.

We met in town. Anto was there when I arrived. He was in good form.

'You're looking well,' I said to him.

'I'd say the same about you but I'd be lying.'

'Yeah I know. I was out.'

'For how long?' he asked.

'I'm all right. I'll be all right.'

'Fuck it,' he said. 'Start the process again. What do you want?'

We sat there and drank. It had been weeks since I'd seen him. He was asking about what I'd been up to and how the work was and everything and I told him it was all fine. It was too early to ask him anything about Patrick so I asked about that girl he'd been seeing and he got talking about how he was still seeing her and he hadn't been out much and he just kept on yapping and it was nice to see him so happy. Then Phil arrived and I got a round in.

Phil hadn't much to say for himself. He'd been buried out in the suburbs and was doing that work–train–sleep thing. He talked about how boring it was and how he was getting old but he couldn't hide that he loved it all. It was fair enough. I asked about all the others and I don't know what they said. I wasn't listening. I was working. I let things go on for a while. I kept buying drinks, saying I hadn't seen them in ages and that, pushed them into drinking faster. I was trying to keep myself calm. I was nervous. Phil started making some stupid joke about living on my own over in the badlands and I tried to turn it somehow to what I wanted.

'The place is fine,' I said 'but I don't much like being on my own.' I got it wrong. They both noticed. It was the wrong thing to say. I'd never say something like that. We weren't girls. They both just sat there looking at me. 'It's all right, I'm not going to start crying or anything. I'm just saying.' Neither of them spoke. I laughed at myself and then they laughed and we went on like before but they had noticed and I had to be careful. I waited a while and then I looked at Anto and asked, 'How's Patrick?'

He was more likely to know and I could read him better.

He breathed in, like he was going to speak, and then paused and then spoke.

'He's fine. He's grand.'

'Any news?' I asked.

'Don't think so, no.'

'That's it?'

'Well what?' he said.

'Nothing's happened to him at all?'

'I don't know. When was the last time you spoke to him?' he asked me. I didn't know if he was avoiding it or what, by asking me questions.

'Ages ago,' I said.

'You should give him a call.'

'You said that the last time. Maybe I will. What about you?' I said to Phil. 'Have you seen him?'

'Eh no, officer,' he said.

Him and Anto started laughing.

'What?' I asked. 'What's funny?'

'If you want to know what's going on with Patrick, why don't you just ring him, rather than putting us through the third degree?'

'Why? What's happened? What's going on?'

'I don't know,' they both said.

I shook my head.

'I'm just making conversation. I haven't seen anybody in ages. I'm trying to catch up with what's been happening.'

'Nothing's been happening,' Phil said. 'Nothing ever happens.'

'Not to you,' I said. 'You're not living in a flat on your own in Dublin 7.'

'What's been happening to you?' he asked.

I thought about telling them that yesterday I saw my closest friend and my girlfriend holding hands but I just couldn't because I didn't know what they'd think.

'Nothing really. It's just a change.'

'We fear change,' Anto said and we all had a laugh about that. It got back to normal. I left it for an hour or two. We were all getting jarred. The two of them didn't go out all that much and I was topping up. It worked quite well. I didn't care any more about what they thought. I just said it to neither of them in particular.

'What's Niamh up to?'

They looked at each other.

'Don't know,' Anto said.

'Catherine was talking to her a couple of weeks ago,' Phil said. 'I haven't seen her.'

'Any news?' I asked.

'Are you starting this shit again?' Anto asked.

'I'm just asking,' I said laughing, keeping it light.

'She's staying in her parents' place. She's applied for a doctorate in Oxford. That's all I remember. May it please the court,' Phil said.

'Right,' I said. I zoned out for a while. The two of them talked amongst themselves. I didn't know what was going on. I didn't know who knew what, what they were keeping from me, why they couldn't just tell me. They had both laughed at me and that wasn't right. And anyway Phil had said it. Nothing ever did happen, so if something had they would all know about it. They would all ring each other up and talk about it. About how I'd fucked everything up and what would I say when I found out. If it was happening they had to know. Maybe it wasn't. I couldn't work it out. I tried to forget about it. They were still talking.

'What's this?' I asked.

'Somebody keyed my car last week,' Phil said. 'I was just saying there's wankers everywhere. Keyed it for nothing.'

'How's your place for that?' Anto asked me.

'It's all right,' I said. 'No real hassle.'

'The whole thing is going to be screwed in a couple of years,' Phil said. 'Things turn around now. Jobs start going and you're left with all these new slums waiting to happen out on the Westside and all these young fellows just hanging around getting pissed off because the immigrants took their jobs and some posh bastard's got a nice car. Give it eighteen months. Joyriding, mugging, the whole lot, it'll all be back.'

'Weren't you in Socialist Workers when you were in college?' I said to him.

'I'm not saying it's their fault,' he said. 'If I was in their shoes I'd probably do the same. You've got all these guys coming up now from one-parent families, with a whole load of half-siblings and no men anywhere. No male figures anywhere.'

'There are no role models for boys. That's absolutely right,' Anto said. He was pissed.

'Who are you going to look up to? Politicians? Sports stars? Fucking musicians?' Phil said.

'I was watching a programme where they were talking about this the other week,' I said. 'The journalist was stopping people on the street and asking them about this exact question. Role models for young men today. What was it?' I asked. I waited. They were both looking at me.

'Oh, I remember,' I said. 'It was *The Muppet Show*. It was Sam Eagle asking a whole load of monsters what they thought about this pressing subject. This subject that's so fucking trite and overstated and boring that a children's programme with puppets is actually taking the piss out of it.'

It was supposed to be funny. It was true but it was supposed to be funny. They both just looked at me.

'What's wrong with you?' Anto said.

'What's your fucking problem?' Phil said.

'I saw the programme. I did,' I said.

'Oh shut up,' Phil said and he went off to the jacks. He was pissed off.

'Why did you do that? He always gets up on his soapbox when he's locked. Leave him alone,' Anto said to me.

I put my head in my hands. I was hammered.

'I'm going mad,' I said.

'Why?' he asked. 'What?'

'Are Patrick and Niamh seeing each other?' I asked him straight out.

'What?'

'I saw them together yesterday and it's been doing my head in.'

'I don't know,' he said. I looked at him and he shrugged. 'I don't know,' he said again.

'Of course you know,' I said. 'Anto. It's me. Just tell me.'

'You're freaking me out, Rory. I don't know what you're talking about.'

'You talk to Patrick,' I said.

'Yeah, so?'

'So he must have told you. He must have.'

He looked at me straight.

'I'm telling you. I don't know.'

It was bollocks. He was too nice a guy to be able to lie properly. He hated doing it. He looked like he was in pain when he was sitting there telling me this. I left it. There was nothing else I could do. He was just trying to do the right thing.

'OK,' I said. 'Don't worry about it.'

Phil came back. I told him I was sorry about before and I got up and left.

# THE VERY MAN

How do you know what to believe? What could I do? I didn't want her any more. I didn't want him as a friend. I shouldn't care. It all made sense. It all hung together so that when I stood back and looked at it, I could see that everything I'd been thinking was right. Nobody was with me. Anto saying he didn't know. Phil just talking shit. Town was too small for Patrick and Niamh to think they could get away with it. They had to know I'd find out and that meant that they didn't care. None of them cared and I didn't know why. What had I done? I spent six years in New York with a whole load of arseholes that I never gave a damn about and they'd never turned on me. In an atmosphere that was much more pressurized and competitive than this, everything was completely out there in front of you. I'd done nothing wrong, nothing different, since I came back and everybody just fucked me over. I couldn't see why.

# 19

I went to work the next day.

'You're better?' the chef said when he saw me.

'I'm all right. I don't know what it was but I think I'm over it.'

'You don't look the best.'

I had been up all night watching telly. Watching nothing but I wasn't able to get up and move and I watched the night tick by on the video clock. I went to bed at ten and then when I woke up it was three o'clock. I thought about not going but I got out of bed and my body took over and I turned up on time.

The guy I was working with tried to talk to me but gave up when I wouldn't. I couldn't. I listened and I smiled at his jokes but I couldn't come up with anything to say and he stopped talking and we worked in silence. I was all over the place. It took me too long to get set up and when the orders started coming in I couldn't handle it. I just stood there useless doing everything arseways. The chef started bollocking me which was fair enough.

'I can't do this section tonight,' I said to him. 'I'm in bits. I'm sorry.'

'You might have told me this three hours ago when I could do something about it,' he said. 'You have to stay on it and try and sort it out.'

'I can't.'

'Just fucking do it. You can't change sections in the middle of service.'

It wouldn't have made any difference if I had a plane waiting to take me anywhere I wanted after I finished work. It wouldn't have mattered if this was the last day I ever had to work in my life. I just wanted to be out of there right then at that moment. I couldn't get through another three hours of this. It was only eight o'clock.

'I can't do it,' I said and I walked.

'Where are you going?' he said as I passed by him. I didn't answer. It wasn't about him. I didn't want to do it but I just had to.

'That's you finished if you go, you know that,' he called after me.

'I know. I'm really sorry,' I said and I thought he was going to laugh.

I didn't bother getting changed, just grabbed my bag and walked out through the full restaurant. I wasn't well. I got a taxi home and had a bath. I woke up when the water got cold. I dried myself off, took the phone off the hook and went to bed and slept until I woke up whenever that was.

This is how I spent the next day. I got up at three and put on clothes and went and bought a paper. I came back and took off my clothes and turned on the telly and ate a fried egg sandwich and drank three pots of tea in front of it, with the paper on the coffee table open but I couldn't read it. I had the remote in my hand and flicked and flicked. I did not watch one single programme. When I went for a piss I thought I should get a haircut but when I checked the time it was after six so I couldn't. I had another fried egg sandwich at eight which was what I wanted and more tea and then I opened a bottle of white wine because I wanted one glass but once it was open I had a second and then I wanted fags so I put on my clothes again but there was nowhere open so I had to get a taxi to the garage on the quays and while I was there I got another bottle of white just to have it and then I went back. I just kept flicking and I drank the wine and I smoked the cigarettes and about halfway through the second I began to get tired and I thought about it and I put the rest in the fridge. I went to bed and as I was lying there I knew that the next day was going to be OK. I felt OK again and it was a Saturday and I could just take it easy and I'd have my shit back together by Monday. New start, get out there and see what I could get from the agencies because by now nobody was going to remember any of the bad stuff. I could hardly remember it myself. I went to sleep feeling better than I had in ages.

I went back into work the following day to apologize to the chef.

'How are you?' he said when he saw me. He was OK about it.

'I'm sorry,' I said.

'You can't walk out.'

'I know, yeah. I only wanted to say sorry. I hope I didn't leave you in the shit.'

'You did. Of course you did. You left at eight o'clock on a Thursday night. There's no point coming back to me now saying you're sorry. I needed you then.'

'I wasn't up to it,' I said.

'I know you weren't. I could see you weren't when you walked through the door. I said it to you.'

'Yeah.'

'So do you want your job?' he asked. 'Presuming I'm willing to give it to you?'

I stared at the ground.

'I think I'll give it a miss.'

'You'll give it a miss?' he said.

I looked up at him. He was pissed off.

'I don't know. I've got a lot going on.'

'Then why . . . ?' he started and then broke off. 'OK well, whatever. See you around,' he said and that was it. He walked off. As I was leaving I met one of the evening boys coming in.

'All right? What's the story?' he asked me.

'I'm finished,' I said.

'He sacked you?' he asked.

'We kind of agreed on it.'

He smiled.

'Back to the office for you?'

'I don't know. Maybe. It was nice working with you anyway.' I shook his hand. I didn't know what else to do.

'We should have a drink,' he said. 'Come around on Monday night. We'll have a pint.'

'OK,' I said.

'I'll see you then.' And I left.

I went out home for dinner the next day. I hadn't been back for ages. I wanted to see Dad, to make sure he was OK. I felt bad. When Shane had said I should go out I said I would but I never did. I rang him one time and he seemed all right but still. I called Shane to see if they were all going to be there and he said they were and then I thought it would be better if I went out midweek when it would be just me and him. But then I was trying to work out what I was going to do on my own all day. It seemed a bit grim so I went and got the train.

They were all there when I arrived. They were sitting out the back drinking gin. The sun was shining but it wasn't warm. They were all wearing coats. All the kids were running around and Shane had brought his dog over which I thought was a bit much. They were running across flower-beds and sliding around on the grass and jumping into the bushes. Nobody said anything, though I could see Dad looking.

'You look well,' I said to him. 'How have you been?'

'Grand,' he said.

'How's the arm?'

'Better. Much better. The cast came off a couple of weeks ago. It's fine.' He held it up and wiggled his fingers.

'Have you not seen him since then?' Brian asked me.

I ignored him, just listened in to Shane and the two wives.

'Rory?' he said. He wasn't going to let it drop. I turned and looked at him.

'What?'

'Have you not been out here in that long?'

'Just leave it,' I said. 'OK? I've had a lot of shit going on.' He shook his head. He started to say something and I interrupted. 'Just drop it.'

Dad spoke up. 'Leave him alone, Brian. Stop.'

Silence fell across the table and then Shane's kid came running over to show me a stone she'd found.

'How was skiing?' I asked her. 'Apart from expensive?'

Dad asked me how I was. I was sitting beside him so I could talk without the rest having to hear. I told him I'd been sick.

'How's Niamh?' he asked then.

I smiled.

'She's no more.'

He looked shocked.

'It's OK,' I said. 'She's not dead. We just broke up.'

'I know what you meant,' he said. 'What happened?'

'I don't know. I was working a lot and that. It just didn't work out. You know, these things happen.'

'Was it amicable?'

I smiled again.

'Not very.'

He waited but I had nothing else to say.

'But you're all right?' he asked. 'I don't want to pry, but as long as you're OK?'

'I'm fine.'

'How's work?' he said then.

I took a deep breath and then just said it's grand. It was too much to be telling him. I didn't want him to worry. He was OK with that and we sat back and joined in with the conversation.

The two wives had made dinner. Roast chicken and stuff. It was good. I hadn't had a proper meal in ages. I hadn't used cutlery in I don't know how long. We started talking about the food that Mum used to make when we were kids. I didn't remember much of it.

'There was the thing with rice and ham and cheese.'

'And the thing with turnips.'

'Where did she get these ideas?'

We looked at Dad.

'I don't know. She never talked to me about it. I just came home and it was there waiting for me. I never even thought about it.'

'Did you ever cook?' Shane's wife Linda asked.

'When she was in having Rory I had to. Before that never. There were days when she was sick when I had to get the dinner but mostly I just went to a chipper. I couldn't boil water really. She preferred to do all that. It wasn't expected of men in general that they would have to do things around the house.'

'Still isn't for this guy,' Linda said.

'I do plenty,' he said. 'I got a cleaner in last year and someone to do the ironing.'

'That doesn't count,' she said. 'You don't do anything yourself.'

'OK, but I have it done. You don't have to do it so what does it matter?'

'Who does things in your house, Rory?' Brian's missus asked me.

I smiled and kind of laughed.

'I do. I do everything.'

'Niamh doesn't do anything?' Brian asked.

'Not much. In fairness I couldn't expect her to seeing as she doesn't live with me any more. I don't think she's in the domestic chores business.'

They were all looking at me.

'When did this happen?' Shane asked.

'I don't know. A couple of months. Six weeks. I don't know.'

'You're some fucking arsehole,' Brian said. Rebecca made a noise like a cat and shook her head in the direction of the children at the other table. He blushed. It was good to see.

'Why's that?' I asked.

'She was a great girl.'

'Did you know her? Because I thought you only met her once.'

'Yeah. Still, I could tell,' he said.

'Because you're so fucking perceptive?'

'Language,' he said.

'Starts at home,' I said. 'Can't blame me for what your kids pick up.'

There was a pause. Me and him were just staring at each other. If Dad and the kids hadn't been there, we would have been standing by this stage. I really wanted to slap him but I couldn't raise it with everybody around. I let it go.

'Did you get a job yet?' Shane asked. I looked at him. He wasn't acting the prick. His face was open and slightly panicked. He was trying to cool it down.

'What's this?' Dad said.

I sat there with all of them looking at me. I turned to him.

'I lost my job a few weeks ago but it's OK. I got another one almost straight away. It's no big deal. It's happening all over the place. I didn't tell you because you were sick at the time and I didn't want you to worry.'

'Who are you with now?' he asked.

I should have just lied. It would have been so much easier. Tell them anything. It wasn't like they were going to check up on me. But I was tired. I didn't want to lie straight to his face so I told him.

'I'm working as a chef in a restaurant.' It was only when I said it I realized that it wasn't true. Brian snorted. I ignored him. Dad looked like he was going to laugh.

'That makes a change,' he said. 'You a cook.'

'A chef.'

'Do you like it?'

'I do, yeah. I don't know if it's something I'm going to do for ever but it's OK for now.'

'Good for you,' he said. 'Fair enough.'

'You mean in the space of two months you've managed to lose your job and your girlfriend?' Brian said. I looked at him. He was smiling like it was a joke, like if I said anything that's what he would say. That he was only messing with me. I didn't care.

'I wouldn't, Brian, I swear to God.'

'Why?' he asked, the smile gone.

'Brian,' Dad said.

'Because there's a whole load of shit going on that you know nothing about. You know fucking nothing about any of it, nothing about me and what's gone on in my life in the past six months so before you start taking the fucking piss . . .' I was getting louder, 'you might want to think about that. Because I can tell you all about it and explain it to you but I don't think you want to hear it. I don't think you want to know.' I stopped. His face was red.

'Do you, Brian? Do you want me to tell you all about it?'

'Not really, no.'

'Right, well then fuck off and leave me alone. Sorry, Rebecca,' I said to his wife and I left.

I was walking down the road towards the train, raging, when Shane came running after me.

'Are you all right?' he asked me when I stopped.

'I've been better.'

'He didn't mean to piss you off,' he said.

'He fucking did.'

'I know he's an arsehole but you know what he's like. He doesn't mean anything.'

'I don't know,' I said. 'He took pleasure from my problems. You saw that.'

'I don't think he meant to. He was just taking the piss.'

'Fuck him. I know what he was at.'

We stood there. It wasn't going anywhere. I was too wound up.

'Are you OK?' he asked again.

'I'm all right.'

'Can I do anything for you?'

'I'm fine,' I said.

'Can I give you some money? Would that help?'

I wanted to say no. I was going to when he said, 'I'll give you a cheque. How much? A grand?'

'You don't have to,' I said.

'I know I don't,' he said. He took out the chequebook and wrote it leaning on the garden wall of a house I used to play in when I was in kindergarten. He handed it to me.

'I'll pay you back,' I said. 'And the other one. I haven't forgotten.'

'Neither have I,' he said. He patted me on the back and it turned into an awkward kind of hug.

'Will you come back?' he asked.

'No, I'm going to go on.'

'You're all right?'

'I'm fine,' I said.

'Any messages for Brian?'

'Tell him he's a cunt,' I said.

'Gladly,' he said and he walked off.

On the train on the way back into town, I should have been thinking about the money, but all I could think was that he'd totally shown me up.

I went to the cash desk in the restaurant at half-ten on the Monday night. I waited at the front until they came out. A couple of the waitresses said hello and the manager just stared but he didn't do anything. When they came out we went to a pub around the corner and got started. Then at closing we went to a club that had cheap beer and was full of students. There was loads of us at first but by the end it was just me and this other guy. He was off the following day so we bought wine in Centra and got a taxi back to his place. He was talking about growing up in Finglas and a whole load of stories about robbing cars and sniffing glue. I just listened and laughed and didn't know if any of it was true but I couldn't say anything. Nothing happened to me when I was a kid. Nothing. I hadn't ever done anything I could tell him, but it didn't matter. I told him about Niamh and Patrick and how all that had happened and he seemed to understand. I liked him. I crashed on his couch and when I woke up in the morning he'd got a fry on the go. It was about two o'clock when I was going to go. I was in bits.

'Do you want to grab a cure?' I said. 'Just the one, like.'

He said yeah so we went into this big barn of a place near his flat. I didn't know where I was. We stayed there for the afternoon watching racing and going into the bookie's and when it got to half-six, I said we should go into town and make a night of it so we got a taxi and went in. We were in Mulligan's which was dodgy because I knew people who drank in there. And then I thought, Fuck them. Fuck them all. This guy was a better friend to me than any of them had been. His name was Declan.

We wanted to drink. It was good. He drank a bit slower than me, so I was able to keep going and he wasn't a prick if you wanted to skip one. He was on for a session and so was I. Then he rang the others from the restaurant and we met them in a club in Temple Bar. I was fucked by that stage. I don't remember much. I was talking to a girl in a big pile of coats and then I fell asleep and then we were all outside and then in a taxi and I woke up in a flat and there were about fifteen people and when I met Declan again it was like we hadn't seen each other in years. He gave me a wrap of speed and I got stuck into that and after half an hour I was back on the beer and ready to go again. People were beginning to crash. I put a CD on and went out on the balcony. The flat was near Islandbridge overlooking the river. Once it got to Heuston it was like any city river full of shit and with grey walls and drains, but here it was like it was in the country, wide and slow with trees hanging over it. The sun was coming up and the sky was pink and blue. I was knackered. I went back inside. Declan was kissing a waitress. I wanted to go.

'I'm going to head,' I said to him.

'Now?'

'Yeah. The sun's coming up. It's late. What time is it?'

'It's twenty past seven,' he said.

'Jesus.'

'What we could do . . .' he said and then he stood up. 'What we will do is finish it properly. Early house.'

'Early house,' the girl said. 'Let's all go.'

Only a few of us went in the end. We went out on the road to get a taxi, but they wouldn't take five and then a bus came so we got on that. It was packed. We stood downstairs shouting and laughing, surrounded by schoolkids and people going to work. We must have been stinking but I felt great.

The place on Capel Street had a queue outside it. One of our lot knew the bouncer and we got in and got a table. It was busy, alcoholics at the bar and shift workers like us on the tables, all fucked. I bought a round. It was all cider. Cider for breakfast. I had a couple more. Everybody was talking but I couldn't keep up. A girl tried to kiss me when my head was turned but she wasn't the right one. There was a girl who I liked, but there was some guy from the pub talking to her and he was tattooed to fuck so I left it. Then I fell asleep. I woke up when somebody spilt a drink down my back. It was just some idiot who was staggering. It wasn't his fault.

When I woke up again, Declan and his girl were trying to get me out.

'We have to go,' they were saying.

'Why?'

'Because you're asleep. Come on.'

'I'm awake now,' I said.

'No. We still have to go.'

'OK,' I said and I tried to get up. The two of them helped me. We walked out. It was Capel Street outside and the sun was shining.

'Where do you live?' he asked me.

I worked it out and pointed. We started walking. I went to get a fag and couldn't find them.

'I left my jacket in the pub,' I said. 'I better get it.' We were on a lane with forklifts. I couldn't remember where it was.

'They won't let you back in,' the girl said. 'I'll get it. What's it like?'

I tried to think.

'It's black.'

'Leather?'

'No.'

'What?'

'No, not leather.'

'I know,' she said. She was getting pissed off. 'What kind of jacket is it?'

'It's black,' I said.

'For fuck's sake.'

'What? It's plastic. Plastic. OK? For fuck's sake,' I said. Me and the guy sat against the wall and she went off. The sun was shining straight on to us.

'It's a great day,' I said to him. 'Declan.' It was Declan.

'It's lovely.'

'Do you have a cigarette?' I asked and that was it. That was the end.

# 20

I didn't know where I was. I felt the sun before I woke. I knew it was warm and I thought I was in bed. I was so comfortable and then I heard someone say my name and I opened my eyes. I could feel the smile on my face as I waited to see the lovely cosy world that I would find myself in. I opened my eyes and I was lying on the footpath with the sun on me and a girl looking at me. I couldn't see her face. I tried to remember where I was and why I was and what was going on and then I saw the girl and it was Róisín.

'Rory,' she said. I smiled to show her I was OK and I tried to think. I sat up. I didn't know what time it was.

'What are you doing?' she asked. I laughed at that because it must have looked crap.

'It's OK.' I sat up. 'I was in the pub and I forgot my jacket and I was waiting for the girl. Me and the guy were waiting and I must have fallen asleep. There's my jacket,' I said as I saw it. It was beside me. 'I must have fallen asleep and then when she brought it back I probably didn't wake up.'

'Why aren't you in work?' she asked.

'Which one?'

'Your job. Shouldn't you be at work?'

'It's OK. I don't have to, no.'

I was waking up. I was more sleepy than pissed and the sun was putting me off. I didn't know why she was there.

'Where did you come from?' I asked her. 'How did you find me?'

'I wasn't looking for you,' she said. 'I was going to pay my car tax.'

'And you found me,' I said.

She kind of smiled.

'I found you. Are you OK to get home?'

'I'm fine. I live really near here. I moved.'

'Yeah. Well I was never in your flat.'

'You weren't? Why not?'

I had forgotten.

'I don't know,' she said. 'Your girlfriend probably wouldn't have liked it.'

'Right. Fair enough. She's gone now anyway.'

'OK. So do you need a hand or are you all right?'

'I'm fine.' I stood up. 'Where are we?'

'Off Capel Street somewhere. Near the markets.'

'I'm going that way,' I said. 'Or that way actually.'

'I'll walk with you.'

I was wobbly. I didn't recognize the street but we walked along.

'How have you been?' I asked her.

'Grand.'

'How's college?'

She wasn't looking at me.

'It's OK.'

I stopped.

'What time is it?'

'It's half-ten.'

'I was asleep on the road for an hour. I must have looked like a fucking bum. Jesus. I mean I know people who work in the courts. They could have seen me.'

She was smiling.

'I saw you,' she said.

'Did I look crap?'

She laughed.

'You were asleep on the street, Rory. There's not any way it can look good.'

I sat down.

'Oh Christ.'

She just stood above me looking at me. I held my head in my hands.

'It's embarrassing, it really is. It wasn't as bad as it looks, I swear to you, I'm not a fucking alco.'

'I know you're not.'

'There was a load of us out and it just kept going and then we were in the early house and I was falling asleep and we left and I left my coat behind and the girl I was with went back to get it and I was waiting with her boyfriend and then the next thing I know you woke me.'

'It's OK,' she said. 'It's nothing to do with me.'

'I know but still. I must look like shit.'

She just shrugged.

'Well thanks anyway,' I said.

I stood up and we walked on. We came to the tax office.

'Are you going to go in?' I asked.

'I can walk you back to your flat.'

'You don't have to. It's just over there.'

'It's fine. You could fall in front of a car or fall asleep again or something.'

It was depressing.

'I'm all right,' I said.

'I know. But I don't mind walking.'

'I didn't know you even had a car,' I said after a minute.

'I brought it down a few weeks ago.'

'You were at home.'

'Yeah.'

The conversation didn't work. We hardly knew each other. I was in bits. I'd messed her around. I didn't know why she was there. We arrived at the gate to my block.

'This is it,' I said. 'Thanks again. Really. I'd still be there if you hadn't got me up.'

'It's no problem.'

'Seriously, thank you.'

I didn't know what I was going to say but I wanted to say something. I'd been drinking for three days but I wanted to tell her something.

'Good luck,' she said before I had a chance and she started to walk off.

'I'm really sorry,' I said.

She looked around and nodded. I walked up to her.

'For everything,' I said. 'I treated you really badly. I'm sorry.' I could hear my voice, thick and ready to break. She stood in front of me.

'You did,' she said. 'But it doesn't matter.'

'It does. It does. It's not fair. You didn't deserve it at all and I'm really sorry and that's all. I'm not a bad guy, I swear to you. I'm just fucked up. Not this fucked up. Not as bad as this looks, but it really was all my fault. My problems and I'm sorry.'

She smiled sadly.

'I never thought it was my fault.'

'It wasn't,' I said again. 'It was me.'

'I know.'

'I'm not trying to give you a hard-luck story or anything. I just felt bad about you. Only about you. Everything else would have happened anyway. That's it. That's all.'

'What's everything else?'

'It's nothing. Nothing to do with you. I've been out for about three days. I'm going to go home and just sleep. Thank you and I'm sorry.'

'Are you sure you're OK?'

I shook my head. I just wanted to talk to her. I wanted to but she said it.

'Can I do anything for you?'

'Do you want to have coffee or something?' I said.

'I have to do this tax thing,' she said pointing back at the office.

'OK. Fair enough.'

'I might ring you sometime,' she said.

'I'd like it if you did,' I said.

'I will, yeah.'

'You have my number?'

'I think so.'

'I can give it to you now,' I said. 'If you want.'

'It's OK. I think I have it.'

'OK. Have a good day or whatever, yeah.'

'Go to bed. You should go to bed,' she said.

When I was going up in the lift I was trying to remember how she had said it, trying to work out if it sounded like she cared or if she just wanted to make sure I didn't die. I was too tired and drunk to work it out. I went in and fell onto the bed and was asleep in minutes.

It was eight o'clock and I couldn't understand why I was waking so early and then I saw that the sun was on the wrong side of the flat. I was thrown. I lay there aching. I went back into my mind to work out why this was and then realized that it was the evening and it all spun around. I went to the jacks and I was standing there pissing when I remembered Róisín. I went back in and lay down and tried to get as much as I could out of the fog and bit by bit it all came back.

There was nothing I could do. I couldn't get rid of it on my own. I went into the living-room and sat on the couch in my underwear and had a cigarette. It was eight o'clock in the evening. I knew it was the drink. The blackness that hung above me. My personal cloud of despair.

It started with embarrassment as I remembered snatches of conversation, stumblings and fumblings with the wrong girl. Shouting on the bus as people looked at us in disgust. What was their problem? They were going to work in the company of drunken, cursing, shouting wasters about to get drunker. Foul language, potential violence, whispered comments about fat schoolboys, ugly women, smelly old lads. Slurring at a barman who thought twice before serving me. Falling asleep at the table. Falling asleep in the sun. Not being able to understand the girl who tried to get my jacket and then the conversation unseen or unremembered, who could tell, between Declan and the girl when they decided to leave me there on the street. He'll be grand. But shouldn't we? He'll be fine. He's just pissed. Who walked by me as I lay there? Who saw me? What they saw was a drunk guy asleep on a side street in a ropy part of town in the middle of the day, his coat lying beside him. Objectively that was all you could say. But what would they think? A bright young fellow who had overindulged after a night of fun with friends. No. Not likely. They would see a drunk. A bum wasted on the street on his own. That's what they would see and at eight o'clock in the evening on my own on the couch, it seemed about right. Because I wasn't having fun. I was on my own and I drank because I could and it made people I didn't know seem like lifelong friends. The conviviality of drink. Buying rounds, passing around cigarettes and joints and laughing at everything. Telling people your darkest secrets to make them like you. Telling them lies to impress them, to make them like you. It was all about people liking you but at the end I was there on the street alone and that's when Róisín arrived.

It was satisfying to think of the pleasure she would have taken out of finding me. I was a mess, my life fallen apart, and she was kind and concerned but nobody is that perfect. At some point she would have to think that I'd got what I'd deserved, that my cheating and lying had caught up with me. She'd have to see it that way. The last time we met I left her in tears and now, with no responsibility or expectation, she had helped me and I left her with me needy and pathetic. Pathetic. You can't respect someone who's pathetic. You can't fancy them. It's very hard to like them.

After a couple of false starts, the words and intentions rang hollow to me. Because it was a Wednesday, this was not the week to start putting my life together again. Next Monday I would start, stay off the drink between now and then, get my shit together. Get my suit cleaned, set up interviews and start working in a proper job again. Get some money saved. Live a quiet life, give up booze, not go out. Read books, go to the theatre, throw the telly out the window. Get a nice house away from the city and start again. My life in the country with a comfortable woman who didn't know about my past as a fucking useless drunk who tied himself in knots with lies. Pumping out children and gardening. It all started on Monday. I was looking forward to it.

But it was only Wednesday. It didn't hang together because if I was going to start on Monday why couldn't I start tomorrow? My new life should start here, right now. Why not? Why not? Because I couldn't. It was too much. I couldn't do it tomorrow and by Sunday I'd be going mad and I'd end up having a couple of drinks to help me sleep and then I'd spend Monday on the couch drinking tea watching cartoons telling myself that Wednesday was a good day to start.

If I couldn't do it tomorrow I couldn't do it and that was all there was to it. I couldn't do it tomorrow. I was stuck and all it seemed I could do was to try and stay away from the world outside because outside the only thing there was for me to do was to drink and I didn't want to drink. Yet. I turned on the telly.

It was the following day which was the Thursday, when I was having breakfast with nothing to do, that Róisín rang me.

'How are you doing?' she asked.

'OK. I'm fine,' I said. 'Embarrassed but apart from that I'm OK. Thanks again.'

'Not at all.'

There was nothing to say. I didn't know what she wanted.

'How are you?' I said.

'I'm grand.' Then nothing again. I was lying on the ground holding onto my head beginning to remember.

'I asked you to ring, didn't I?' I said.

'You did.'

'I'm sorry. I was just depressed after the drink. And you finding me in all my glory.'

'Do you want to meet for coffee or something?' she asked.

'It's OK. Really it's fine. You don't have to. It's very kind of you, but I'm fine.'

'I'm not being kind. I just wouldn't mind meeting you.'

'OK.'

We made an arrangement. I didn't know what she was doing but it would get me out of the house.

I was there before her. I waited for five minutes on my own. I was beginning to think she'd been winding me up when she arrived. She touched me on the shoulder and asked did I need anything. I said I was OK.

She sat down and I asked how she was and she asked how I was and then when that ran out we had to start talking. I kept asking questions about everything, her course, her family, her car, because if I stopped I knew she'd ask me. I couldn't keep it up. When I asked how much she spent on petrol on a trip to Monaghan she just laughed and said, 'How are things with you?'

'They're OK.'

She smiled and hesitated before speaking.

'What happened to you?'

'I don't know. Just. Things changed.'

'I'm going to be honest and you can tell me to get lost if you want, but you were so completely together and in charge of yourself and now . . .' I liked the pause, 'you're not.'

'I know.' I looked at her. I looked for any trace of irony, to see if she was taking the piss, if she was enjoying seeing me squirm but I didn't see it.

'Small things add up,' I said, 'and then you lose momentum and it's hard to get going again.'

She asked what I meant so I told her. I told her the lot, completely straight, including everything about her. No lying or anything to make me look better because she was sitting in front of me listening and she had asked to hear it so I told it. I thought I saw her react at one point when I told her about going back home to Niamh after the first night with her. I thought she was going to say something but she didn't and I just kept going until the end and then I told her again that I was sorry about messing her up and she shook her head.

'I'm fine,' she said. 'You're the one who's messed up.' She didn't say it angrily.

'Yeah,' I said. 'That's about it.'

We were sitting at a counter in the window of a place near Christchurch. The window was fogged up. The traffic outside was jammed, just not moving. I could barely see the faces of the drivers looking in at us as we sat beside each other in silence. She put her hand on my knee after a minute and I looked at her.

'I'm going home this weekend for Easter. Do you want to come with me? Get you out of town?'

'OK,' I said and I laughed once and then she laughed and said OK.

'Why?' I asked.

'Be good for you,' she said.

'What's it to you? At the end of it all? Why would you care?'

'I don't know,' she said. 'I probably shouldn't.'

'You shouldn't,' I said. 'Really you shouldn't.'

'I'll pick you up at four from your flat. I'll give you a ring.'

'OK,' I said and she stood up and kissed me on the cheek and I held her for a second and then she was gone.

I couldn't understand it. I thought maybe it was because she was young or naïve or she was setting me up for something terrible but I couldn't believe any of it. I didn't understand why she would want to help me when I had been bad to her. It didn't make any sense but then maybe she was just good. Maybe she had forgiven me and was helping me because I needed it. Maybe she still cared for me despite everything. Maybe I would find out when I went with her. I couldn't understand it then though.

She rang me before she came over.

'Are you ready?' she asked.

'You're sure you want to do this?'

'I wouldn't ask you if I didn't.'

'I'm ready,' I said and she turned up five minutes later.

We drove out into the suburbs on the Northside, then onto the motorway and when it came down to two lanes again we were in the country. It was a good day. The sun was shining and clouds were blowing across the sky above the fields. I thought about it and I remembered that it was April.

'Who's going to be here?' I asked her.

'My parents.' I felt unease creeping into my stomach.

'Do they know I'm coming?'

'I told them you were coming.'

'Do they know about me?' I asked.

She looked over at me quickly, smiling.

'What do you mean?'

'Do they know about you and me and all that?'

'All what?' she said. She was messing.

'How I took advantage of you and then became an alcoholic?'

'I told them. My father is going to sort you out.'

'You didn't tell them. Fuck me. Please tell me you didn't.'

'I didn't. I told them I was bringing a friend with me. That's all.' She was quiet after that for a while.

'I'm sorry,' I said.

'You have to stop apologizing.'

'I'm sorry.'

I watched the life come back into her as we got closer to her place, as we got off the main road and onto bouncy bog roads going up and down over drumlins, as the smell of shit and silage filled the car. I listened as she told me what we were going to do that night and the next, as her accent got stronger while she drove through back roads where she knew every corner, every tree, every pothole until we turned into a farmyard.

'You're a farmer's daughter,' I said when she stopped the car. There was a dog barking beside my door.

'I am,' she said.

'Who's this guy?' I asked pointing at the dog.

'That's Rocky,' she said. His teeth clicked off the car window.

'Are you getting out?' she asked me.

I looked at the dog and looked at her.

'I don't know if I want to.'

'He won't touch you,' she said.

'I'm scared shitless,' I said.

'You'll be grand,' she said and she got out and the dog went over to her wagging his tail.

Her parents were in the kitchen when we walked in. They both hugged her and then they looked at me.

'This is Rory,' she said and they said hello and shook my hand and we sat down and had tea.

They talked about how she was and what had been going on and all that. I sat there trying to look normal and pleasant and kept my mouth shut. It didn't seem like a good idea being there. The conversation went on around me until they all got up and Róisín showed me to my room. We had dinner and it was fine. When her mother asked me what I did I told her I was in advertising. Róisín looked at me with a half-smile that I didn't understand.

'But I'm not working at the moment,' I said and they just let it go.

They went out later. I sat with her in the living-room in front of a fire, drinking tea, and watched a film on telly. They had satellite. I felt OK. She was beside me but not close enough to be touching. I didn't know what the story was. I didn't know what she was expecting. It was easier to do nothing. If she made a move on me it would be fine. I wouldn't mind but I thought I'd prefer if she didn't.

'This is nice,' I said after a while.

'Good,' she said. 'You see. You don't need to drink to have a good time.'

'I just said it was nice,' I said and she laughed.

'We'll go out tomorrow night. There'll be a bar if you need it.'

'Sounds good.'

I went to bed at midnight. Her parents were still out.

'I'll see you in the morning,' she said on the landing and we went to our rooms.

I knew it was late when I woke. I felt great. The aches were gone, the gloom had lifted. I went downstairs and she was there in the kitchen with her mother.

'What time is it?' I asked.

'Nearly one.'

'Country air or something.' I was embarrassed.

'Do you want breakfast? Or lunch?' her mother asked. I looked at her and she laughed.

We went out after I ate. There were fields at the back of the house with cattle grazing on scrubby-looking grass. There was a lake at the bottom. We walked down to it and then along by the edge until we came to a boat. She was wearing boots. I got in and she pushed it out.

It was warmer than it should have been. I rowed and she sat at the back with her hand trailing in the water.

'You're lucky to have this,' I said.

'I know. You can take it for granted.'

She talked about when she was a kid with her brother out fishing on the lake every morning in the summer holidays. She pointed out houses on the hills around where her friends used to live. We went down the lake until it narrowed and she showed the way through a gap to another bigger lake. I took the oars in as we drifted through the gap, rushes brushing the sides of the boat. As we came through onto the other side, the water was completely still, sheltered by the reeds. We sat there in the silence, the sun shining down on us and listened to the sound of the birds, the engine of a tractor in the distance. There was nothing else.

'It never changes,' she said. 'I go away to Dublin and nothing stays the same, everything keeps changing, things keep happening and I come back here and it's always like this, exactly like this. Like it was when I was six.'

We sat and listened to the emptiness. You could smell the water, feel the sun, listen to everything growing around you. Neither of us spoke until the boat began to drift towards the shore. I put the oars back out and asked her where we were going.

We pulled the boat up on the far side of the lake and walked up the hill to a church with a round tower and a graveyard. We wandered around separately. I walked along the walls of the church, read a notice in Irish on the side of the tower which I didn't understand, walked through the gravestones, sunken and worn smooth by wind and rain. The same names over and over for three hundred years until the modern ones in black marble with photos scanned into the stone, and poems that rhymed.

'It's nice,' I said to her when I found her.

'I like it,' she said. 'And there's nothing else to show you around here. This is all there is. Fields and lakes and this.'

'It's OK. It's all very nice.'

'And there's a disco in Clones tonight.'

'Are we going?' I asked her.

'I am. You can come if you don't fall asleep.'

'I'll do my best.'

We went back down to the boat and she rowed for a bit with me spread out in the back watching my fingers plough a furrow through the cold water.

She rang her friends when we got back to the house. I listened to her talking, the half-sentences and in-jokes and constant laughter of people that knew each other for ever. We had dinner with her parents. I could see them trying to figure out what the story was between us. I didn't know myself.

Two of her friends picked us up later to bring us in to a bar in Clones. She introduced me and I kept my mouth shut and let them get on with it, talking and laughing and shouting. I sat in the front seat and looked out the window as we bounced along. The buzz of a Saturday night crackled in the car. We arrived in the bar and it was packed. There was a mix of local types and young farmers and people who obviously spent their weeks in Dublin. They all seemed to know each other. Róisín stopped five times between the door and where we sat down. There were the two girls who picked us up and then another two and one of their boyfriends and then later another two guys arrived. They were all OK. They were all young. I tried to keep up. I laughed at jokes I didn't understand and smiled a lot. I was like an exchange student. I didn't mind. I talked to a couple of them and they asked who I was and how I knew Róisín. They didn't seem to know or care really.

After we went to a nightclub beneath some hotel, a big barn of a place full of guys in football shirts drinking pint bottles of cider and the smell of Red Bull in the air. We sat along a counter on the top floor overlooking the dance floor. The girls went and danced and me and two of the guys sat there looking out over the crowd, all of them, all types mixing together and dancing in bouncing swaying unison. It was just fun. The guy beside me started talking. He was talking about a girl who was here that he didn't want to meet. He'd gone out with her for a couple of weeks and then she'd shifted somebody else and he still liked her and he knew she would be here but he didn't want to meet her because he didn't know what he might do. He was hammered. I wasn't. I asked him how old he was and he said he was twenty and I told him all of this wasn't going to matter in three weeks and he nodded but I knew he didn't believe me.

I went down and found Róisín and the others and danced beside them. She laughed at me, how shit I was, but I kept going beside her. When it got too hot I asked her did she want a drink and she nodded. We went upstairs to the bar. We stood leaning at the counter drinking. I could feel sweat between my shoulders.

'It's not exactly hardcore,' she said to me, into my ear. I could feel the heat off her body.

'I like it,' I said. 'You don't get Fields of Athenry in Dublin too often.'

'It was the dance mix,' she said. 'It's not posey anyway,'

'It's definitely not that.'

We stood there with the music pumping, people milling around us at the bar.

'Why are you doing this?' I asked her.

'What?' she said.

'Me. Why did you bring me here?'

'Here? There's nowhere else.'

'No, I mean up here. To your house. To your family and your friends.'

She shrugged.

'I thought you might like it.'

'I do like it. It's all great but I don't get why you'd want to bring me here.'

She smiled at me like I was stupid.

'The state you were in, someone had to do something with you. You were a mess.'

'Yeah, but why you? You hardly know me and . . .' I stopped. I didn't want to say it there in her place with her friends around us, on a happy Saturday night. It seemed wrong but I had to. 'I treated you like shit,' I said. 'What do you care what happens to me?'

She shook her head.

'No, Rory. I know you a bit. I liked you a lot when I met you and yeah, then you were a prick but you said you were sorry and I believe you. I think you are sorry. I think you are an OK guy who just lost it. So I brought you up here to get you away for a weekend. It's not anything more than that. Why wouldn't I?'

'Most people wouldn't.'

She laughed. 'Well I'm not most people,' she said and then I hugged her and held her. I looked in her face and said thanks again and she let go. She held my hand and then squeezed it and then let it go and went back downstairs to the dance floor.

There were about seven of us in the car on the way back, driving at about seventy through the back roads staying away from the guards. I was thinking it was the kind of car that you hear about every weekend going into a tree and everybody dying. They dropped us at the end of her road and we walked the rest of the way in pitch darkness, her holding onto me showing me where to go. I kissed her when we were at the kitchen door and we went inside. When we were on the landing she kissed me outside the door to my room. She went off to her own room and I fell asleep feeling happy.

I was up in time for lunch. It was Easter Sunday. They'd all been to mass. I came down and she was setting the table. I ate until I couldn't move and then we went into the living-room and had tea and read the papers all afternoon. Nobody spoke. When she went into the kitchen, I followed her and asked when she was going back and she said she was staying until Tuesday. I said I thought I'd better go and she said she'd give me a lift to the bus. I packed my bag and said goodbye to her parents.

She left me at the bus station in Monaghan. We said goodbye in the car.

'Ring me when you come back,' I said to her.

'I will,' she said. 'We can do something next week maybe.'

'Yeah, let's do that. Thanks a lot,' I said.

'Are you sure you want to go back now? You don't want to wait and come with me on Tuesday?'

'No. It's fine,' I said. 'I better.'

'You can stay,' she said.

'It's OK. I want to go back.'

She tried to find a way to say it.

'You won't get too low if you're on your own?'

'I don't think so,' I said. 'I'm OK. I've got people I can ring if I do.'

'Well do.'

The bus pulled in and I said goodbye and kissed her quickly and went and bought a ticket. She waited in the car until I got on and then drove off.

Why would she do it? What reason could she have? She could say what she had said. It wasn't a big deal. I had stayed in her house. That was all. She saw that I was in trouble and she helped me. I tried to believe what she had said but there was a gap that I couldn't bridge. It made no sense. It was just stupid and I didn't think she was stupid. The way she carried herself, the certainty with which she spoke, the clarity to herself of her own logic. Not stupid but maybe unworldly, inexperienced. She could be all of them. In ten years, given the same circumstances, would she do it again? Probably not. She hadn't lived. She hadn't been let down by people she put trust in. She hadn't seen how you have to look out for yourself. She believed in forgiveness, its power for all involved, she could wipe the slate clean, forgive and forget, which most people would never do. The thought of a world waiting to corrupt her and take that away from her made me feel protective. I knew what it was like. That was where I was from. She was from somewhere totally different. She was ten years younger than me, we had almost nothing in common but it didn't matter. It

couldn't stop me feeling a loyalty towards her, a need to defend her from what would inevitably happen, a responsibility to pay back her faith in me which had come unasked and undeserved. A love. It made no sense but when it came, I couldn't stop it.

As we came into the suburbs I could feel myself waking up, like I had been asleep. The traffic that slowed as we got towards the centre, the streets full of people going out on a bank holiday Sunday, laughing and smiling on a dry, warm evening in April. I didn't want to go back to the flat.

When we got to Dublin, I walked across Talbot Street and towards the flat, then changed my mind and turned and crossed the river at Tara Street. I didn't know where I was going. I walked down Grafton Street with drunk schoolkids in not enough clothes hanging onto each other screaming at the hilarity of everything. Along Dame Street full of English boys on stags making lechy comments at the English girls walking the other way, all of them loving it. I went up towards Christchurch, crowds of people walking out of the hotels past me down towards the centre and Temple Bar. A whole city given over to drinking, enjoyment and company. The thrill of what might lie ahead that night, what could be done, who could be met, the feeling that tonight, if you tried hard enough, if you kept going and pushed and really believed in it, that tonight could be the best night you ever had. It was there as real as the air I breathed. It could change your life. I could feel it. I knew what it meant. I walked down towards the river ready to go home.

# Acknowledgements

Thanks to Marianne Gunn O'Connor, Imogen Taylor, Cormac Kinsella, my parents, and Sarah, the Binchy and O'Connor families and my friends for their help and support.